Reverie

by Zee Lacson

ISBN 978-1-7351358-1-6 (Paperback Edition)

Some characters and events in this book are fictitious. Any similarities to real persons, living or dead, is coincidental and not intended by the author.

Editing by David Rutter
Front Cover Art by Zee Lacson
Book Design and Layout by John Lacson

Printed and bound in the United States of America
First Printing 2020

Visit www.reveriethebook.com

for

my Dad,
Eduardo V Laureola Jr.
(1964 - 2006)
who had the wisdom to insist I take up
Fine Arts in college but supported me
when I took up Engineering anyway.
I miss you constantly.

my amazing children,
Cale & Caden
who had to share their mother
with fictional characters.
I can't imagine better characters than you.

my brilliant husband,
John
who made this happen.
You are my favorite dream.

I'm mad.

I'm crazy.

I'm insane.

I must be if I'm here. Feeling what I'm feeling.

This is not some rabbit hole I've fallen in. There are no talking animals, psychedelic colors that flavor the environment in acid-trip rainbows, or fuzzy blue caterpillars. Instead, I feel the damp chill of my clothes, tension in the air, and fear that is real.

I shiver, though I can't be sure if it's just because I'm cold. My shirt clings intermediately to the back of my neck. Every inhale causes it to rub against me like a handful of tiny needles slowly ripping through my skin, seemingly sharp and unrelenting. I press the bottom of my palms to my eyes, pushing out errant tears. The pressure reminds me that there are other things happening. There are other things that hurt. The purpling bruises on my side. The raw scratches on my arm. The sores on my feet thrusting against my shoes. They all meld in a slur of fresh, throbbing ache.

The smell of stale air and wet tile saturates the air and invades every breath.

It is a unique combination of suffocating hopelessness that makes the tight enclosure even smaller. Hollow sounds echo unnaturally within the empty room. It makes the steady drips of water louder. My heart is crashing in waves, so loud in my ears that it blocks out the water. It's an overload. I can't stop crying. I can't stop feeling.

My senses insist this is happening … here and now.

Somewhere in the other real world ... somewhere far from here, where things make sense ... I must be unresponsive to everything. There is too much going on inside of me to have anything left.

Here, the high windows reveal little. There are no shadows or movement. The stillness watches me while I wait. I'm waiting because he told me to. He's the reason I'm pulled to this place. Alone in this prison of choice.

I flinch at the rhythmic pops and snaps in the distance.

Was that ... Gunfire?

It's begun. The next few minutes will determine his fate ... and by extension, my own. Do we even stand a chance? Did we ever?

I can't just stay in this huddled position while our future is being decided. I need to do something. I need to see. It's not what he wants but It's not going to matter anyway if we're both killed.

What happens then?

The uncertainty that holds me in place now drives me to motion. I extend a shaky hand forward into the dim light. Trying to find a semblance of courage, I will the rest of me to follow.

It is a step closer to him. Am I also a step closer to the end?

A door bursts open. I am no longer alone.

New World

"Maybe we'll take a side trip to Hollywood."

"That's a seven-hour drive, Dad. Do you want to drive seven hours?"

My father and I were walking down a terminal of the Sacramento International Airport. Our plane had landed 15 minutes ago and he already identified as a local. At this rate, he'll be in tight pants and ironic glasses by the afternoon. I'm going to be living with California's newest oldest hipster.

He reconsidered his proposal, rubbing a free hand over the bald spot on his head. "Maybe when you drive …"

I laughed. Right. I hate driving.

"So we'll see Hollywood in roughly, what, never?"

He threw an arm around me, the weight of it familiar on my shoulders. "I bet we can get Locke to take us." I grinned. "I bet we can."

We met my favorite brother, Locke, outside security. He was the youngest of my three older brothers and the one with whom I spent most of my time. He always knew the best parties, the latest trends, and the coolest games.

I saw him only during long holidays since he moved away to college, but he was just at the house in Illinois last week when he volunteered to drive Dad's X5 all the way here. I contemplated joining him on that road trip but I'm a bigger fan of airplanes than I am of cars.

I've never gotten sick in the air but I've thrown up in every vehicle that anyone in my family has owned.

He wore his cropped hair under a tattered green baseball cap. Dark stains were evident around the collar of his UCLA shirt and under his arms. He handed me a bottle of pop; then took over our luggage.

"Here ya go, sis. They didn't have anything non-carbonated but I figured you may want something to drink."

He was right. The air outside was ridiculously hot, even in the shade of the parking garage. I wished that I had shorts on instead of my jeans. I pulled my hoodie off and tied it around my hips, grateful for the tank top I had underneath. My hair was too short to pull back properly but just long enough to annoy me. I tucked what I could behind my ears and promised myself for the hundredth time that I'd finally do something about this someday. Maybe just shave the whole thing off and start over. Like we're starting over here.

I took a swig of the pop but instead of refreshing me, it only made me more thirsty.

"It's, like, a hundred degrees out here!"

"Good call," Locke replied. "It's a good 101 degrees last I checked."

Dad whistled. It was a solid sound of appreciation. I groaned.

"It'll be even higher tomorrow."

Great. It was hardly ever this hot back home. I'm going to need to get the sweat glands under my arms surgically sealed if I have to deal with these kinds of insane temperatures. I fervently wished that this wouldn't be the kind of weather I'd have to suffer through when school started in two weeks.

The smelly new girl. Awesome.

"Isn't it supposed to almost be Fall?" I complained. Dad laughed. "I think it's great! No more shoveling snow! No more salting the driveway!" My brother chuckled as he loaded the empty SUV with our luggage.

"Dad," I argued, "You hadn't shoveled snow since I was, like, 5. Liam's done it for you since!"

"Regardless," Dad continued. "It is such a relief to be able to chuck the bulky winter coat!"

"What are you complaining about anyway?" Locke asked, getting behind the wheel. "You love summer weather." I faced every available vent in my direction, hoping for reprieve in the form of cooler air.

"A 100 degrees isn't summer weather, Locke. That's the temperature in hell."

"Don't be a crybaby. It's just a heat wave. It's not like this all the time."

It was more than just the weather.

I've lived my entire life in the same house. The same room even. Everyone I know, I've known since I was a child. I had thought I would be more intimidated at the prospect of starting everything all over in someplace unfamiliar, but I was energized at the prospect of redefining myself.

"Hey, London," my brother addressed me, breaking my trance. "How are your friends handling you leaving abruptly?"

We had hit a stoplight and Locke glanced at the rearview mirror as he spoke. I saw Dad tense at the question and I knew he would be listening especially closely to the answer. This was a big move and he was worried about scarring me emotionally or something.

"They used me as an excuse to throw a party."

"Was it a good one?"

"I didn't know half the people that showed up and we ended up having to hire a cleaning crew to restore the house to a more familiar condition."

Locke laughed in approval. "Excellent."

Dad hadn't shared the sentiment when he saw the condition of the house the following morning. My friends chipped in for the service and sent Dad an apology cake. He ate the cake.

"They're a good group, your friends."

And yet I was feeling relieved that I could leave them all behind. I closed my eyes and tried to convince myself that the nausea I was feeling was motion sickness and not residual guilt. How could I be pleased to leave such a good group of friends? There was absolutely nothing wrong with them.

If there was nothing wrong with them, then something must be wrong with me.

The humidity added that extra unhappy element to the long drive from the airport. It turned out that it really was motion sickness that was making me queasy. We pulled up to the small three bedroom bungalow when the headache started. I waited until Locke shut off the engine before I opened the car door. A wave of hot air greeted me.

I grabbed my pack from the seat next to me and tried not to collapse on the front steps. The movers have already been here. Locke had taken care of everything on this end for us. The rooms were filled with moving boxes that I had meticulously labeled and color coded back in Illinois.

As I followed Locke to my room, the light reflecting from the sterile white walls made it difficult for my eyes to focus on anything. The air in the house was significantly cooler. Demonstrating unusual foresight, Locke must've had the A/C running all morning. The sweat on my skin cooled uncomfortably.

He kicked open the door to my room and dropped the luggage unceremoniously on the hardwood floor. My old bed, sans the sheets, was already set up in the middle of the room. Also white. Big surprise.

I sat on the bed. Three boxes lined the other wall. I had two windows with no curtains, letting the sun in and causing unrestricted vertigo. I groaned, closed my eyes, and lay down.

"Dramatic much?"

I scoffed. "No. I think the heat is getting to me. I'll probably be normal after lunch. I just need to get used to it."

"Speaking of which," he said. "What should I pick up? What are you in the mood for? Tacos? Pasta? Pizza?" I almost hurled at the mere suggestion of greasy fast food. I didn't really feel as if I could keep anything down but maybe part of the problem was I haven't had anything decent to eat all day. "I need something cool. Get me iced tea and a mandarin salad or something like it."

He made a sound that I translated to amused disbelief. "Since when did you eat salad?"

"Since the weather hit 100 degrees," I retorted.

"You got cash on you?"

I opened my eyes to look at him in exasperation. He spread his arms open. "Hi. Hello. I'm your brother, Locke. Broke college student?"

I laughed. "Fine." I found my wallet in my pack and threw him a credit card. My aim was off but he plucked it from the air anyway.

The name on the card was mine but it wasn't really my card. Dad paid the bill. In an attempt to prevent our home from regressing into a frat house, I had been left in charge of the household. I did all the groceries and most of the cooking. Grocery shopping for four grown men is, if I may coin the term, a defining experience. My father understood this. The card was meant to mitigate the struggle.

I had unlimited freedom on that card but I knew the unsaid rule was it was to be used for household expenses, school, and emergencies only. I was fairly responsible. As long as I stayed under the radar, I could get away with high-end art supplies every now and again.

"I'm going to gas up on the way too," he was saying. "You aren't super hungry yet, are you?" I made a non-committal noise only because I didn't want to have to move my head.

When he left the room, I lay back down and curled up in a fetal position. Even with my eyes closed, the sun's bright light was bothersome. It sent shooting pain through my brain. I placed both arms over my face to block the offending blaze but the damage was already done. I was definitely feverish.

Maybe a cold glass of water would help.

I was either nauseated or we were experiencing an earthquake of extreme magnitude that didn't seem to affect the furniture. I stumbled down the still unfamiliar stairs. My grip on the rail was the only thing that kept my body upright.

I heard voices outside when I made it to the ground floor and knew that Locke hadn't left yet. I headed straight to the kitchen sink with all the intent of drinking water directly from the tap.

I threw up when I got to the sink. Every breath between episodes only made it worse because the smell of vomit induced more vomiting. The stench lingered in the air like drunks at closing time. I threw some cold water on my face. It was good. I cupped some in my hands to wash my mouth off.

I thought the worst was over until it was as if someone had tipped our new house on its side. I gripped the edge of the counter to keep from falling but lacked the strength to hold myself up.

I fell to the floor.

Contact

My eyes must've been closed for a long time because they were trying vainly to adjust to the light when I finally opened them. Everything was blurry. There were voices that I didn't recognize all around me … and they were shouting. Shouting at a very low volume. It was like trying to listen to an argument from another room. I couldn't make out anything they were saying even when I strained to listen.

I was lying flat on my back looking straight up but nothing above me made any sense. The more I tried to focus, the more the images eluded me.

Something uncomfortable was over my face. I tried to lift my arm but couldn't move it. Panic. I tried to talk, but I couldn't get my mouth to work. What comes after panic? That's where I was. The after-panic stage.

One of the unidentifiable shadows came close to my face. The voice was calm and commanding. There was no calming me. I still couldn't understand what it was saying and the more I failed at trying, the closer I got to hysteria. I may have started to hyperventilate, but I couldn't tell because I was paralyzed.

Then as I tried to scream, everything went black.

My body convulsed. I was shaking. I was bound tightly in the darkness and being tossed about like a rag doll. I was convinced my eyes were open. They were open, but I couldn't see, I couldn't see anything because there was nothing to see. Everything was just … gone.

Is this what it feels like to die?

The first light I saw was not as blinding as I thought it would be in the unending black. It was a wisp of color, swirling in poetic motion around me. Along with the impossible visions, there were sounds. No more muffled shouting but the clear notes of twittering birds and rustling leaves. I was breathing easily. A cool, soft gust blew my vision into perspective. In the next second, I had all my senses returned to me.

I was lying down, but it wasn't on my bed. It wasn't even on the kitchen floor. I sat up slowly, using my hands to bear most of my weight and found myself sitting on … pine leaves?

Oh, I know where I am. I'm in a Disney movie. Winnie the Pooh is going to round the corner any minute now …

It seemed to be late afternoon already. Maybe even early evening. I sat there for a time trying to remember how I went from our kitchen to the middle of the Hundred Acre Woods. I was still wearing the same jeans, light green tank top, and hoodie tied around my hips. My Chucks were on my feet, the laces half-tied as always. An empty candy wrapper in my pocket. No phone. That must still be in my pack.

I considered various circumstances ranging from kidnapping to schizophrenia to death. Each scenario becoming more elaborate and far-fetched. It didn't help my anxiety to see that I was alone.

I pushed myself up and noticed, with relief, that at least my head no longer hurt. Around me were no visible pathways. No indication of how I ended up here in the first place.

"Hello?" I said first in a whisper and then again in a yell. There was a slight movement in the trees as a response. I startled a little brown furry critter that was hiding in the leaves. I was expecting a squirrel but instead of a twitchy nose, the beady eyes that met mine were accompanied by a disproportionately long beak. It screeched at me.

I stumbled back in surprise, tripped over absolutely nothing, and fell hard on my tailbone. The unpleasant sensation that ran up my spine momentarily distracted me and I closed my eyes instinctively against the pain.

The round squirrel-bird protested one more time before escaping back into the undergrowth. It generated a series of movements through the foliage, rippling away from me until everything was still again.

California is so weird.

I sat there for another minute, feeling like I respawned from the last save point on a video game. When I dusted myself up the second time, I decided that the best direction would be the one away from little creatures that yelled at me.

I had to step through a mix of pine and moss before I found the faintest suggestion of a beaten path. The trees seemed to turn a more impossible shade of oversaturated green the further down I went. Only the sounds of distant birds and fast-moving invisible creatures periodically interrupted the quiet.

Time didn't seem to have any affect on my surroundings. I just kept walking. Long enough that the soles of my feet were indented with pebbles. Long enough to realize that the trickle of sweat down my back meant that this could not just be a crazy dream.

Someone had once said that insanity is doing the same thing over and over but expecting different results. This wasn't working. I needed to try something else.

I tested my Chucks on a sturdy looking tree. My feet slipped out from under me on the first step. I tried to twist around to protect my head and landed on my back in a tangle of ferns. Leaves tickled my cheek.

From my vantage point down on the ground, I spotted what looked like a break in the trees at a distance.

The forest opened up into a wide clearing overlooking a grand area. The sun bathed the meadow in a soft yellow glow. Wildflowers spotted the grass with pastel color, a contrast to the intense emerald of the trees. The air was delicately perfumed with honey and spice. It was a breathtaking painting but this impressionistic masterpiece ended abruptly, like an unfinished canvas.

Where the grass ended, it was just an open sky. Flat earth. I was standing at the edge of the world. I walked as close as I dared to the brink. It wasn't a safe drop. The rock was uneven and jagged.

Further down was proof that it was not the end of the world as I had feared. Fringes of civilization meant that I wasn't alone. The visible edge of a town was the logical way out of this mess. I studied the cliff face to find a way down. It looked just about as promising as my attempt at tree climbing.

"Are you trying to kill yourself?"

A shiver ran up my spine. Whether it was one of relief that I wasn't alone or fear that I wasn't alone, I couldn't tell. Both? His accent was not one I could identify. It was almost British but on a different melodic scale. I turned, not certain what to expect.

He stood almost a full head taller than me, his back to a tree, and his arms crossed over his chest. He was comfortable in the stance like he had been planted on the spot. His expression was both derisive and concerned. An inane combination that he managed successfully.

I inwardly withdrew. Wrestling with my emotions left me silent.

When I didn't answer, he pushed himself off the tree and walked toward me. A mess of light-colored hair fell over suspicious eyes.

"Hallo?" he asked more tentatively as if more than one word would be too much for me to understand. He'd recently been in a fight, made evident by the cut on his lip that cracked when he spoke. It made him look formidable. He was a few feet closer before I took one step back and he stopped.

"You be 'right?" His voice was softer now and his eyes, darkened underneath from lack of sleep, bore into mine. They were golden with flecks of green. Like they couldn't decide what color they wanted to be.

I shook my head a fraction. "No," I finally said when I could trust my voice. I had to clear my throat, "I don't think I am."

He didn't deviate far from his position, but it felt like he was much closer to me. "Who are you? What are you doing here?" His tone hinted that I was trespassing. He leaned slightly forward and a glint of dark metal tucked into the band of his pants caught my eye.

Alarmed, I took another step back and was reminded how close I was to a different kind of danger. Loose pebbles skittered down the rocks. I saw him tense in response.

"I think it's a fair question," he said. I looked up from the descending gravel to his face. He looked like he won a recent fight whereas I'm fresh from throwing up in my kitchen sink. Yeah, not an even match. He wouldn't even need a weapon.

I swallowed. "I'm not exactly sure where here is, to begin with." That was too honest. I realized, with chagrin, that it wasn't the smartest thing to admit. I was aware that I lost a small advantage by providing more information.

"But I'm sure Dad will be looking for me," I added belatedly. It was a feeble attempt to balance the scale I had thoughtlessly tipped.

He looked entertained. "Am I scaring you?"

"No," I answered too quickly. Demonstrating that I was, in fact, scared. I was doing everything wrong. The tension rose between us. He took a step back. I didn't relax.

"Unless you're known to come this far in the wops, you won't likely be found, eh." He shrugged casually. "This is sort of my turf," he continued. "If you want to find your way out, you'll have more luck if you stick with me."

The what? W.O.P.S? Where? What? And did he actually say turf? "Your ... turf." He shrugged again. I mirrored his stance by crossing my arms over my chest, risking a step forward.

"Is this, like, a gang thing?" I knew I should still feel some kind of danger but now this was all rather absurd. The last forest gang activity I've ever heard of was a band of Merry Men. And they wore tights. I lost my fear and stared at him in disbelief.

He snorted dismissively, mumbling something under his breath that was too fast for me to catch.

"Not even ow." He abruptly turned his back on me and started to walk. I stayed where I was. He stopped, looked at me over his shoulder and said, "Coming?"

I looked longlily toward the distant town. There was hope in sight but no way to get to it. He was right. I could wander around indefinitely. Maybe I'll be eaten by a bear. Maybe I'll find the cottage of a cannibalistic witch. The latter may not be all that bad. At least there was cake involved. I looked back at him. He had no cake but he was probably my best chance out of here.

Hoping that I wasn't heading toward some kind of human trafficking ring, I followed.

Dangerous Ground

I kept pace with him but lagged a few steps behind. It offered false security. He didn't say anything. He just kept walking. I just kept following.

It grew marginally darker as we walked deeper into the forest. We stopped at a small creek. It was little more than a trickle of water that cut through the trees. Narrow enough to jump across. The water was tempting but I didn't think it was all that clean. The smell of wet leaves was strong. It was still humid but cooler under the shade.

"I need to know where you're from then I'll know where we're going," he said finally. He spoke slowly and softly, almost condescendingly. Like he was speaking to a child. He spoke with the bearing of a man but he was still a kid, a boy on his way to being one. It was really his eyes that made the difference. They had a haunted look. He'd seen more than he should or perhaps having seen such things made him older. He didn't look at me, but rather walked toward one of the trees near the brook.

"Um ... I don't really know," I played with the empty candy wrapper in my hands. The plastic made a soft audible sound with every twist and crinkle. It was inexplicably therapeutic to me at the moment.

He reached up the tree for a couple of small green fruits. A thin, delicate silver chain wrapped around his wrist caught my eye. It shimmered like a mirage. I stared at it, wondering if it was a trick of the light. "I can't remember how I got here," I admitted haltingly.

He tossed me one of the fruits.

I almost dropped it.

He tore a bite off the fruit he was holding but spit out the bit. He then squeezed it in his hands and started to suck out the pulp. Like a menacing fruit vampire in dark jeans.

"Did you hit your head at some point?" he asked. I followed his lead with the alien fruit and bit into it tentatively. It had a very distinct smell but not particularly identifiable. The skin was bitter. The pulp inside, in contrast, was rather sweet. Reminiscent of the Mexican guava that Dad thought was a creative way to introduce me to new cultures.

International, magical fruit. How extraordinary. I wasn't in the Hundred Acre Wood. I was in Narnia. The summer version.

Hitting my head and losing my memory were distinct possibilities taking into consideration how muddled everything was. I shrugged. "Maybe. I don't know." He sat against the tree. He had a stern, defiant, puzzled look on his face when he addressed me, and it never seemed to go away.

I sat on a rock, maintaining space between us.

"You don't know."

"No," I put my lips to the opening I had made on the fruit and sucked again. I had to squeeze it a bit to coax more of the pulp out but was rewarded with sweet flavor. Though I wasn't really hungry, the fresh juice was what my parched throat needed. Safer than possibly contaminated creek water anyway. I was also trying to reconcile the sensation of eating a thick skinned pear with the flavor of, I don't know … a pineapple-guava??

It gave me something to do under his scrutiny.

"What's your name? Or don't you know that either?" he asked sarcastically.

I bristled at his tone. "London." I meant to say it more forcefully but instead, it was an ambiguous offering at best.

"London?" He snorted. "Did they name you that so you never forget where you're from?"

I rolled my eyes. He almost smiled, but stopped himself. "This is the first time I've ever seen you around here," he said. He hadn't told me his name, and I didn't want to have to ask for it. I asked a different question instead.

"And how long have you lived here?"

He laughed without humor. It was loud and brief. I jumped at the sound, and he looked like he was surprised himself. "You must be mental. I don't live here." The way he said that made me feel incredibly stupid.

Feeling stupid in front of a boy. What a novelty.

"Where do you live then?" I challenged, feeling more irritated. It felt as if he hadn't answered a single question of mine since we'd met.

He gave me a look of guarded disbelief. Juice from the fruit had run down his left arm and collected by the wide band of his watch, staining it a darker brown. He tossed the hollow fruit skin from his hands, wiping his arm on the side of his shirt.

He plucked two more off the tree with one hand, bit off a chunk from one to spit out. A fresh line of juice ran down his arm again. He gestured at his chest, his eyes never leaving mine. "Paradigm?" he said it like it was a question. I tried to make out the print on his shirt, but it was missing in several places and I didn't want to gawk. It made me uncomfortable.

"Paradigm?" I repeated. That was an actual question.

"Yeah, of course, you'd have never heard of it. It probably doesn't even exist in your world." He mumbled something about privilege and ignorance. Though I didn't understand what he meant and why he would think that a dark shirt and jeans were obvious indications of his origins, I didn't think any institution for teenagers was likely a positive thing. Especially if the teenager was alone in the forest with a weapon. He must've escaped some sort of correctional facility. Fantastic.

"What? Did you just move here?" he practically spat out.

Finally, something I could answer with certainty. "Yes."

He relaxed. "Well, that does explain things. We'll just head toward the main and you can call whomever you want for a pickup."

That was going to be a fun ride home. "You said your dad was looking for you," he prompted. I could see that he thought I was lying.

"Yeah, he just won't be very happy with me when he finds me." Another smile tugged at his lips. His smiles were notably disarming. "Oh, you do come out this far into the wop wops," he declared with humor.

I still didn't know what that meant, but I also refused to dignify it with an answer. "Do you have a phone on you I can borrow?" I asked, wondering why it wasn't the first thing I thought of.

"Nah. No signal either, even if I did."

Of course not. That would be too easy.

My stomach was queasy again. I wasn't sure if it was unfamiliar fruit or unfamiliar emotions. I sensed the gaze of my self-declared guide. I looked away and concentrated on the sticky juice all over my hands, feeling guilty but not understanding how this was my fault.

After a few moments, he tossed the whole sticky mess of fruit near the trunk of the tree he took it from and wiped his mouth with the back of his hand. "It's a hike from here to the closest thing to a phone so we'd better get a move on if you want to get to your dad before he involves the police." I was all for not escalating the situation. I rinsed off the gunk on my hands in the brook and wiped them on my jeans before I followed him again.

"Why are you here?" I called from behind as we continued our hike. He stopped walking, turned to look at me and waited for me to catch up. I stopped where I was, a good distance from him.

"Listen," he said tiredly. "If you have questions, you need to come a little closer." I weighed the idea and decided that if he wanted to do anything, he could have and would have already. He seemed to be genuinely trying to help me find my way out.

He continued walking when I fell into step. He didn't answer right away. I didn't ask again.

"I come here when I don't want to be found," he finally said.

I should have left it there. He was doing me a favor. If he was in trouble, the less I knew, the better. Plausible deniability.

Of course, I asked. "Are you hiding from someone?"

He met my eyes and returned a half-smile that served him well. "Temporarily."

"Why?"

He looked away, the smile still on his face, and his voice low. "I don't get along with people very well."

"Big surprise," I muttered.

He gave me a sidelong look. "Judgmental much, Miss Congeniality?"

I shrugged. "I can just see how you wouldn't really get along with people."

"What would you know about getting along with people?"

His comment stung.

"You don't know me," I said defensively. He barked a laugh, "And you know me? You don't even know my name, London." He said my name, heavy with emphasis, driving home his point.

I blushed. He was right. While I had been offended, he seemed more amused. It was the more mature response. I looked at him pleadingly. *Please don't make me ask,* I thought desperately, feeling more and more humiliated.

"I'm Ethan," he said, as if reading my thoughts. I nodded, acknowledging his save quietly. I didn't feel like talking anymore.

"How old are you, London?" He asked, breaking the silence further down the path. I didn't respond. Where was he going with this? "Fifteen, maybe?" he suggested with much doubt. It's the lack of makeup. Everyone always thinks I'm younger than I really am.

"17," I finally answered then thinking it was polite to ask, "You?"

His word tumbled out, on its own accord. "16." There was wistfulness. A hint of sadness that caught my attention. It wasn't that he didn't want to be 17. It was that he didn't want it to end.

"You don't want to be 17." It was a statement.

He shrugged but responded anyway. "What's there to look

forward to for a bloke like me? Homelessness or the defence force? Pardon me for not being enthusiastic about my options."

I was feeling profoundly lost. Lost in the forest and lost in this conversation. It was like he was speaking a different language.

Dad once told me that sometimes, the only way out was through. I needed to find familiar ground.

"Why are those your only options?"

He looked at me strangely, "Oh, I do suppose there is the life of crime …" He said uncommon things so nonchalantly that it only confused me more. Suddenly, I felt like there were more pressing things I should question.

"Where am I?" I asked in a voice close to tears.

"You're pretty deep in. It's actually not safe here. If you know what's good for you, you shouldn't come back this way again." He considered what he said, possibly realized that it sounded more like a threat than a sincere warning. "You just never know what you'll find here with you."

My sense of direction was never a strong point, and I had no real reference to go by, so all that information was useless. I just knew I had never been here before. I knew that. Right?

"Is that why you carry a gun?" I tried to act unconcerned about it, as if a teenager carrying a weapon is something I was used to.

"A gun?" he repeated. He looked honestly perplexed. I gestured at the band of his pants where a bit of black metal was almost hidden by the folds of his shirt. Understanding dawned and he reached for it.

He pulled out a butterfly knife and flipped it expertly open with a flick of his wrist. The twisted blade was longer than what I would've thought a pocket knife should be. He handled the uniquely shaped gray handle with such ease and comfort that I didn't doubt his skill to use it.

"Not even," he said, unperturbed. He saw the look on my face and flipped it shut, tucking it into his pants in one smooth motion. "She'll be 'right. It's just a toy."

"A toy?" His flippant remark bothered me. It was obviously not a toy.

"Granted, it's not your typical Switch …" His face had changed. "Maybe calling it a toy isn't that." He twisted his hands slowly in front of him as if grasping for something that wasn't there. The chain on his wrist twisting along, hypnotically. "It's a … medium … freedom of expression … release of emotions …"

I thought about what ways a knife can be a tool of emotional expression and I tensed. I've seen enough documentaries. He was unstable. Dangerous.

He noticed the change in atmosphere. He watched the emotions I wasn't bothering to hide play across my face. He took a step back.

When he pulled the knife out again, I cringed. He reacted. I couldn't tell if he was angry or disappointed. He looked at me in such a way that all I could do was stay where I was, fixed under his scrutiny.

Without even blinking, he flipped it open and tossed it in the air. It was defiance. I couldn't bring myself to see how high it went. I was fixed, looking into the conflict in his eyes. My breath came short and shallow.

He stayed rooted in place but caught the knife behind him with his right hand. In the same motion, he brought it forward, spinning between his fingers.

The metal was fluid in the confidence of his hand, reflecting the little light beaming through the trees. The blade cut the air with melancholy sighs, dancing to unheard melodies as if magic moved it. Beautiful. Spellbinding.

It would have captured my full attention if it weren't for the power behind his eyes. His eyes were searching mine, looking for something. The green and gold struggled with each other. He tossed the knife up into the air again, taking a quick step toward me as he did. I still hadn't moved, even when all there was left was that look in his eyes and the impossible faint smell of laundry detergent on clothes that looked like they hadn't been washed in days.

His arm came up close to my face. There was a sharp gust of wind near my cheek. I blinked. He leaned back and I saw that he had the knife secure in his grip, the blade folded safely inside. Tucking it back into his pants he looked away.

My knees were weak, threatening to buckle. It wasn't fear anymore.

It was sensory overload. I was captivated by the emotion that he commanded, utterly attracted to his violent control.

When I caught my breath, I saw that he was already steps ahead of me, moving forward as if I wasn't there. As if he was in this world alone. Even the forest remained silent and the only sound was the quiet light between the trees.

His loneliness echoed deep inside me.

"Ethan ..."

It was the first time I said his name. It pulled me out of the free fall my emotions were taking and stopped him in his tracks.

I didn't know what else to say. He was not dangerous; just troubled. I had unintentionally judged him. I was wrong. Unfairly wrong.

With a certainty I didn't know how I had found, I knew that he was not the savage, unstable teenager I had thought he was. Despite what could all be textbook warning signs, I could see that there was also nothing textbook about him. He was someone much more.

"I'm sorry."

His eyes found mine and held it for an immeasurable amount of time. His expression softened slightly and he smiled. It was just a little tug on his lips. His eyes were sad but mercifully forgiving. "She'll be 'right." Then he inclined his head, an invitation to walk with him again.

Reality

We didn't speak much until we got to the edge of the preserve, where there was a road that I didn't recognize. My relief turned into unrealized regret.

"Well, you really can't get lost from here. Across the road is the lot for the main entrance. The office is there too." He checked his watch. "They're open for another hour and a half. They should have a phone you can use." I nodded but didn't say anything.

"I doubt I'll see you again," he said indifferently. The disappointment surprised me. There was a lump rising in my throat.

"You're not coming?" I asked, knowing the answer. He blinked. "It's probably not a good idea."

It wasn't a surprise considering how badly I'd behaved.

He gave me a mock salute with his index finger. "It was … interesting."

Interesting. Sure. That's what it was.

I stepped on the road, still staring at his face, memorizing his features. The subtle gust of wind was my first warning. It was quickly followed by the sound of an engine. I turned toward the speeding truck coming round the blind corner. I heard his voice sounding like a soft echo in contrast to the roaring in my ears. Comprehension came slowly and without fear or hope. I knew that even if I moved at an inhuman speed, there was no way I could get out of the way fast enough.

There was a flash of blinding light.

Awareness

The first thing I was aware of where unrelenting beeps.

Beep. Beep. Beep.

I didn't feel that something this annoying was in any version of heaven. I hadn't made it to heaven. After all the times my annoyed Biology lab partner has told me to go to hell, It's finally happened. This was your fault, Melody Carter. I'm damned because I didn't submit that stupid summary in time.

I had expected hell to be more like sitting in a tight school bus that smelled of gym locker and tacos, less like the Starship Enterprise. Something wasn't adding up. Have I been abducted? Was probing in my near future?

I opened my eyes.

No Aliens.

By some miracle, I wasn't reduced into roadkill by that truck. I had survived and I was lying in a hospital bed, not a spaceship.

I'm probably in a coma or paralyzed for life. It would explain the beeping.

If I braced myself for the worst, then maybe I could handle anything less than that with more finesse.

No sharp pain. Just an overall ache. I was a giant bruise. This was good. Feeling was good. It meant I still had a body and limbs to feel. Nothing amputated. I had an itch on my arm and it was a little difficult to breathe. My lips were chapped. A burp had died in my mouth.

The light hurt but it wasn't as bad as it had been. I turned my head to the side, gratified that at least I wasn't in any kind of brace. I was right about the beeping. Medical equipment I didn't know how to read monitored all sorts of bodily functions.

How long had I been unconscious?

I turned my head the other way and saw someone standing with his back to me, on the phone. Did Ethan decide to stay after all? When my eyes finally focused, I knew, even as the hope danced through my head, that he had not.

"Liam?"

I didn't recognize my own voice. I sounded like a chain-smoker at the end of the chain. Weak, hoarse, and in dire need of a mint.

Liam spun around. "London!" Then into the phone added, "Just right now. Yes, that's probably best. No, I don't know. Talk to you later." He put the phone down and was at my side.

"What are you doing here?"

"Hey, kiddo" my brother said, ignoring my question. "How are you?" He pulled a chair up to the side of the bed and sat down.

"I don't know." I was confused. "What happened?"

He laughed without humor. It was that big brother bark.

"You almost gave Dad a heart attack, that's what happened."

I tried to sit up but he held me back down and instead pressed a button. The upper half of the bed started to rise up and help me in position. He handed me a cup of water. I took it with my left hand and started to sip. I was feeling a bit dizzy still.

"Doctor said you had a fever-induced seizure." I could see the worry lines on his face. Only 27 and the man looked like he was 40. And a half. My poor brother. He worried way more than was necessary.

"Dad found you on the kitchen floor, doing the Exorcist. Thrashing around, foam coming out of your mouth, the works. You were burning up badly and wouldn't respond to anything he said. He just called 911."

Kitchen floor?

"What about the truck?" My voice was getting stronger now but I was disoriented.

Liam looked almost as confused as I felt. "The truck?" Then as if trying to force pieces of a puzzle together said, "Oh, well Locke had already left with it. Besides, I think Dad did the right thing calling 911 instead of trying to take you himself. Dad doesn't panic well."

I closed my eyes, trying to make sense of what he was saying. He launched into his well-practiced lecture mode. "London, you had a fever of almost a hundred and nine! That's fry-your-brain level and just plain irresponsible! Flat out stupid."

I remembered being in the new house. I had motion sickness. I was feverish. I threw up all over the kitchen sink. Yes, I remember that.

But what about the forest? What about the boy?

Dammit, I should've asked for his number.

"I didn't know." It sounded like a lame excuse. "I mean," I tried to explain, "I thought it was just motion sickness and the heat, you know?" I heard him make a noise of disapproval. "I've never had a seizure before, have I?"

He was still visibly upset. "You never had a fever of a hundred and nine before either. You usually take better care of yourself," he added with concern. "Is this about the move?"

I knew it would come to that. It seemed to be the foregone conclusion that men in my family liked to make.

"No, this is not about the move. I didn't do this to myself on purpose. It's like I've been telling Dad if I really didn't want to be here, I'd have moved in with Chase or you." I shifted in place, dislodging a stray hospital gown tie from under my thigh. It left an itchy red line on my leg. "Why are you even here?" I asked.

He seemed to believe me, however reluctantly. "Dad is completely freaked out. I flew in as soon as I could. Locke is back at the house with Dad, but they're on their way now that you're awake." He leaned back on the chair.

"I doubt you'd move in with Chase. You wouldn't be able to stand the mess." He grinned. I took another sip of water. The nausea passed. My disorientation was largely mental.

"I'll never understand how someone that obsessive-compulsive can be such a slob," he continued as I struggled to reunite my mind with my body. "I chalk it up as classic middle child behavior," I said absentmindedly. This was not the first time we've had this conversation. "How long have I been here anyway?"

"They took you in the day before yesterday. You've been kinda out of it the whole time. Sometimes, I thought you were awake but you were talking in your sleep. The doctor said it was normal. That your brain was trying to protect itself."

I had been asleep. I had dreamed.

I was really struggling with all of this. On one hand, everything that Liam was telling me made perfect sense. I had allowed myself to get so sick, trying to deny that I was. My body had not been able to take it any longer. It had shut down. I'd been unconscious. Between the soaring fever and the drugs, it's no wonder that my dreams were dynamic.

The real problem I could see was that I didn't want to accept it. I didn't want to believe Liam.

I should've been relieved that I wasn't hit by a truck, but I was absurdly too upset to recognize my fortunes. The tragedy is that the only boy I had met that was remotely interesting wasn't even real.

I thought that I had braced myself for the worst but I had not anticipated this. He had been all in my head. It was ridiculous to be overwhelmed by this. Ridiculous to be affected by a dream.

"You'll probably have to stay another day or two," Liam continued. "I know the doctors talked about having you take some tests to make sure the fever didn't cause any kind of damage. Well, no more than usual anyway." He grinned teasingly at me.

I blinked back the tears.

I tried to act normal to reorient myself. The doctor came to check on me. She was a sharply dressed woman who was both nice and stern. I received a lecture on the dangers of high fevers. There was a list of ways on how to prevent it from happening again. After listening to my take on the incident, she suspected that I suffered a migraine that might have triggered it all. She launched into a detailed explanation of what a migraine was and even involved a 3D model of a brain to help illustrate her lecture. I glazed over when she started talking hemispheres and just nodded every third sentence.

She asked me random questions that were supposed to test my brain functions. I left out mention of my hallucinations.

It … and he … had become a more personal experience, and I wanted it to remain that way.

Locke and Dad arrived sometime between flashcards and the questionnaires. I was doing well right up until they started asking questions on current events. She claimed it was to test my memory but I suspect it was to shame me into doing better in my U.S. Government class.

"She lives in her own little world, Doc. She thought Al Gore was an impressionist painter," Locke teased.

"I never thought that."

"In fairness, I may have heard that said about him before." That was Liam's version of standing up for me.

"I never thought that."

"Moving on," Dad urged.

"I never thought that," I mumbled, unwilling to let it go. Locke winked at me. I glared. The doctor moved on.

When all the tests were done and it was revealed that I was no worse for wear, I received more lectures from both Dad and Locke similar to the one I had heard from Liam and the doctor.

I toyed with the idea that maybe the truck did hit me and I was in hell after all.

Dad left the room to speak with the doctor while Locke drove Liam back to the house to help unpack a few things before he flew back to Chicago in the morning. My brothers … men of action.

With nothing to distract me, my thoughts returned to him.

Every detail of his face down to the fresh cut on his lip. The way his hair couldn't hide the intensity in his eyes no matter how much it covered. The wrinkle between his brows. I could see that clearly. I could see him.

He didn't feel like part of an elusive dream. He felt so real that my heart started to race at the thought of him. I had to take deep breaths when the monitors threatened to go off.

He was literally a dream guy. So what? That wasn't crazy. Everyone had one.

I accepted this feeble line of logic. Not only did I accept it, but I held on to it in desperation. It would be my defense for how I was feeling. It would be my extremely thin cord to sanity.

I was excited to go back to sleep. If he wasn't real, dreaming about him would be better than nothing. It was easy to convince people that I was tired and just wanted to rest. I had them shut the lights and draw the curtains. I closed my eyes and lay in bed thinking only thoughts of him.

When I finally did fall asleep, He was not waiting for me in my dreams. Not that night nor in the nights that followed.

Colors

I was cutting up onions in the kitchen when Dad came home from work.

Since I got home from the hospital, I was banned from doing anything remotely tiring. Dad even had me stocked with a new set of high-grade watercolor pencils, a sketch pad, and three boxes of Gobstoppers.

It was an open invitation for me to hole myself in my room for extended periods of time.

I had initially accepted solitude with enthusiasm but after producing repetitive drawings of my one elusive dream, I was beginning to feel that art had become counterproductive to the restful state that I was trying to achieve. I spent days dreaming with my eyes open and nights in frustration.

Liam and Locke had gotten most of the things unpacked and put away. That meant I had only a vague idea where things were because my brothers are disciples of the principle out of sight, out of mind when it came to mess. Their idea of unpacking was to take things from the box and stuff them randomly into cabinets. Complete with packing material.

"If it protects the stuff in transit, it can protect it in stasis," was Locke's declaration when I confronted him about it. I found extra blankets beside canned goods in the pantry. Nice. Thanks, bro. All that time and effort I spent color-coding everything was completely ignored.

Being the youngest can suck sometimes.

I was also banned from cooking. That meant an uninterrupted stream of takeout food for the past week and a half. While it bothered no one else, it bothered me. I like pizza just as much as the next teenager but there's only so much of it I can stand consecutively. I needed something that didn't come with its own jingle.

Locke had finally flown back to Los Angeles for school. Since school started a week earlier for him, I was left home alone while Dad went to work. No more bouncers in the kitchen.

One of the perks about the small college town where we now lived was the environment. There was a grocer right next to the not-a-Starbucks cafe down the street. A little further down was a home improvement store, a bank, gelato, and a used book store that sold things like yummy smelling candles. It was a good 20-minute walk one way but the weather had cooled significantly in the past week and it was good to be outside.

"Should you be cooking?" Dad asked disapprovingly as he dumped a load of colored folders on one end of the counter. A few red ones spilled to the kitchen floor.

"Locke used to ask me the same thing but now he enjoys my bacon-chicken casserole," I answered defensively, putting the knife down and wiping my hands on a kitchen towel. I gave Dad the customary kiss on the cheek and helped him with his escaping office supplies.

"You know what I meant," he said, trying to rebalance the folders before finally just deciding to spread them all over the space I had recently just been able to clear out.

"Dad, the whole overprotective thing has peaked." I tossed a loose paper on top of his pile and started on the tomatoes. "School starts in three days. Surely by now you've decided I'm well enough to go to school, right? And if I can go to school, I can cook a dish."

He reluctantly agreed with me. There was no way he was going to keep me home from school.

"Take it easy in school, OK?" It was as if he needed to lecture me on something, no matter how inconsequential or unlikely.

I rolled my eyes. "Yes, Dad. Because there's a real danger that I may just join every single extra-curricular activity available to me," I said sarcastically. "I think you're confusing me with Liam, the overachiever. I'm the quirky yet lovable daughter that you just adore. "

He huffed at my disregard for his attempt at parenting. I smiled innocently at him. The true beauty about being the only girl on top of being the youngest was that I had leverage. I was brazenly his favorite. I could get away with anything. There hasn't been a single confrontation with him that hadn't gone my way at some point.

It was entirely understandable that Dad would have a soft spot for me. I was told repeatedly growing up how much I looked like my mother. I was the strongest link he had left to her. There was nothing he could deny me because there was nothing he would deny her.

My brothers learned quickly not to begrudge me for it. Instead, they found ways to use my clout to their advantage. It was no coincidence that most of the toys I "wanted" as a kid ended up in my brothers' hands.

"I could always skip school, stay home and paint some color on the walls of this house," I teased. He gave me his version of a parental disapproving look as he pulled out a book from his bag.

"Leave it," he said. "I've forgotten what white looked like living with you." He put on his reading glasses and headed toward the third bedroom, his converted office. This was the universal sign that the conversation has come to a close because he was heading down some intellectual road in his mind that only he traveled.

"My room is my domain," I reminded him before he retreated completely. "I get to do whatever I want in there."

I heard a grunt of some kind. "Dinner will be ready in half an hour!" I yelled through his closed door.

I visited the local home improvement store the following morning. I left right after Dad drove to work. I decided that I would not live in a white room out of boxes any longer. If I have to start school on Monday, I will wake up to my room. Not a room that cries asylum.

I think maybe it was just too close to the truth. I was losing my mind. I didn't need to be reminded of it in my own room.

I found myself standing in front of rows upon rows of paint chips. They had every conceivable color and shade. From sublime neutrals to glow-in-the-dark Martian Puke. An overly enthusiastic sign advertising color matching options loomed over the entire section.

Excuse me, can you color match my indecision.

My last room was the default baby pink I had since I was born. Since before I was born. My mom had painted the room herself; I instinctively knew it wasn't something I should undo. I tried plastering the walls with all sorts of photos, posters, and artwork to make it work for me, but it never really did. Pink was not me.

What *was* me?

I rolled the Gobstopper in my mouth. Maybe they'd color match that. It tasted like purple.

I contemplated going for the deeply dramatic look. but I wasn't sure how long I could live in a room that was swatted in Dark Plum and Black. Reds were too much emotional chaos. Orange was too bright. I stayed away from the neutrals. That was like conforming to me. It was pointless to paint if I did that.

After more than half an hour, I finally narrowed my choices. I held four different paint chips that were all shades of blue. Blue was a versatile color. Just like a favorite pair of jeans. It was casual, comfortable, and worked with anything. It was calm enough to be the dominant color for a bedroom and deep enough to elicit the artist in me. It made sense for me to gravitate toward it.

Blue Jeans. That was the way to go. Definitely.

The associate and another customer were arguing over what looked like a large plastic funnel. I played with the color chip in my hand while I waited for help at the counter.

It was the wrong color.

This was stupid. It shouldn't take me this long. I shut my eyes tightly to shake the feeling when I suddenly saw the right color. The perfect combination of colors that both saw my soul and reflected it. I was instantly energized. I abandoned the blue and scoured through the greens. The green and the gold.

The harmony I found in his eyes.

I plucked out what was labeled as Goldenrod. One color would not be enough.

I ran with this, not having the faintest idea how to make it work. I pulled out two more paint chips. One hint of green and a light shade of brown. Inspired, I brought my choices to the counter with confidence. I ordered two gallons of the Goldenrod and a pint each of the remaining two colors. It would be just enough for my little space.

I also had to add a few extra things ... lightweight painter overalls, an extendable roller, a paint tray, painter's tape, a plastic drop cloth, a sponge, and a smaller paintbrush. I handed the cashier my credit card, thinking that it was somehow going to be denied.

The card company would laugh at my choices, call my father, and in the span of 30 seconds, Dad would be on the other end of the phone yelling at my financial choices while the IRS descended on me in full riot gear.

I said keep the walls white, he'd yell. *Just leave them white!*

The transaction cleared. I exhaled. The universe approves.

It took me twice as long to walk home. Paint cans were unforgiving, digging into my hands and killing my circulation. I did not think this through. When I could finally see our new home in the distance, it was the push I needed to pop the favored red Gobstopper in my mouth and grit through the pain.

Finish strong, London! You've got this.

I was winded by the time I got home. My hands were numb. They were reminiscent of Polar Vortex winters in the Midwest. That was one way not to miss Illinois. I dumped the purchases near the back door and took a long drink of cold water from the kitchen. It was lunchtime.

I was eager to get started. I grabbed a banana and took the

stuff up to my room. I would consider myself the one-trip-or-die-tryin' kinda gal, but this time I made the extra trips. My hands deserved it. I was going to need them.

It took me a couple of hours to move everything to the center of the room, roll out the drop cloth, and tape off the edges of the wall. I wanted to do this right. I dug out my speakers and set them up outside the room. This called for an old school glam rock playlist. I popped a couple more Gobstoppers in my mouth and faced the blank canvas that was my bedroom.

Feeling like I was embarking on some kind of adventure, I stepped into the overalls and got to work. As I slathered on the first coat of Goldenrod paint, I thought of him.

I remembered how he looked standing by the tree. The first time I laid eyes on him. I remembered his confident stance, the square of his jaw, the smile that played on his lips, and the mystery in his eyes. The more I thought of him, the more feverishly I painted. I heard the timbre of his voice. I indulged in the scent of his proximity. I had caught a glimpse of his intangible soul in his analogous blade. Dangerous, misunderstood and bursting with potential. Tempered by beauty.

I lost myself in my daydreams that I hadn't noticed that the speakers were silent until I was done with all four walls. It was a nice, warm color but it was incomplete. I didn't stop to restart my playlist or wait for the paint to dry. Even as I threw the second color of paint on my walls with little rhyme or reason, I saw nothing in front of me but the gravity of his eyes. The eyes that held me in place and yet brought me to heights I had not imagined in just one afternoon.

In just a dream.

It was like working blind. I didn't see the colors I was working with. Just the colors I wanted it to be. Conventional painting techniques were forgotten. First going one way then another.

Blending, skewing, transforming. The colors were kinetic, without pattern. Unpredictable and could not be contained. I existed simultaneously in two realities. One dancing in the presence of magic and the other desperately working with imperfect materials to recreate it.

It was my goal to merge the two worlds. To create a portal in which I could travel easily between the two. Or, if given a choice, exist only in the other.

"What do you call this technique?"

The intrusion yanked me from my trance. I spun toward the door and saw Dad standing at the entrance with a slightly battered pizza box in his hands.

"Oh," I said, startled, "Hey, Dad. Home early?"

He shook his head. "Early? It's past seven, Sweetheart. I tried calling twice to tell you I was going to be late, but you didn't answer."

I didn't even hear the phone. I love that he wasn't even remotely worried.

"Sorry."

He nodded absentmindedly. "It looks good," he said, indicating the walls. I followed his gaze and saw my walls as an outsider would for the first time. Visible strokes of color blended together at some points and announced their individuality in others. It was a motionless ballet of colors, yet in constant dance. In spite of myself, I smiled. It turned out better than I thought I could do.

"Not what I was expecting, but it's good," he said.

"It wasn't what I was expecting either."

"Ah, I see you employed the Let's-See-What-Happens-When-We-Do-This technique."

"It's a London staple."

"I think it's a London invention," he teased affectionately. "Pizza?"

Now that I had been pulled back into this reality, I felt hunger stabbing at me. The thought of takeout pizza, which had been disgusting to me only two days ago, was inviting now. I had gone through the day with nothing but a banana and a box of Gobstoppers to sustain me.

"I'll meet you downstairs."

I closed the door and got out of the splattered overalls. I had paint caked on my hands and even some in my hair. It didn't look as good on me as it did on my walls.

The sun had almost disappeared on the horizon, throwing the room into another brilliant kaleidoscope of color. I looked back at my work, feeling both triumphant and an aching sense of longing at the same time.

I followed Dad downstairs for dinner.

It took me longer than I thought to pull out all the tape, clear the drop cloth, store the paint, and put my room back to working order. I left my belongings in boxes for now. They would have to wait another day.

I spent more than an hour in the tub soaking all the paint off. I prefer the efficiency of showers but tonight, sitting in water and letting the warm liquid do most of the work was significantly more appealing. The warm soapy water still had laboring left to do on the stubborn traces of paint under my nails, but I got out of the tub when it threatened to be a bed.

It was past midnight by the time I collapsed gratefully into bed, smelling of soap in a room that smelled of fresh paint. The moon bathed my room in soft light that would've been beautiful had I the awareness to see it. As it was, I was asleep before my body had even warmed the sheets.

Unhealthy

I was sitting on a bench in the middle of a crowded shopping mall. Unnaturally bright fluorescent lights were almost enough to make the scent of retail mixed with fresh pretzels a visible haze. It was all strangely disorienting. I had green cotton candy in one hand and was watching shoppers I didn't recognize do their business. The candy melted into sweet satisfaction in my mouth.

"Aren't you dead?" I recognized his voice before I turned to look at him. Ethan was standing beside the bench like a fixture. His head cocked to the side and one eyebrow hiding under his messy hair.

Just as I remembered him. No, he looked better. There was only a suggestion of the cut above his lip. It looked like he had at least washed his face earlier that day. He had on an old olive-colored army jacket open over his dark Paradigm shirt, sleeves folded up to his elbows.

"You aren't that lucky." I offered him some candy. He kept his hands in his pockets and shook his head a fraction, watching me in suspicion. I was thrilled, grinning at him. Somehow, someway, he was here. It wasn't the fever. It wasn't drugs. He was just as vivid as before. Maybe even more so, now that I was relaxed and not lost in the middle of the Blair Witch Project.

I was immensely grateful that I wasn't sitting in my jammies.

He considered me for a moment before sitting beside me. Suddenly, we were alone. Everything around us melted into unimportance.

"OK," he said, "What's going on?"

"You're a figment of my imagination," I said brightly. The bench gave way a little as he leaned back, crossing his arms across his chest and stretching his legs. "I'm a figment of your imagination?"

I popped more candy in my mouth. It melted on contact and was made sweeter by his presence. "Uh-huh," I nodded.

"You have a sadistic imagination, then."

"It's quite difficult to control," I admitted gamely. He snorted and I watched the muscles around his jaw tighten. He twitched without moving, a wild creature that looked out of place outside of his forest.

"How come we're at the mall today?" I asked him. He didn't answer right away. He looked at me for a long time like he was deciding whether I was worth his attention. "Since I'm a figment of your imagination then shouldn't you be able to tell me what's going on?" I shrugged.

"I have no control over these things. I'm just a participant." I had been trying to hold on to this for weeks. I had been trying to prove that he wasn't just part of a dream that was too quickly forgotten.

"Of course you are." He deliberated another moment, took a breath in surrender and said, "I'm here because this is what normal kids are supposed to do."

"You're pretending to be normal?" He nodded.

"Are you succeeding?" I probed teasingly.

"I think I'm failing miserably," he said. He was being wry. "But it wouldn't be the first time."

We were both silent for a while. I happily ate my candy. He watched me happily eat my candy. I couldn't measure time passing. There was a lot I wanted to ask him, at the very least to hear his voice, but it was a comfortable silence, where I could be content in just his presence.

"You like lolly," he said as I squished the remaining amount into a small ball and popped it in my mouth. I tossed the rolled-up paper into the bin beside me and brushed my hands on my jeans, the same ones I've had on all day.

"Most candy, I guess." I thought about the box of Gobstoppers that were ever-present in my school pack and the Tootsie Roll stash I kept in my desk. Candy kept my energy level up.

"I like candy. You like to play with knives. I really don't think you should be judging me."

His eyebrows furrowed. I smiled.

Without warning, he reached out and grabbed my hand. His touch was warm and strong. There was an urgency that I couldn't identify. His eyes flared when we made contact but he recovered quickly and pulled us both to our feet. "Come on," he urged. "Let's get out of here." It wasn't up for debate.

He pulled me behind him as we made our way to the exit. I didn't pay any attention to the stores we passed or the distance we covered. I was wholly absorbed by the feel of his hand on mine. A sensation that I shouldn't feel in a dream. I shouldn't be able to feel the thrill that ran up my arm in goosebumps, but I did. I felt it amplified.

The unfamiliar mall opened up to a city street and beyond it, a park. The yellow sunlight, a contrast to the artificial lights inside the mall, bounced off the paved roads and made them shine like they were embedded with little diamonds. A breeze tempered the warmth with the smell of fresh grass. I smiled wider and he glanced over his shoulder at me, still not letting go of my hand. "We're going to have to cross the street. Don't rabbit."

My heart skipped a beat. I nodded even if I couldn't honestly promise him that.

We crossed the street without incident. When we got to the park, I thought he would stop but he kept going. He walked us past a couple of people walking their dogs, the fountain, the kids in flip flops on skateboards, the old lady knitting, the gravel walk, and the monument of some unknown hero. He dragged me willingly along. The way the park sloped, I almost couldn't see the mall anymore. He walked through one of the bushes that lined the path when he let go of my hand. The ghost of his hold remained on my palm and I cradled it to my chest unconsciously. His eyes still on me, he sat at the foot of one of the trees.

He pulled out his knife, opened it without me even seeing him flick his wrist, and balanced the two halves of the handle with his fingers. He wasn't watching what he was doing. He was watching me. I sat cross-legged on the grass across from him. "I take it that you've given up pretending to be normal?"

He continued to twirl the knife around his hand as if the motion was soothing to him. "It was a lost cause anyway," he admitted. He mumbled something else to himself, and the words seemed to bother him. He continued to stare. I waited.

"I can't suss this out," he said after a while.

"Maybe we make up the rules as we go along," I replied brightly. It's a London staple, I almost said aloud. I expected him to raise his eyebrows as he often did but they knitted together in concentration instead.

"Hmmm." That was all he was inclined to say.

Flip. Flip. Flip.

The knife was making quick somersaults in the air. This was slightly more awkward than the mall for me but suited him better. I shifted a little and pursed my lips, thinking of something to say. "So …."

He didn't help. The intensity of his stare made me fidgety. *You're in a dream, London. Whatever. Just go with it.* "No Paradigm today?" I asked.

I thought talking about something uniquely associated with him would soften him up but he looked increasingly confused and frustrated. As if everything I said exasperated him. "No," he said slowly, in contrast to how fast the knife was flying through his fingers. "But then," he added. "Not much time left for that anyway, eh?"

"Is it military then? Or a life of crime?" I raised both eyebrows innocently, an invitation to let him know neither answer would surprise or scare me. He snorted and a smile finally tugged on the edge of his lips. He didn't answer. "What do you hate about it," I prodded. "The authority?"

The knife flew up in the air and he caught it by the hilt with his left hand. "I don't get along well with people, remember? Can you imagine how much more that would apply to people who are telling me what to do?"

"Aren't there always rules? I would imagine the Paradigm would have a whole lot in place."

He seemed to accept my line of questioning without difficulty. Almost as if he was expecting it. "The 'rules' in Paradigm aren't there to streamline you and make you into some sort of human lemming. It's not a big deal if you break them." I can tell that he's broken a lot of them.

"In the force, you aren't a person. You're a soldier. You have to be just like every other soldier. If they don't like the way you tied your boots, you get beat up. Brilliant."

I shrugged. "Then you should just make sure you tie your boots right."

He gave me a look of long-suffering. "I suppose the loss of one's personality and identity is not considered a big waste, is it?"

I scoffed. "Don't be melodramatic. It's a job. You just have to meet expectations when you're on the job. When you're not, you're still you. I mean, if you have a strong sense of yourself, I doubt even the military can take that away from you, right?"

He rolled his eyes. "It figures a chick like you would love soldiers to the days."

"What's that supposed to mean?" It was hard to react when I didn't know if I was being insulted or not.

He was enjoying this. "She'll be 'right. I don't even know.'" I seethed at him. How was I supposed to react to a gibe that I couldn't understand?

"Look, don't get all worked up about it now, eh," he said. The knife stopped spinning and was just rocking from one side to the other in his light grip.

"Why not?"

He lowered his chin and looked at me through his lashes. The half-smile playing maddeningly on his lips. "I'm not sure my psyche can take it." His gaze was compelling. I was instantly hypnotized.

This boy was a balance of contradictions. He was rugged and fascinating. Far, far more interesting than any high school kid back in my sheltered world. His hair fell over his eyes, designed to conceal as much as possible. He was unassuming in his stance but bold in his word. He hunched when he spoke like he was sharing a secret. He's likely the type to leave his dirty clothes on his bedroom floor and has never put the toilet seat down.

Frankly, He wasn't what I was expecting to dream of. What about those dark-haired hunks with the six-packs and rippling biceps? Why aren't I dreaming about them?

But his eyes ….

"What color are your eyes?" I asked.

Surprised, he fumbled the blade. It bounced off his hand toward him and the ultra-sharp edge slit a gash on his arm even as he flinched out of the way. He swore.

I was on my feet and beside him before I knew it. I knelt down. "Are you OK?" The knife was on the grass, not a stain on the blade.

He looked up and his face was close to mine. Nearly as close as it had been in the forest. I smelled the hints of laundry detergent and soap but this time blended together with something else; a slightly musky scent that I couldn't place. It was pleasant. Incredibly inviting.

"She'll be 'right. Happens all the time." I took a look at the gash and saw that he was right. It wasn't deep. His blood was content to stay close to the wound and not make a mess.

"A mere flesh wound?" I asked, settling down beside him. Close enough that our hands were almost touching. A blade or two of grass between us. "That's what you get for playing with sharp objects."

He picked up the knife almost reverently, flipped it shut and stuck in back into the band of his pants. "Small price to pay," he said without looking at me.

He unfolded the arm of his jacket to cover up the wound. His forced nonchalance made me believe that he did so to hide the evidence more because he was embarrassed by his lapse rather than because it actually hurt. He kept one leg raised and rested his injured arm on it.

"Do you get cut up a lot?"

"Not even," he shrugged. "Back when I was green, sure." He shifted and pulled out a silver, unadorned Zippo lighter from his pants pocket with his right hand. It matched the chain on his wrist. He flicked it so that it opened and a tiny flame responded to the action. Without closing it, he danced the lighter through his fingers like it had a mind of its own, the flame chasing behind a second late.

"I like having something to play with when I think. It helps me focus," he mumbled. We both watched the flame before he shut the lighter and made it bounce in the air. This wasn't for focus. He was showing off.

"You know they sell these things called fidget spinners," I made quotes in the air just to be even more obnoxious. "Maybe you've heard of them?"

He gave me a withering look, recognizing that I had just rained on his parade. I laughed. His show was now less impressive than he had intended.

"You smoke?" I was surprised because I didn't smell it on him. I was usually sensitive to it.

He shrugged. "Used to. Honestly though, I only rolled a durrie because I fancy carrying around a lighter."

"That doesn't make sense."

"Don't you think it's a bit mad to have a lighter when you don't smoke? I felt like I needed to justify having it on my person."

"I suppose your lighter may be the safer alternative to your knife." He snorted. "Unless you're sitting in the middle of dry pines and you drop it. Start a forest fire. Devastate nature. Kill all the wildlife.

"Incidentally, that's about the same time I stopped smoking," he said casually with a smile. It was difficult to tell if he was serious.

He spun the open lighter like a top on his thumb and index finger. "At least, with the knife, the only one that gets hurt is me."

"Maybe what you really need is a set of chopsticks. Like the fidget spinner, they too can come in a variety of colors."

He shook his head. "Where's the fun in that?" Where's the danger in that, is what he didn't say.

"Maybe you'll poke your eye out?" I offered. He grinned. The lighter settled on his knuckles, he looked at me full in the face. "What is all this attention about my eyes?" He was teasing.

I smiled back at him, lifting my chin in mock defiance. "Maybe I need a closer inspection to figure out what color they are. Poking an eye out helps us both." The smile on his lips was the only hint he gave of his intentions before he leaned toward me deliberately, completely filling my vision.

"I like my eyes where they are," he said in a low voice. "Maybe we can compromise. Is this close enough for you?"

The air was charged with emotional electricity. I was shocked by the current but I couldn't move. His breath was strong and steady, blowing his scent directly at my face. I was light-headed, afraid to say anything because I'd be incoherent. Surely start stuttering. Babbling.

The mischief danced in his eyes. The green was almost alive, swimming in the gold. A blend of such incredible color. I realized, with regret, that I could never capture that in paint. Regardless of how well I thought it had originally turned out.

I swallowed. "Um," I finally whispered, feeling far from being able to participate in conversation. "They aren't blue ..."

He leaned back and settled into his original position. Still close but not nearly as intense. "When you can't figure out what color it is, it's thrown into the catch-all category of hazel."

Hazel. When you can't figure it out. I smiled at how his eye color could be a metaphor for himself.

"Now," he began in all seriousness, not a trace of a smile. "Let's learn more about you."

Learning about me wasn't nearly as interesting as learning about him but as dreams go, isn't that what it's all about? I sighed. As long as he was around while I sought self-enlightenment, I wasn't going to complain.

"What do you want to know?"

The open invitation made him think. I could see him considering and discarding several questions at a time. The crease between his eyebrows getting deeper. I was relaxed under his scrutiny, a far cry from our first meeting. He set his jaw, took a deep breath, and let it out slowly. He visibly relaxed.

"What color are your eyes?" he asked finally, a touch of humor back on his face.

I looked at him strangely. "What do you mean "what color are my eyes"?" They weren't remotely as confusing as his. One boring color … the same color as everyone in my family history. Never deviating.

"It's a simple question, eh. You shouldn't get your panties all up in a bunch." He was definitely amused.

"They're fairly easy to figure out. They don't fall into the can't-tell-what-it-is-hazel category. Why would you even have to ask?"

He closed his eyes, leaned back and the smile played across his lips. "When you're color blind, it's usually safer to ask these things rather than to assume."

"..."

When I didn't answer, he opened one eye to look at me. "What's the matter? Are you prejudiced against the color impaired?"

"The color impaired," I repeated, mocking him. He nodded.

"How does that work?"

He opened both eyes. "Not the way it should, I suppose." I laughed.

"I mean, how do you see colors?"

"In plaid. Sometimes, checkers. Occasionally polka dots."

"Wait. What?"

His eyes crinkled and for the first time, I saw a flash of his teeth when he smiled. He was obviously having fun at my expense. "It's not a deal," he said. But it was to me. I've never met a color-blind person before. Everything about him was exceptional. "Do you see color at all?"

He rolled his eyes. "Yes, I see color. I'm not a bat. Just sometimes not the right ones."

"You mean, I can tell you my eyes are any color and you'd have to take my word for it?" I brightened at the idea of being able to exchange my eye color in this pleasant fantasy I've created.

"I know they aren't red," he said. "To me, they're brown but they could well be blue or gray." I sighed. I wasn't a good liar to begin with and I didn't want to lie to him.

"They're brown," I conceded.

"Why is that a bad thing?" he asked, noting my disappointment.

"Brown is boring," I whined a little. "Not exactly the prettiest color in the world, you know? No fascinating shades like blue. No mystery. No enchantment. The plain, boring mud brown."

He was thoughtful "Not necessarily. Brown is warm, comforting and strong. It's the color of nature." He tapped the bark of the tree he was leaning against for emphasis. "It's hot chocolate on a snowy day. The coffee that wakes you up in the morning. Sweet syrup on plain, boring Vanilla ice cream. Really, who wants to eat a blue chocolate bar anyway?"

He leaned closer to me and stared right into my newly deemed wonderfully colored eyes. "I like brown. I think brown is a rather pretty color." If he couldn't hear the hammering of my pulse, I was sure that it was sending palpable vibrations across the space between us.

"Is it your favorite color?" I asked teasingly. There was light in his eyes. "It is now." My heart took off, chasing the breath that he effortlessly took away.

"And is hazel your favorite color?" he asked me in return. I swallowed. "I like blue." He leaned back again and closed his eyes in mock pain. "Ah, the story of my life." His sigh relaxed the atmosphere. I collected myself.

"If you're color blind, how do you know the color of your own eyes?" I asked.

"Because it's on every single one of my documents since I was a child." I heard the unsaid, obviously in his tone. At the same time, he looked as if he doubted that information. His reaction was confusing and challenging to interpret. I wasn't navigating this conversation successfully.

"You have any siblings, London?" he asked before I could backpedal.

"I have three older brothers," I replied. "No sisters." He started to play with his Zippo again.

"Your poor mother," he commented.

"My mom died when I was really young."

"I'm sorry," he said automatically, tensing a little.

I shrugged. "I don't really know much. Dad doesn't usually talk about her." I played with the end of my shoelace, not meeting his eyes. "She probably couldn't take all the testosterone. Dad and brothers raised me. It was like being in a wolf pack." I laughed at my own description. "I learned all the things necessary for a young lady to survive in this world."

"Such as," he prompted.

I left my shoelace alone and considered his question seriously. My brothers each had their own set of expertise and each one did their best to recruit me to their respective camps. "Such as the secret to every Zelda game ever made." Chase's obsession with old school video games and his need to transfer his fluent geek language to me happened early on in my life. "Why Star Trek: The Original Series still rocks and the subtle genius behind every comic book."

Locke's influence came later. "I also learned how to throw a successful party, say the right things at family gatherings and strategically park yourself by the food at the buffet table."

Liam may have been the most successful because as dad's right hand, he dominated over us all. "I was taught how to load, aim and fire a gun, but none of them have ever owned one and for every lesson I was given, I received an equally lengthy lecture on why I shouldn't be near one." I rolled my eyes at the memory. "They're all just protective."

"Did your dad give you a hard time when you were lost in the wops?" he asked.

I didn't know what to make of that question. "He almost had a heart attack, I was told." I did not continue.

"Hmmm," was all he said.

"What about you?" I asked before he looked deeper into my hesitation. I was afraid that if I became fully aware that I was dreaming, it would all come to a stop. It took me this long to get here; I wasn't ready to leave. There was much more I wanted to know.

"I'm never lost in the wops."

I rolled my eyes. "I meant, any siblings?"

He answered slowly, but without hesitation. "I don't know. I don't think so."

It was an odd thing to say. He continued as if analyzing his own words, which made little sense to me. "I've been in Paradigm since I was 7, picked up for trying to swipe some rum from the dairy. I don't remember."

"At 7-year-old?"

One side of his mouth curved upward. "It would probably explain why I don't remember much." My eyes were wide in disbelief. "No one claimed me from holding so they transferred me to Paradigm. Unless you're admitted with full papers, you just have to assume that you're alone." He shrugged like it was nothing.

I didn't realize that he was an orphan. Considering the tight relationship I have with my family, I couldn't imagine not having that in my life. I'd have no anchor. I'd go insane.

"Wow."

That was my eloquent response to his revelation.

"Is that hard to deal with?" I asked.

"I play with knives and set things on fire," he admitted gamely. "Your presence here is clearly an indication of my unstable mind."

I gave him the most sarcastic look I could muster. "Gee, thanks. Thanks a lot." He reached over and wrapped his arm around my shoulder like we were buddies and squeezed once. It was hard to pretend that I was trying to be upset with him.

"She'll be 'right. I'm starting to enjoy your company." How could my face feel flushed and my hands feel this cold at the same time?

"It's not really all that uncommon. Some people even have it worse. Likely, I think it's just me," he said generously, looking away from me and staring at the lighter that resumed its gymnastics between his fingers. "There are choice programs out there. Most other kids get by without being half as messed up. Focus on the right things. Build the right bridges. I'm the hogan that falls into every open manhole."

Flip. Spin. Flip.

"Others eventually learn how to swim instead of sink, while you willingly allow yourself to drown. It's easier that way, eh. Not much effort involved. What others achieve, you call stupid. You think it was never meant for you so you don't try. Not worth the disappointment. Why reach out when every hand that you've held only slaps you across the face or belts you in the back?"

His head was down. I couldn't see his expression properly. I saw his eyes tighten and couldn't even imagine the memories in his head.

"You cuss at the real people trying to help you, start fights for no reason, miss lessons, do drugs, and run away. You always come back at the end of the day. At the core of it all, you know that it's because you're a right coward and don't want to admit it. Nowhere else to go."

He sighed. "Then at some point, you have to stop blaming the system and the gods. You realize that you're only here because you allowed it to happen. You closed your own doors. Cut all ties. Until you run out of excuses. You can only hold out a little hope before you decide that there's nothing meant for you." The lighter closed with an audible click.

I had pulled my legs up and wrapped my arms around them

while he spoke. His voice sounded empty and hollow, a shell of strong emotions that have been snuffed for his own safety. It affected me so much that I wouldn't have been able to stop myself from crying if he said anything more. He took a deep breath before facing me fully, a tight smile on his face.

"You're still here," he said.

I lay my head on my hands and said honestly, "I don't want to go."

He studied me for a moment and said quietly, "I don't think I want you to either." I smiled. He shook his head and closed his eyes. "This can't be healthy."

"No," I agreed. "I don't think it is."

Mode Of Transportation

I didn't move even when I realized that I was awake. I kept my eyes closed. The lingering images in my head dissipated along with the dream. What remained was a weak contrast to the vibrant state Ethan was alive in. It was as if I had left something behind but couldn't remember what it could be.

I opened my eyes in submission, knowing that both he and sleep would evade me now. I stared at my newly painted walls. I had been proud of how it turned out just a few hours before but now, fresh from seeing his eyes again, the art was unsatisfactory, flat, and lacking. Even when the first rays of light filled my room, I didn't move.

"Rise and shine, sleepyhead," Dad's muffled voice came from behind my closed door.

It was Sunday.

"It's my last day of freedom," I yelled back. "Leave me alone!"

Being Dad, of course, he ignored me. He opened the door

and popped his head inside. "Get up. We have things to do today." Years of reading the laugh lines on his face alerted me that he was up to something. I was instantly suspicious. "Now I know I don't want to get up," I said, making a show of pulling the covers around me tightly.

He sighed.

"This was supposed to be a surprise but I really don't want to start the day arguing with you." He crossed the room and sat at the foot of my bed. "We're going to buy you a bike."

A bike.

He waited for my reaction, as if he expected me to jump right out of bed in excitement. What was I? Eight? I hadn't owned a bike since I was 11.

"Like a bicycle?"

He sighed again. I'm so confused.

"Why?"

Clearly disappointed, he explained, "I don't think you noticed, Sweetheart, but this is essentially a bicycling community. Every road has a designated bike lane. Every store has a place to park your bike. More than 80 percent of the student body rides a bike to school."

"You so made that number up," I accused.

"You'll never know," he said with absolute confidence. "The point is, hardly anyone drives a car around here unless they have to. You don't drive. As I see it, you could walk everywhere … or you can ride."

I thought about this. A bike. My own means of transportation. I don't have to take the bus. Hold the phone. I didn't even have to learn how to drive.

It's as if I was made to live here.

It took two full minutes for my brain to process this. I was not a morning person, and Dad knew this well. He waited patiently.

"We're going bike shopping?" I was seeing the appeal. This was like buying a car small-town style. We were going to get me some wheels.

"Yes, we're going bike shopping." This man of infinite patience.

I smiled. Seeing my genuine delight, he smiled too. "Wow. Thanks, Dad! You're the best!"

"This is what I'm saying," he declared under my hug.

It used to be that a cool bike was determined by the number of accessories one can attach to it. Neon spinners? Glow in the dark paint? Rocking it.

We walked into a store that spoke about low profile cantilever brakes and carbon alloy frames.

"What do you plan to do with your bike?" asked a man who introduced himself as Richard. Richard looked more like a salesman than a man who actually biked anywhere. He had the practiced smile and the friendly-but-not-overly-familiar voice down pat. His slightly crumpled button-down shirt tucked neatly into pleated khakis.

I was hoping to host a cooking show on it, Richard.

"... um ... pedal?" That was a genuine effort not to sound sarcastic. I still earned a warning look from my father.

Dude. I tried.

Richard wasn't fazed. "I sure hope so! Are we thinking we're going to be tackling mountain trails?"

I was appalled. "Yeah, no."

Dad laughed. "She needs it as her primary source of transportation … to and from school. That sort of thing."

Richard was delighted. Progress made thanks to the adult in the room. He started to lead us to another area of the store. Dad walked next to him, and I lagged behind, running my fingers on metal and ringing all the bells I walked by.

"Pavement riding then," Richard was saying. "I suppose speed isn't as great a factor as durability and stability."

"Yes to stability," I chimed in from behind. "Can we call that the deciding factor?"

They both ignored me.

"She'll need some good grip on the tires and strong brakes …"

I rolled my eyes and popped a Gobstopper in my mouth. We walked past an honest to-goodness unicycle. A unicycle. They actually sold them to the public. Who knew?

What started as a discussion over roads turned into Richard asking Dad about his car. The two were now in animated conversation over the challenges of being a Bimmer owner.

Well played, Richard.

I found a chair by a stack of magazines. I sat and pulled out my phone. This seemed to be an opportunity for some time-sink mindless phone games. "I'll be over here in case you need me …"

They didn't need me. Not until it was time for me to return and agree to everything that they pre-decided was best for me. Because, you know, it was my decision, right?

I did have an actual say in the color, though. The sleek light gray with the most minimal of stickers won over the red, white, and blue contrast that yelled #1 Patriotic-Citizen-of-the-Free-World.

Dad sprung for the fee for it to be assembled in-store. He also threw in a fancy bike lock and helmet to match.

Let's be honest. It's technically Dad spending on the bike; so it's not as if I had any right to complain. Not that there was anything to really complain about. Admittedly, it was a pretty epic-looking bike.

We had lunch at the neighboring pancake house while we waited for my bike to be completed. The weather-worn sign in front identified the place as "Caden's". It was a small corner restaurant with cream-colored clapboard and green trim. The tables had a little laminated sign advertising free wifi.

An older maternal-type server, Cindy, chatted us up while she filled our glasses with water. Dad was enjoying this small town camaraderie.

"Well, glad you found your way to us," she said. "Did you need a minute or did you know what you wanted to order?"

"Phad Thai?"

"Sweetheart, this is more of a breakfast place," Dad started to say with a laugh. Cindy interrupted him.

"Chicken or Tofu?"

Dad stopped speaking. I met his baffled look with a triumphant smile.

"Chicken, please."

"Honey," Cindy said to Dad, "We serve all things your appetite wants. If it isn't on the menu, we've probably got something even better." She winked.

I think I found my favorite restaurant.

"You can ride your bike to and from school. You'll have more flexibility with your schedule and exercise to boot. I don't care if other kids don't wear it but you have to wear a helmet."

I rolled my eyes. "Yes, Dad, I will wear the helmet," I assured him as I juggled to contain the Pad Thai on my fork. Looking cool had never been my forte.

"You're going to have to learn the rules of the road," Dad warned between mouthfuls of steak and potatoes. I nodded. "I've never had a problem with rules."

I had gone almost the entire morning without thinking directly of Ethan. Dad's casual reference to authority brought back both the pleasant and uncomfortable thoughts. I had been so excited to see Ethan in my dreams again that I didn't pause to consider the ramifications.

He had evolved into more than just a two-dimensional idea of a perfect guy. He was far from perfect. He was hard to read. Obviously conflicted. He was so different from who I am, yet I related to him instantly.

Of course I could relate to him - he was my dream. It didn't explain why he confused me so much. Why he felt like a part of me, yet a completely different entity.

I went beyond being satisfied at the idea of him being a representation of my dream guy to desperately wanting to believe that he truly existed as a person. Not an idea but a flesh and blood individual.

Maybe he does. I argued with myself, wanting it to be true.

What if?

What if there was someone just like him? Someone I could even meet in school tomorrow. What if these weren't regular dreams but some kind of precognition? A distorted perception of a similar future event. People talk about it all the time. Déjà vu.

There are movies about this sort of thing. TV shows.

Great, I thought. *I've willingly volunteered to be an episode of Black Mirror.*

But I couldn't stifle the excitement that maybe I would meet someone like him in school. The idea took root in my mind so quickly that before I had finished my meal, I was convinced of it. School had never been so desirable to me before.

We took the bike home by lashing it to the top of Dad's X5. I spent the rest of the afternoon reacquainting myself with balancing on two wheels and learning routes.

What they say about never forgetting how to ride a bike was an outright lie to me as I wobbled down the road. I blame the 20 extra gear speeds that I've never had to deal with before. It used to be that the bike went as fast or as slow as I pedaled. This monstrosity had gear shifting, dual braking, and a fancy suspension. At this point, riding that damn unicycle was infinitely more plausible.

Dad questioned aloud if the bike was a good idea.

"Maybe we should just return it," I suggested, gripping the brake handle in panic and falling over.

"Can't. I think you scratched it." He lifted his phone and took a picture of me, half on the ground, the frustration all around me being the perfect photo filter. I growled at him. He smiled. "Immortalized."

"#WhyIMurderedMyFather"

"#ParentalPrerogative," he retorted.

Despite Dad's doubts, by dinner time, I was confidently rolling downhill and effortlessly pedaling up. I didn't fall when I turned, and I enjoyed the feel of the warm wind whipping my face. No motion sickness here. This monstrosity was my new crush. I was already more in love with this bike than I was with any car I've been in.

"Best idea ever," I yelled as I blew past my father. This time, I smiled for the camera.

We had leftover pizza for dinner and I was ready for bed before nine. I convinced Dad that I was just tired and needed a good night's sleep to prepare for my big first day of school.

An hour and a half later, I was still restlessly awake on my bed, staring at the walls that were a lame representation of Ethan's eyes. Eyes I didn't see even when sleep finally took me.

Institution

With all the fuss of the first day of school, one would think that I would be a bit less distracted. The mismatched socks and backwards shirt were indications that my head wasn't on particularly straight either. I had arrived early on my new, slightly scratched bike, skipping breakfast because I was too nervous to eat. Not so nervous about the different environment but the possibility of the new people I would meet.

The new person I hoped to meet.

I started out less graceful than I would've liked with my pack being a new factor that I had not previously practiced with. By the time I was two blocks from the house, my confidence returned. My world's promise looked incredibly bright. I was flying.

I was the first one at the office. It was probably a good thing because everyone I met was friendly, not yet overwhelmed by the rush of the school day. The administrative official was a tall, thin woman with platinum blonde hair and sporting a funky necklace that contrasted her otherwise neutral attire. She was surprisingly sweet. She had a good sense of humor and did her best to make me feel welcome right away.

I was handed my schedule and a few sheets of loose paper, a couple of which covered the basic code of conduct, dress code and orientation rules. Others had important information and numbers, a list of events and organizations. One was a map of the campus. I stuffed them all in my pack.

The school was significantly smaller than my last one. There was only one main building other than the gym. The office was up front past the doors that would be locked during school hours. Everything was efficiently laid out. Most of my classes were on the second floor. Even someone like me couldn't get lost.

I paid little attention to the entire experience.

I had some ludicrous fantasy that the first boy I'd bump into would be him. It would be kismet. Instant attraction. He'd have had dreams about me too, and we'd have found each other in this big, bad world.

Not so much.

It wasn't him. The first boy I met had longer curly reddish hair and freckles. He smiled at me, albeit confused, as I looked at him half in accusation and half in disappointment. Not my boy.

Trying to be as subtle as possible, I was searching the faces of all the guys that I passed, who possessed the slightest similarity to him. One was the right height and nothing else. Another had the same build. Maybe the same hair.

But no one had his eyes.

Not one.

I was already feeling dejected. Reality had sunk in. This wasn't a fairytale. This wasn't a dream.

I scanned my classmates quickly while I walked into my homeroom. I already knew that I would not find anyone remotely like him.

The enthusiasm that began in earnest yesterday had crashed before the first period even started.

I am a mediocre student so I found a seat near the middle. I didn't need to stay up front under the scrutiny of all, and I learned that teachers pay more attention to what students are doing at the back of the classroom than anywhere else.

At least they did back where I grew up.

I smiled tentatively at the girl sitting beside me as I took an empty seat. She had long blonde hair, blue eyes, a fantastic tan, and the most complementary shade of blue eyeshadow. She looked back at me in surprise and gave me a once over.

"New girl," she concluded aloud. I braced myself. She was probably a cheerleader, and I was probably sitting in her best friend's seat.

To my surprise, she smiled widely. "I'm Brieann," she said in a melodic voice.

"London."

Her eyes widened. "Wait. Are you *from* London?"

Every single time.

My polite smile was well-practiced. "No. My parents are just weird." That was my standard answer when I didn't want to go into detail. She smiled despite her disappointment.

"I'm from Illinois," I added.

"I think I've been there once," she said hesitantly.

"Chicago?" I offered in question. No one knew Illinois. Everyone knew Chicago.

"Oh, then yeah. But just the airport."

Of course.

She opened her mouth to say something when a boy with wavy brown hair had come up behind her, turned her around, and gave her a kiss full on the mouth.

Not going to lie. I was a little grossed out.

"Tristan," she said in mock protest. He grinned at her. She had enjoyed the kiss but gave him a playful swat anyway. I kept up my polite smile to stop from rolling my eyes.

"Tristan, this is my new friend, London." Before he could even get a word out, she gave him a knowing look. "But she's not from London."

I almost laughed at her seriousness. While part of me thought this should all be irritating, I was mostly entertained. If anything, it was a distraction from my otherwise melancholy mood. Tristan flashed me a smile and nodded in my direction while he grabbed her by the waist, pulling her toward him. Not doing much to ward off his advances, she introduced me to a few people in her immediate circle of three other girls and two guys.

I was greeted with variations of a polite "hey"; then they went right back to doing whatever it was they were doing before Brieann interrupted.

The girls were very different from each other, yet still looked very much alike in all the ways that the world would see them. They both had coordinated clothing, matching makeup, and perfect manicures. I already imagined the stereotypical weekly sleepovers and hours on the phone talking about guys.

One guy had dark hair and facial structure that guaranteed a career in modeling. The other had his rumpled hair longer precisely the way he had intended it to fall. He had the air of someone that cared that he looked like he didn't care. I was beginning to feel like this was the wrong kind of crowd.

Social self-preservation ... was this going to lead to a Mean Girls type of situation if I continued to consort with them?

While the rest of the group seemed to ignore me, Brieann decided that I was even more interesting than a make-out with Tristan. I didn't think Tristan agreed as he drifted away to watch a video on another guy's phone.

I tried just pulling out my own phone and sinking into my seat but she moved her chair to face mine and gave me her full attention. I was starting to feel like a helpless rodent under the gaze of a playful but lethal tigress.

No sudden movements.

In fairness, there was nothing about her that was particularly terrifying. She was polite, maybe a little overly friendly, but she also seemed sincere.

In 15 minutes, my impression of her shifted radically. I decided that I liked her.

I really needed to stop judging people on first impressions because I never seemed to get it right.

A man walked into the room with a stack of papers in one hand and a mechanical pencil behind his ear. He had thick-rimmed hipster glasses and a neatly trimmed beard. Probably to make him look older than he was. "OK, class ... find a seat and park your butt down on it. I need to lord over you all."

There were the sounds of metal scraping on the floor, kids talking over each other, and eventually, butts being parked.

"Welcome to your Junior year. This is home base. I'm Mr. Jacobs. Some of you might know me as Mr. Jacobs, your homeroom haven but others may see me as Mr. Jacobs, your Trigonometry god. Fear not. I respond to both ..."

He passed out the papers and started to go over the school year's expectations with various coming events and activities.

It was the same one I received at the office. I absentmindedly doodled around the edges of the handout. I already knew that I'd be avoiding anything that I wasn't required to attend.

I had Brieann with me in another class before lunch and welcomed not having to explain my name to every person I met. She enthusiastically fielded questions like my personal PR advisor. Most people didn't spare me a second glance and seemed to only greet me to indulge Brieann. Others asked the expected precursory getting-to-know-you questions and talked about teachers and their reputations.

The morning droned on monotonously.. New classes, new teachers, new faces but still all the same. Events that were easily forgotten the moment they happened.

At lunch, I sat with Brieann's crowd. Although gratified that I didn't have to sit alone, I was out of place. I sat at the edge of the table so that I wasn't between people whose names I couldn't remember.

My eyes wandered around the cafeteria. Though by this time, I had well accepted that my version of the day's events were not going to go the way I wished, there was a small, stubborn voice that refused to be crushed. I wanted to leave the gates open so I could feel somewhat justified should the impossible happen. I still hoped. Hoped I could say, 'See? I wasn't crazy! He does exist!'

Just like every high school everywhere, the cafeteria was segregated into little factions. Not quite as distinct as the bigger cities but still there. I didn't detect outward antagonism, and no one I've met had anything bad to say about anyone else in particular. But certain people still banded together.

I eyed a small group of kids that looked like they would be the most rebellious. They weren't looking destructive, but they didn't sport the same homogeneous attire the rest of the school had adopted.

He wasn't there. The stubborn voice in me mumbled a bit before eventually quieting down.

He's not real.

"How was the first day of school?"

My father walked into the kitchen, dropping his bag and travel mug on the counter.

Disappointing. Crushing. Disheartening. Frustrating. Hopeless.

"Not bad." I was convincing. "I made a friend." I sounded like a kindergartener.

"Oh?"

I rolled my eyes. He was digging for information. Specifically the gender of my new friend. I thought about giving him a hard time but that probably wouldn't end well for me. "Yeah, she's the only one whose name I actually remembered. That's a big deal."

Dad looked relieved but took the opportunity to launch into a lecture anyway. "How many times have I told you? It's important to remember people's names. It makes an impression. The trick is to relate their names to something familiar -- that way it'll help you remember."

Argh. Parenting. "Are you even serious with that right now? When 20 people machine-gun their names at me, I don't have time to relate their names to something familiar. Gimme a break, Dad. It was my first day. I have all school year to remember their names."

"Have you decided on any extracurricular activities?"

Does my father even know me at all?

"Absolutely." He looked so hopeful that I almost, almost felt bad for him. "None."

His expression sagged but he didn't seem surprised. Maybe he did know me after all.

No matter the disappointment, you always hope. And boy, do I know that feeling.

"London …" he began. I cut him off with a well-practiced whine. One of the more powerful weapons in my teenage arsenal. He grimaced. "You know that's the proverbial nails on chalkboard to parents everywhere, right?"

"You realize that's just motivation for me to utilize it, right?" I retorted. He snorted. "Look," I bargained. "Can you please just give me a chance to at least see what they have to offer before I commit to anything just yet." He looked at me doubtfully, probably knowing that I was simply employing a delay tactic. He nodded. He would probably try again in a week.

I escaped to my room before he decided to parent other aspects of my life.

Slap In The Face

The next couple of weeks in school saw progress. I learned the names of most of the kids in my homeroom class and Brieann's small group of friends. I wasn't comfortable enough with claiming them as my friends just yet. Other than Brieann herself, I wouldn't really be talking with any of them. I was still the new girl.

The Abercrombie and Fitch model wanna-be was a boy named Sam. He was quieter than Tristan but just as charming, in his own way. He wasn't currently attached to anyone in the group, but I had the feeling that he preferred it that way. They called the boy with designer hair, Echo. It wasn't his real name but I don't think anyone knew what his real name was anymore. He was just Echo or 'E'.

Amanda and Raven were the other two girls. They took turns flirting with Sam and E. They excelled in it and even flirted with Tristan when Brieann wasn't looking.

I didn't have the camaraderie that I had back home. I wasn't expecting it, and that fact didn't really bother me much. I almost welcomed the change and wondered if deep inside, I actually didn't want anyone knowing me at all.

It was easy for me to blend in with the crowd. I understood how to balance the scales and maintain harmony in a group. Dad skipped over the mandatory birds and the bees talk when I came of age and instead focused on how to diplomatically befriend a clique. The results of which allowed me to maintain friendships with the president of the Epsilon Alpha Math Society, as well as the captain of the football team. On paper, it was an idealistic balance.

Not so much in my head.

Instead of being happy with the number of friends I have, all of whom are nice and worthy people, I may as well have had none. They weren't friends with me. They were friends with the part of me that I portrayed for their approval. Collectively they could make up the perfect ambiance in which I can be myself but I needed to be with different individuals given different situations.

To be able to reveal myself to another, I would risk losing that connection.

I didn't want to be that homogeneous person anymore. It was tiring. I wanted to be me without having to worry about the approval of others.

I also needed to be certain who I was in the first place.

In the meantime, I kept to myself when I didn't need to be with Brieann so I could figure it out without being influenced by others.

I had so far been able to escape Dad's insistence that I find something to do with my free time other than being holed up in my room. Whenever a lecture loomed on the horizon, I hung out at the park adjacent to the school with my stuff and continued to create art that was always related to my source of obsession in one form or another. I did homework whenever I got home.

I've never been so ahead in my schoolwork. Ever.

I also couldn't avoid Brieann without hurting her feelings and causing complications. And this was California after all. Unhampered by snow and cabin fever. There was always something to do, some reason for Brieann to invite me out.

There was talk of the carnival coming down for Oktoberfest. On the third Friday of September, Brieann's crowd made larger by four others headed out for burgers after school. An action-fueled, no doubt, by the insatiable appetite of teenage boys. I had decided, to my peril, to join them because I had already bailed on the last event gathering. Doing so too many times in a row would make it necessary to field unwanted questions. Also, it would be something to show for with Dad.

"You are coming to Oktoberfest." It wasn't a request or a command. It was a statement of fact. I opened my mouth to argue but she held up a perfectly manicured hand. "You're going to want to be there," she insisted. Then announced with natural flourish, "We're going to have a booth!"

The announcement was greeted by excited clamor that I could not understand. I didn't bother to voice my confusion. She would explain. I've learned that my lack of reaction usually is enough to tip her off.

She rolled her eyes. "Oktoberfest is epic, London!"

"Everyone will be there," Raven added. Yes, well, I see everybody in school every day anyway; so what's really the big deal?

"It's the biggest event in town. Bigger than Christmas! The whole town sets up. Every food place has a stall so there's literally everything to eat …"

People started to talk over each other and voices overlapped.

"Who's supposed to headline? How many bands ... "

"There are rides … games … the horror house is choice ..."

"A Love Tunnel," Amanda added in the middle of giggles and hoots. "This year," Brieann commanded with flavor, "we don't just attend. We get to be part of it.

"And," she added with smug satisfaction, "I don't think anyone in school has one. Not even the seniors!"

"The basketball team had one last year," E pointed out.

Tristan threw a crumpled up burger wrapper at him across the table. "Eff that! It was a faceplant."

I looked at Tristan questioningly. "They sold drinks and stuff," he said in explanation. "It was a glorified lemonade stand."

The wrapper ball he had thrown at E came flying back at him. "Whatever, dude! We made over $150!"

"Making money is not the point," Brieann said with authority. "We have to be, like, the sickest booth there ever was in history."

"What should we do?"

There was an excited babble of ideas and opinions. It was punctuated every now and then with compliments on Brieann's ability at securing this celebrated status for the group. I didn't participate, obviously missing the enthusiasm that was practically radiating in pulses. Instead, I zoned out as I often find myself doing. I doodled on my napkin.

"What do you think, London?"

Leave it to Brieann to put me on the spot.

"I'm game with whatever you guys decide." It was a non-committal response I had apparently used too often as she whined. "Come on! Don't you have any ideas? I want something totally center stage!"

"And you're going to ask her?"

It was that statement coupled with the venomous way it was expressed that caught me unprepared. I looked at Amanda dumbfounded. It was evident by the tone that she meant it darker than a joke. A girl sitting next to her, whose name I hadn't remembered yet, giggled. Brieann gave her a rotten look but before she could say anything in my defense, Amanda continued talking about me as if I wasn't even in the room.

"How can anyone like her come up with anything tight?"

Was I being pranked? What's happening? I looked around, hoping to find a solution or escape. None was forthcoming. This was exactly what I was fearing would happen if I stayed in this group. It's a scene right out of Pretty Little Liars. I've made a massive effort not to antagonize anyone. Why is she suddenly picking on me? Instead of finding a smart way to counter her belittling words, I was busy thinking back trying to remember how I became her target. I didn't say anything in defense.

"Unless we put up a rotten tomato throwing booth … that might work." There was more giggling and this time even Tristan let out a bark of laughter. Only a few people, including Sam and E, just kept silent.

I flushed.

"WhatDaFaqisWRONGwithyou?" Brieann was enraged.

"I'm just saying," Amanda continued unrelentingly. "Having her around is like wack community service, and I think we've paid our dues. Could we just stop pretending already?"

I couldn't take it anymore. I grabbed my pack and stood up, trying not to cause a scene as I did so.

I was vaguely aware that Brieann was protesting. I was out the door before my fury erupted into angry tears.

Escape

I didn't know where I was going. I just pointed the bike away and kept on pedaling.

I was both furious and humiliated. Swear words and things-I-should've-said swirled around in my head like a messy toilet flush. Grounding my teeth, I redirected all my rage to speed. Angry tears leaked from my eyes, and I was grateful that I was moving too fast for anyone to really notice.

Not that anyone would.

The bike lane ended at the highway crossing before all my fury had burned out. I was not yet ready to turn back. Instead, I got off the bike and walked with it under the highway overpass. Alone, under cover of the bridge, I sat on the dusty grass and let myself cry.

I understood why this happened. I was convinced of it because I gave them no other reason to hate me. By not immersing myself into the group as I would have done back then, I had inadvertently alienated them. Liam had often warned me that lack of action is an action in itself.

It was naive for me to believe that there would be a different outcome to this. There was a reason why it took me years to make the friends that I had made, and why I continue to hide from them even now. There was a reason I had maintained a front. There was a reason why I never let one person see me for who I think I am.

I've learned that life is easier when you are who people expect you to be. It's easier not to disappoint when you're placed into a category with predetermined characteristics and goals. Why would I assume the rules would be different here? Because I'm older? Because no one knew me? Because it was a clean slate? Because it's a small town?

It didn't make a difference. Well, maybe it's only worse.

I'm ridiculous. Immature. Childish. Impossible. Utterly laughable. I'm lame, I'm boring, and I'm fully aware of it. How could I expect anyone to accept that version of myself? Why is it so important to me that they do? Why don't I have a problem with myself? Instead of wanting others to accept my lame self, why can't I just easily embrace the same things others do? Why can't I be normal? Why don't I want to be?

I stared at my hands, still in tight fists. I suddenly wished they weren't empty.

I could see the appeal of Ethan's butterfly knife.

I smiled involuntarily as I do whenever I think of him. I had scoffed at him about his aversion to authority and yet I struggle with the same issue. Not authority but conformity. Should this surprise me at all?

I recalled a dim image of what seemed more a memory than a dream. I hadn't understood his struggle then. It seemed clear to me because, at that time, I hadn't realized how hard it would be.

How can I be me when there are so many rules to follow?

It was exactly what Ethan was asking me. The one person who could understand me before I could understand myself. And he's all in my head.

One more thing that made me even less normal than everyone else.

My anger was ebbing. Without me being aware of it, longing replaced all my resentment. If only I knew where to find him. If only I knew how. If only I had him to run to at a time like this, it would make the unfair world so much easier to live in.

If only he were real.

If only.

He would be the one person I would want to be with right this moment.

I hadn't dreamt about him in more than a month. It didn't matter if he was in my daily thoughts. I couldn't force myself to dream about him. Maybe my unconscious mind knew when to stop. That was probably a good thing because the rest of me was inclined to embrace mental sickness completely just to hear his voice again.

I wanted to scream, but what would that really accomplish? It would just cause someone to dial 9-1-1. It's either a murder is being committed, officer, or it's just some teenager being all angsty. I kicked at the dirt, feeling like a trapped animal. The move had held so much promise. Ultimately, I had just simply moved from one cage to another. And he didn't exist in either of them.

The ringing of my phone startled me. I didn't identify the noise immediately and in that same moment, I had the irrational hope that somehow, beyond all reason, Ethan was calling me. I went searching for it in my pack.

Caller ID indicated that it was Dad. I sighed. I didn't think my network provider offered a program that involved mental calls from imaginary friends.

I popped my last Gobstopper in my mouth to disguise the emotion in my voice. I answered the phone, feigning cheeriness. "What's up, Dad?"

"Where are you?" He didn't sound too worried. Just curious.

"Under a bridge."

I'm honest. I just don't provide a lot of details if I can get away with it. Dad was used to my obscurity, and his self-defense mechanisms taught him not to ask for more information. "Stay away from trolls. It's almost seven; are you coming home soon?"

I looked up at the sky and finally noticed how low the sun was. I had been in solitary longer than I realized.

"Yeah," I said getting up. "I'm on my way home now."

I was surprised by how far I found myself from home. I hadn't realized that I had covered such a distance in a short amount of time. Dad had called me one more time before I finally made it home.

I staggered into the house, feeling like my legs couldn't hold up my body weight.

"Where were you?" Dad asked, dumping his dinner plate into the sink. "Alaska?"

"Felt like it," I mumbled.

I threw my things at the bottom of the stairs and collapsed on the couch. I didn't feel like moving again. Ever. Being this tired is good because it distracted me from all my emotional frustrations.

"I don't think I have the energy for dishes tonight, Dad. I'll get them in the morning."

He shrugged. "It doesn't matter to me either way, Sweetheart. I'm telling you, it doesn't make sense to run the dishwasher when it isn't a full load."

My response was automatic. "So gross."

He looked at me more critically. "Why don't you go upstairs and get some sleep? You look done."

I nodded numbly knowing that it would only be worse in the morning. I didn't have much of an appetite anyway.

I took my time in the shower for two reasons. One, because I swear that I could feel every particle of dust and grime layered on me and fused to my skin with dried sweat. Positively disgusting. Two, because the hot pulse of the shower was very, very good on my weary body.

I stopped when I was in actual danger of drowning.

I barely even made it to my bed before I fell asleep.

Free Will

The aches in my body didn't go away. There was burning in my legs as I stood, facing a clearing that I recognized. I didn't dare breathe. I didn't have enough energy to eat but suddenly, I was capable of more. I wasn't aware of the pain anymore. Not when I saw him.

I found him crouched in a ready position, as if in battle. He was alone in the middle of the clearing overlooking the city. He had the sleeves of his shirt rolled up so high that it was over his shoulders. A sheen of sweat covered his arms and darkened the neck of his shirt. His pants hung low down his hips. I saw his jacket flung to the ground with a half-empty water bottle that had its label peeled off, his watch discarded on top. The glint of silver around his wrist complemented the blade that was spiraling in the air.

He had a grey kerchief tied around his eyes.

The knife fell toward him, no longer spinning, blade down. It was as if he was unaware of its position. I knew better. When it seemed the hardened metal would inevitably bury itself into his left thigh, he caught it by the hilt with his right hand, his left arm tight across his chest, his head low.

I exhaled. He heard me. In one fluid motion he straightened up, cocked his head toward me and the knife was gone from his empty hands, tucked unseen into his pants. It was the product of years of practiced concealment. He ripped the blindfold off his face. I waited for his eyes to adjust.

"Hi." I held myself in place.

His expression went from disbelief to suspicion. I was hoping for a different kind of reaction. My smile had been of its own accord, fueled by excitement that he obviously didn't share. It was a blow to my already wobbly self-esteem. My smile faltered. He didn't move and neither did I.

"I thought we determined that this was unhealthy," he said guardedly.

"I determined that I didn't really care."

"Mature," he noted.

"I've been known to be," I quipped.

He regarded me for a moment, sighed, then walked toward his jacket. He wiped the sweat off his brow and ran his fingers up his hair, further exasperating the already rumpled look. He turned his back to me and pulled his sweat-stained shirt off. My eyes widened at the sight of no less than half a dozen, various sized scars on the skin of his back. He threw his jacket on over his bare back, obstructing my view. He took a swig from the water bottle. By the time he turned around, I was composed.

"Why are you here?" he demanded, still on the defensive. He left his jacket open and I was momentarily distracted as he tightened the band on his watch. When I looked up at his eyes, they were furious. Flustered, I fumbled for words.

"I thought …. um …. you liked …. didn't want me to …." I heard the hurt in my voice and tried to control it. "I couldn't … " I took a deep breath, closed my eyes and tried again. "I've been trying -- I thought --" Before I could stop it, tears threatened my vision. "You don't want me?" My attempt ended in a whisper.

Even my dreams rejected me.

I heard him groan. "Bugger," he said in surrender. "Don't do that. Stop. I can't take it." I wiped my eyes with the back of my hand quickly as if speed would dismiss the action. I didn't want to stand here begging to be in his company. I didn't want his pity. That was humiliating. The shame gave me strength. I balled my hands into fists at my side.

"You know what," I declared in a shaken voice, "It's fine."

I looked up at him haughtily and tried not to process the pained look on his face. "Just forget it." I turned in a huff to walk out of the scene and into the safety of the forest. My ego was damaged, and I wanted to save face and escape.

"Hey, stop! Don't …" he called after me and caught me by my upper arm. I pulled my arm away, and he released me immediately.

"London, please don't." It wasn't his pleading that stopped me but the sound of his voice saying my name. I stopped but didn't turn.

"I'm … sorry," he added quietly. "Please? Stay?"

I took a deep breath to steady myself, tried to hold on to my anger and turned to face him. The expression on his face was so completely apologetic that it was as if I had imagined the hostility earlier.

"Look," he continued when I didn't say anything. His brows gathered tightly in confusion.

"I just don't understand what's going on here."

He was standing so close. As easily as it had surfaced, my anger dissolved. I could feel the heat radiating from his body. His eyes looked more green than gold today, probing mine, searching for answers. He smelled muskier, the barest hint of laundry detergent lingering. I went from one extreme emotion to the other and my mind was reeling to catch up. I barely made out anything he said after.

"You show up out of nowhere … disappear in a blink of the eye. You aren't real," he lifted his hand and tentatively brushed his fingers to the side of my face. I instinctively leaned my head to his touch. It was electric but irresistible. "But you are. I can touch you. I can feel you." He dropped his hand. "I don't understand," he repeated, shaking his head.

"I don't either," I whispered.

He looked at me through his lashes and damp, messy hair for what seemed to be a long stretch of time before he spoke. "If this is the road to insanity, I can see why so many people opt for it."

He ran his hand through his damp hair again. Almost nervously. "Now what?"

I shrugged. I really didn't care as long as he was part of the story. "Were you done or did you want to put yourself in unnecessary harm's way a little longer?" He looked away but had a smile on his face. "No … no, we can walk." He bent over to pick up his discarded shirt and rolled it into an untidy ball under his arm.

"Why do you do that?"

"I told you, it helps me focus." He walked toward me and I fell into step with him.

"Well, yeah, but why do you have to do it blindfolded?"

"It's not always well lit when I need to use it. I like to be prepared."

There was something foreboding in his tone. "You've used it against ... people?" I was almost afraid of his answer.

He nodded slowly but didn't look at me. "It's saved my life a few times."

My stomach was in knots but I needed to know. "So, like, just in self-defense, right?"

He turned to look at me. There was something in his expression that I couldn't place but there was also the honesty I was searching for. "Sure, but that's not always an acceptable excuse, eh?" He mumbled the last part of his sentence that I almost didn't catch it.

I never really believed that it was a harmless thing to him. He had such respect for it. Yet, earlier, when he became aware that someone was watching him, the first thing he did was hide it. He didn't brandish it in front of him to ward off an unseen attacker. Instead of using it to protect himself, he was protecting it. He was a mess of contradictions.

We found ourselves back near the brook and strange trees. I watched as he hung his shirt on a low branch and threw some water on his face. I sat at the base of the tree and looked up at whatever blue sky I could see between the leaves. It was a beautiful day. I stuck my hands in my jeans and found a lone individually wrapped Tootsie Roll mini. It was slightly disfigured, but I figured it shouldn't affect the taste. I unwrapped it.

"This is nice," I mused. "I see why you like to escape here. Far away from school and all that crap."

His hands froze half way to his face and he looked at me strangely. "School's done," he said.

"Really?"

"You're surprised that I'm not as dumb as I look," he teased. I wondered how seriously he thought that.

"No, of course not." I'm cursed with some sort of mutant

ability that insults him with every statement I make. "Sorry, I just have thoughts of an upcoming Trigonometry test terrorizing my dreams." He stood up, wiped his face with the sleeve of his jacket and half smiled. He maintained the strange look on his face.

"You don't like Math?"

"Oh, I like Math just fine," I corrected. "It's Math that isn't fond of me."

He didn't laugh but held his head to the side in a manner that I've come to understand was an invitation to continue.

"My brothers and Dad are all Math geniuses. My dad just got a new gig at the University teaching Calculus. There's a bit of pressure for me to meet certain standards." I shrugged. "I don't really have a problem with it. It can be fun, I guess in a solve-the-puzzle sort of way. I'm just not a fanatic like the rest of my family."

He smiled encouragingly. "I've never been a fan myself," he said. "I like … History."

History? I absolutely loathe history. It was the licorice of subjects. The only thing worse would be World Language Arts. That would be the gross flavored Bertie Botts Every Flavor Beans of the bunch.

He studied my expression and he smiled wider. "I take it you don't like History." I shook my head and stuck out my tongue in exaggerated disgust. "What's to like? History is practically just a meaningless garble of names and dates to remember for no other purpose than to answer an exam."

The conversation paused before he concluded, "You failed a test, eh?"

I glared at him.

"You failed your last test, didn't you?"

Suddenly, he wasn't attractive anymore. I bit my lip and turned away from him. I heard him snicker and I flushed.

"Whatever."

"Hey, now, don't be like that." He cupped my chin with his right hand and forced me to look at him. There was a crinkle at the edge of his eyes and the smile was nothing less than unfair temptation on his lips. I was instantly captivated. So much for lack of attraction.

I rolled my eyes to save myself from melting in his arms. He let go.

"What can you possibly like about it?"

He shrugged. "It's interesting."

So not true.

My disagreement made him grin. I didn't see him take his knife out but it was there … dancing in his hand effortlessly as he spoke. "It's not the monotonous names and dates that capture me. Your exam results notwithstanding, History is more than memorizing names and the correct sequence of events." I snorted. I didn't think he needed me to elaborate on my feelings over his statement.

"The way I see it it's a fascinating account of how different people react to different situations." He found a spot beside me, lower on the ground so that his head was actually lower than mine. "The same person can react differently to the same situation depending on what point in their lives they encountered it."

I tried not to tune him out. He had taken on a lecturing tone. It was the trigger that would automatically launch my brains out of my head to wander. Instead of imagining what it would feel like to run my hands in his hair, I forced myself to focus on his words.

"I don't get it," I finally admitted.

He could tell and wasn't all too surprised by my admission.

"OK," he tried again. "Let me break it down to simple needs. Let's say you're hungry. Someone offers you a sandwich and you take it."

"Because I'm hungry?"

"Well, I'd use lolly as an analogy but you'd always take lolly," he teased.

I sneered and stuck my tongue out at him, a practice born out of many childhood arguments with older brothers. "So you eat the sandwich," he continued, ignoring my glare. "15 minutes later, the same person offers you a similar sandwich. Do you take it?"

"Am I still hungry?"

"How many sandwiches do you need before you aren't hungry anymore?" he asked innocently, but also not innocently. He was baiting me.

"So I'm not hungry?" The knife stopped spinning. He put a fist up to his chin in a convincingly natural move but I could tell he did so to hide a smile. I let that one slide.

"If I'm not hungry," I clarified, "then no, I don't take the sandwich."

He took his hand away from his chin and opened it, palm up at me. His face open in a happy expression of arriving at a conclusion unanimously shared. "There you go! You've reacted differently to the exact same scenario because it was introduced at different times. Once when you were hungry and once when you weren't." He looked almost delighted with himself. I rolled my eyes.

"Everyone in history acted the way they did in relation to when events occurred in their lives. Heroes aren't determined by who they are but by circumstances forcing them to act the way they did. They didn't have a choice. We're all just pawns forced to live lives dictated by events beyond our control."

What he said hit a nerve with me.

"Predictability is not the same thing as not having a choice. Saying that we are what our environment makes us is just an excuse people give when they don't want to own up to things they did."

I expected him to dismiss my argument but instead he was more excited that I was engaging him in this discussion.

"Do you believe in destiny?" he asked.

"Destiny?" I repeated.

He nodded once, his eyes alert. "God? Some Supreme Being that holds our predetermined future? Do you believe that we're more than just random happenings?

"Do you believe in purpose?"

I didn't know where he was heading with this. "Sure. I believe that there's a reason for everything even when we don't understand it right away."

He clapped his hands once in triumph. "Therefore, you can't believe in free will."

"As a matter of fact, I'm a big proponent of free will."

"If you believe that everyone has a purpose to fulfill, then you believe that no matter what that person does, they will inevitably fulfill that purpose. There is no such thing as free will."

I shook my head. "You're assuming that one can't exist in the presence of the other."

"They can't," he declared without doubt.

"Yes, they can!"

He laughed, "Your argument loses merit when you revert to 'can too' as a rebuttal."

You started it, I almost fired back, feeling like I was a kid in a schoolyard argument.

Almost.

"No," I refused to be sidetracked. There was something important happening here. This was more than just theoretical discussion. There was a deeper meaning unrealized. I was convinced of its presence.

"You assume that there exists only one destiny that a person is meant to fulfill. That's a faulty presumption. I believe that we have more than one destiny. I believe that our decisions lead us to a maze of events that fulfill different destinies. Our choices will determine what our own future is. The power to decide what actions we take give us the free will to choose which destiny we want for ourselves.

"The trick is finding the best destiny."

His eyebrows creased and he looked like he was about to argue. "And even if there was only one destiny," I added before he could begin. "Even if all choices ended the same way; it's still up to you to dictate the manner in which you get there. That is still exercising free will. "

He shook his head, bemused. "That's what you believe?"

He asked without irony but I was suspicious, thinking that he was baiting me again. "Yes. What do you believe?" He didn't answer but met my look appreciatively. He grinned.

"You're quite opinionated, did you know? Particularly for someone who does not appreciate the complexities of History."

I shrugged, still feeling the unease that I had missed something.

Repeat Offender

"How's the flesh wound?" I jutted my chin toward his left arm. He shrugged. "It's old news. She'll be 'right. I've had worse."

"Hm," I agreed thoughtfully.

"Eh?" he asked.

I hesitated but he had been honest with me and I wanted to know. With the least intruding tone I could manage asked him softly, "I saw the scars on your back. What happened to you?"

A shadow came over his eyes immediately and a hostile look clouded his face. His blade was still. He looked very, very dangerous.

"Sorry. Never mind. None of my business."

After a beat, he sighed. He spoke equally as soft. Reluctant. "I didn't have a choice childhood." I met his eyes and saw that they were still dark, but more resigned than angry. "When no one is there to protect you, other people ... take advantage of that.

Sometimes the people that are supposed to be helping you.

"And people can be genuinely cruel when no one is watching them." He held the hilt of his knife tightly, channeling all his anger in that one tight hold. He didn't elaborate further.

The cruelty he spoke of was alien to me. The more I knew of him, the further apart our worlds seemed to be. I never doubted the love my family had for me. They were my safety net. Even if the rest of the world was cruel, I knew I could find solace at home. They may not always agree with my choices but there would be acceptance in the differences. There was respect. There was love. It was a privileged life. A life so different from his.

The silence between us was causing a rift. He was falling into his own ugly memories and I felt I knew too little to fall with him. He'd seen so much violence in his life. Did he have a choice in that matter? Was he merely surviving in an environment that shaped him into who he is now?

"Are you part of a gang? Like a drug thing?"

He blinked twice, gave a little laugh and furrowed his brow. It was a combination of emotions. I translated it as amused disbelief. He considered me a moment before answering. "What is it about you and gangs?"

I shrugged. "They always say gangs are the reason for inner-city crime and juvenile delinquency so I just assumed."

"No, never a gang thing. Not a drug thing. Not anymore"

"So you stopped." Problem solved.

He shrugged. "I'm a bit of a control freak. Drugs make you lose control so in the long run, it wasn't compatible with my personality."

"Why would you even try in the first place?" Say no to drugs. It was ingrained in us since grade school. At least in the world I knew.

It was taking him considerable effort to speak. I could've ended the conversation. Maybe I should've. I didn't want to. I was also under the impression that despite the difficulty, he wanted to tell me anyway.

"It seemed like a good idea at the time. There were things I wanted to forget and drugs seemed to be the easy way out short of hanging myself."

I shuddered. There was such bitterness in his tone despite his attempt to control it.

"I thought drugs were super addictive. How did you stop?"

He spun the knife in his hands so fast that it was a blur. "Do you know how you detox?"

I shook my head, wondering if I really wanted to know.

"They stick you in a room with nothing but a cot and a toilet. The door is even padded. There are no locks on the inside. You stay there until you can't tell if it's night or day outside. Someone comes by twice a day to check if you're still alive. They take away your shoelaces. After a while, you're sort of forced to deal with things another way."

I tried and failed to control the shaking in my voice. "So what stops you from doing drugs now?"

He laughed bitterly. "There is no way I am going through that again. Doesn't help that I'm walking the thinnest line possible for a repeat offender. I can't have a serious record. That'd be the end of it. One more ..." He shook his head as if to erase the thought. "Generally, it's fairly easy to stay out of the box but not so much when you're high. I'm not risking it. I'd rather ..." He gave a half shrug. "...die." He concluded. His knife stopped spinning, caught in the grip of his hand. "Why not, right? I would but I was too much of a coward to go through with it all the way."

He stopped talking and closed his eyes. I felt a lump in my throat.

He looked vulnerable but at the same time, unapproachable. I got up, crossed the ethereal distance between us, and knelt in front of him so that he'd be forced to look at me. He turned his face away from me, his eyes still closed. I reached out with one hand and placed it on the side of his face. He didn't move.

"Stop it. That's not true at all. It takes much more to keep on living." I said, trying to keep my screaming emotions in check. "I'm glad you're here with me now."

He opened his eyes and turned to look at me. His expression was serious and thoughtful. He didn't reply. He just continued to stare. He was studying me carefully and it was making me self conscious.

"Do you know what else is madly unsettling about this whole thing? You are too easy to talk to."

I released the breath I didn't realize I was holding. "How is that a bad thing?" He guided my hand away from his face, piercing me with eyes that were neither green nor gold.

"I've been a muppet about the entire thing and I couldn't afford to be anymore. It was time to put a stop to it. After our last …encounter, I decided that you were right. I should be able to follow the rules without losing myself.

"I think the trick is that instead of forcing everything about myself on everyone, I need to share everything about myself with only a select few.

"Or one," he said softly.

I held his gaze but didn't reply. I was awed by his candor. There was courage behind it. I didn't reply -- not because I couldn't agree, but because I didn't have the eloquence to do so.

He turned away from me and continued. "To be honest, I'm not doing it for them anyway. I'm doing it for …" he hesitated. "To be a better person," he amended. "The rules, the training, the authority … they aren't there to suppress you. Just to guide you. It's just easier for me to pretend that they're the enemy. That defying them is something noble instead of something foolish.

"So …" he took a deep breath and gave me a surrendering smile, "I made my choice. Out of my said free will. While I still have choices. I signed up for a new kind of destiny. Completed all the tests. All my paperwork is in and I ship out for Basic Training in two weeks."

"I'm impressed," I said, only because I didn't really know how I was supposed to react.

He shrugged. "Let's get real. It's months of not using my brain, physical training, and pointless yelling anyway."

"So nothing out of the ordinary?" When in doubt, use humor.

He smiled that half-smile of his. "I should be used to it by now?"

"Not using your brain? You should be an expert. Physically, you may need some more training," I teased. Teasing was good. Teasing was light.

"Ow. Uncalled for," he complained. I laughed.

He was serious again before the laughter faded. "It's unreal that at a time I'm struggling for something, you would appear and in five minutes, I've learned more about myself than eight years of therapy. You force me to face myself in ways I've been avoiding. A blink of the eye and I've accepted my future and am committed to making it work.

"Another blink and you're gone."

He was looking up at me with such intensity. There was longing, desperation, frustration, questions, answers, distrust, loyalty. Complete vulnerable honesty in his look. It was not fair that he could express such emotion in such depth without having to say a word. And yet, to respond, I would need years.

"Don't blink," I whispered.

His eyebrows came together and his lips parted.

Epiphany

I was startled awake by a door closing, muffled but distinct. Dad had gone to bed. The digital clock by my bed told me that it was a little past midnight. He had stayed up to watch the "Late Show."

Back to reality.

I shut my eyes again, knowing that I wouldn't be able to find him again in sleep. Of course, I would dream of him tonight. Of course in the height of all my anger and confusion, he would swoop into my dreams to save me. I opened my eyes, still seeing him in my mind. I thought about what he said.

I was dissatisfied with how I had to be in front of others. I wanted to be true to others, But at the same time, I wanted to be accepted for the person I knew I was.

I'm not a two-dimensional person. Given the right mood, I can cook up a great meal. The next day, I can enjoy pizza delivery. I can listen to Heavy Metal and love ballads in the same afternoon.

I am the responsible daughter and also the eccentric artist. The comic book lover. The sushi addict. The obsessive-compulsive maniac. The terrible driver. The geek. The slacker. The punk. They're all me.

And then some.

If I thought of myself as someone worth knowing ... someone who has something to offer, then I shouldn't feel like I have to prove myself to everyone.

Just the ones that mattered.

Instead of forcing everything about myself on everyone, I need to share everything about myself with only a select few.

Or one.

I shivered at the memory.

He was not there every time I wanted but when I needed. It is not a coincidence that he was struggling with the same things I was. Not a coincidence that he came up with an answer when I had finally forced the question.

Of course I would dream about a guy. A great looking guy that actually seemed interested in me.

Definitely a fantasy. And not a creative one at that.

But why can't I make sense of half the things he says?

Because it's a dream, you idiot, I thought to myself sourly. *Dreams don't make sense.*

The physical ache that had so quickly brought me to sleep was nothing to the intangible ache in my heart. I didn't sleep.

I finally got out of bed when I heard Dad stirring. I didn't feel like facing the day just yet, but had I a choice, I'd probably just want to induce a coma. Stay away from reality. Stay with him.

Not the most rational of choices.

Of course, if I were to be honest with myself, rational choices did not exist in the same universe as he did.

Dad had left early for work, not bothering with breakfast other than a cup of coffee. My legs still ached from yesterday's impromptu bike trek. I decided to stay at home. It would also decrease the chances of bumping into anyone I knew from school to zero.

I attempted to find some lame show on Netflix to watch mindlessly in the family room, just hoping to remove myself from this reality, but it wasn't remotely effective. I wasn't in the mood to do any homework; so I grabbed a chocolate bar as I headed upstairs. With few options left, I pondered the blank sheet of art paper on my desk. There had to be a better way to find an outlet to all this emotion.

I don't know how long I spent over my drawings. Instead of nursing the inexplicable emptiness away from him, it only fueled the ache and made me yearn for him even more, accelerating my spiral down to ...what? Incurable insanity? I looked down at the latest sketch in accusation and disgust.

What was that term again? Oh, yeah. Unhealthy.

I jumped when the doorbell rang.

We haven't gotten a single visitor since we moved, and my heart leaped at the outlandish idea that maybe he was standing outside my door, summoned to me by my echoing want and frustrated art. The combination of both must have been the divining spell that would finally call him to me. I walked to the door with my nerves on edge.

I looked out the window and my heart sank. Not just because it wasn't him waiting for me but also because it was Brieann standing there. She was alone. I struggled with what to do next. Had anyone else been with her, I'd have feigned deafness rather than answer the door.

I looked quickly down the road as I opened the door for her, thinking that this may all be a prank that could end badly for me and live forever on YouTube. All I saw was her car parked in our driveway. She stood there looking both worried and vulnerable.

"Brieann," I said. As if that was any kind of greeting.

"Hey, London," her voice was a tad higher but still musical. "I tried calling you loads."

I shrugged. "My phone died." It was a transparent lie, and she knew it.

"Oh." She chewed the bottom of her lip and started to play with her hair. "Can I come in? I was hoping I could talk to you."

What could I say? No? Thinking that I would regret this conversation, I still opened the door wider so she could come in.

"Thanks." She smiled tentatively at me and walked inside.

I shut the front door and led her to the kitchen, the well-trained host in me taking over. "Did you want a pop or something?" I asked. She shook her head and sat down at the breakfast counter.

"London, I'm sorry. That was all just total bull," she began.

I tried to shrug it off. "It wasn't you, Brieann." It made no sense for me to be mad at her, even if the child in me wanted to cry foul and say that it was her fault for exposing me to the wolves. It would be easy to say it was everyone else's fault but my own.

"I know," she said kindly. "But it still shouldn't have happened. Amanda was off base. I think she was just trying to show off. She can be a total bitch."

I laughed without humor. "You think?"

"She's not everyone, you know."

I looked away. "I don't know, Brieann. She's right about me not fitting in with all of you. I'm not like any of you. Why do you keep insisting I hang out, anyway? So you can have someone around to always talk about? To pick on behind my back?"

When I looked back, Brieann looked horrified. I suddenly felt guilty.

"Of course not, London!"

"Then why else?" I demanded, refusing to back down.

She bit her lip again, and I knew that I had offended her, But my feelings were justified. My questions deserved an answer.

"It's not like that. It really isn't." Her voice shook with emotion. "I really wanted to be your friend. I thought you were interesting and fun and different. I don't really have a best friend, and I thought that if you hung out with me often enough, you'd want to be mine."

"What do you mean you don't have a best friend? You're friends with everyone in school, Brieann! Everyone loves you!"

Her laugh echoed with the lack of humor mine had earlier. "I have 'friends' like Amanda. I'm not stupid. I know she talks about me behind my back like she talks about everyone. I have 'friends' like Tristan, who only pretends to hear what I'm saying so that he can keep other guys away from me. I'm just a prize to him. A status symbol." She had tears in her eyes. "Those are the kind of 'friends' I have, London. Each one of them wants something from me. And if they can't get it, I'm useless to them."

She spoke about her life in a harsh new light that I never considered. I had thought her to be privileged and without want. She was friends with every kind of person in school; how could she feel alone and out of place?

How could she feel the way I've always felt?

I had not seen my similarities with her. I hadn't realized just how much we had in common, this perfect cheerleader and I. There was a solid kinship defined by this revelation. A revelation that was too honest not to be sincere.

"I'm sorry," I said. For lack of a better thing to say.

She waved me off. "It wasn't you, London."

I smiled. She did the same.

"I have to warn you," I said lightly. "I am not the most sensible person to be friends with right now."

"There's a better time?"

I laughed. "It's probably too late."

She shrugged. "Better late than never?"

I'm not big on the whole sisterhood solidarity thing, but I gave in to a hug. It just seemed right. "Thanks for being my friend," she said.

"Thanks for wanting to be mine."

Later that afternoon, Brieann sat cross-legged on my bed, looking wide-eyed at the different sketches cluttered all around my room. Each one pertaining to him in one way or another. The product of a fixated mind. She held up the first one I made of him. It was a rough pencil sketch. I drew him at an angle, facing away from me. Even in my drawings, his expression was somewhat troubled. Brooding about things I was too sheltered to fathom.

"Is he your boyfriend?"

I paused over trying to organize my supplies. How can I even begin to quantify this relationship? How can I begin to describe him?

I automatically thought of him as his own person, separate

from my consciousness, or rather, subconsciousness. He was not just a part of my fantasy or an escape. He was autonomous. As if he existed in some reality other than the one in my head.

A 16-year-old rebel reluctant to be on his own. He's seen more misfortune than I could even imagine and yet can find some kind of satisfied fascination in something as mundane as History.

He tempted fate and risked danger but only when it exposed him and no one else. So much anger in him tempered by his amazing sense of control. There was assurance despite the fear. Determination against all the desperation within.

He was nothing like me. He was his own person. What was that person to me?

"It's, um, complicated."

"Do you like him?" I laughed at the question. Gesturing wildly at the sketches around me I said, "Oh, it isn't obvious?" Brieann giggled but continued, "Does he like you?"

I thought about how his hand felt on my cheek. How his eyes bore into mine. My heart started to race. *If this is the road to insanity, I can see why so many people opt for it.*

"I think so," I dared to admit.

"So what's the problem?"

I didn't answer.

She pursed her lips thoughtfully. "Did you leave him behind?"

I considered that. That was a valid explanation. It would mean I'd have to explain less. It would mean I'd sound less like a nut job. The prospect was appealing. As if sounding less crazy made me more normal.

In a way, I did leave him behind. When I wake up and he's gone. I'm gone.

I nodded slowly, convincing myself that it wasn't a lie. "You could say that."

She nodded sagely, assuming Illinois, as I knew she would. "Well, that must suck."

"Absolutely," I agreed emphatically.

"Do you keep in touch?" Will the questions end? Probably not.

"In a way." I could not elaborate. She looked at me quizzically. "Well, that's a good thing."

Is it? I nodded absently, "I just wish it could be more."

She looked sympathetic. "You must miss home." I suppressed a rush of guilt. "Not really," I answered honestly. "Just him."

She picked up one of my earlier sketches and studied it, "He's kinda cute in that rugged indie kind of way. What's his name?" I flushed. Having someone else confirm something I had been thinking was validation that I didn't realize I was looking for. He was definitely cute. I wasn't the only one that thought so. Does that make me less crazy?

"Ethan."

She giggled.

When she didn't stop, I had to ask, "What?"

She started to laugh. "I'm sorry," she said. "It's just such a dorky name, no offense." I frowned, taking offense anyway. "I think that's actually the name of the Probability teacher on the senior's floor," she explained. For a horrified second, I wondered if they were one in the same. How cruel is this world?

"Not the History teacher?" I asked hesitantly, unreasonably afraid of the answer.

Brieann shook her head, her laugh receding. "Nah, their History teacher is the same as ours." I pretended not to care to cover my relief. I was being ridiculous about this.

"I wish I could draw like you," she said, holding up an inked watercolor. "Hey, maybe for our booth, you could make, like, people's caricatures! They do that in Six Flags and stuff."

"Yeah, that would be sick but I'm just not fast enough for that." She pouted. Another idea shot down.

"You know," I began thoughtfully. "We need to play up our strengths. You and … the rest of the girls really know your … cosmetics." She looked at me blankly.

"Seriously, I've overheard Amanda comment on other people often enough to know she feels like she could do a better job." Brieann scowled. "So why don't you make the booth like, I don't know, some kind of make-over booth?"

She turned the idea over in her head and I could see that she liked it. "Maybe the guys could set up some kind of camera and take 'after' pictures. Maybe pictures of couples and stuff? Like a souvenir." I was unprepared for the enthusiastic hug and delighted scream that assaulted me.

"Oh, London," she practically screamed in my ear as she hugged me so tight that she lifted me off the floor. "That is a sick idea! Wow! Yeah! That's perfect!" She released the hug but held on to my upper arms, jumping up and down in comical excitement. "I knew you'd think of something! I knew it! Oh, this is going to be great!"

We spent the rest of the day planning the project. I have never seen such enthusiasm. It carried her through the afternoon. We didn't talk about Ethan again until right before she left.

"Hey, Brieann. Are the girls going to give you a hard time if we continue to hang out together?" She smiled affectionately but shook her head. "Nah, I don't think so. If we don't make a big deal out of it, no one will." Still, I worried how Brieann's sudden show of affection would affect Amanda's building contempt for me.

"I'd appreciate it if you didn't say anything about Ethan to the others." I was more and more uncomfortable with her knowing as much as she did. Half-truths or not. "It's just really, really personal to me."

She looked like a kid that was entrusted with an important secret. It didn't help my confidence. "Long-distance relationships are so hard." With another quick hug, she bounded out the door and into her car.

She has a good heart, I thought to myself in consolation. *She won't do anything to intentionally hurt me.*

Unintentionally was another matter. While obviously good-natured and pure-hearted, she was a product of her environment. I had a sinking feeling in my stomach.

Oktoberfest

Come Monday morning, Amanda studiously ignored me as if Friday afternoon never happened. True to the high school code of ethics, I did the same. We all sat together for lunch where Brieann revealed the booth idea amidst general approval. The boys clustered together to talk about camera equipment and setup while the girls masterminded hair, make-up supplies, and getting sponsors.

To her credit, Brieann didn't overstate our relationship as I feared she might. She continued to sit by me in all the classes we had together, just as always but did not hint that our friendship was any deeper than it had been before my emotional explosion over burgers and fries. I liked it that way, and she seemed to sense it. She didn't mention Ethan to anybody.

So it went for the next week and a half with the expectations for the booth becoming exponentially larger by day. When Oktoberfest arrived , it seemed as if the booth was the experience and the fair only secondary.

I had difficulty concentrating for other reasons. Ethan. I would find myself staring into space and going over the conversations I've had with him. It was ultimately distracting. Even during my Trig test, I found myself smiling between problems despite not knowing what I was doing.

I originally had thought all the commotion over the fair to be annoying but as it turned out, the commotion worked to my advantage.

I failed my Trig test.

No one cared. Not even Dad. When I told him, I received nothing more than a furrowed brow and a shake of the head. He took a bite of dinner then steered conversation toward the upcoming festivities. He was more than pleased that I was participating. He had volunteered with the town committee to chaperone the event. It was part of his overall plan to assimilate into the community.

I was so grateful to be spared his guilty lecture that I finally threw myself into the preparation.

Because I had absolutely no talent in the makeover department, it fell on me to design and distribute fliers during the fest that advertised our booth. That suited me fine because it meant that I wouldn't have to be in close quarters with the rest of the group in a charged atmosphere.

Oktoberfest was indeed as big and beautiful as was described. It was a three-day event, starting on Friday and ending on a Sunday. School was out early Thursday in preparation. No one complained.

It took up the entire area of the fairgrounds and spilled over to the front of the town hall and even some stores. Every restaurant in town had a representing booth, including home-based businesses and specialty items that normally aren't sold. The mouth-watering lemon bars from Mrs. Harris' kitchen and Farmer's Market special roasted corn received the same acclaim.

I enjoyed a treat or two (or maybe five -- who was counting anyway?) as I made my rounds. Washed them all down with sweet iced milk tea. I had to keep my strength up, after all. The sugar lifted my spirits and, despite my initial apprehensions over this affair, I found myself having fun.

The air was filled with excited screams from the many death-defying rides and the unrestrained laughter from the toddlers on the kiddie rides. Typical carnival music played in the air and blended with the muffled announcements from the numerous game booths from one section of the park. It was perfectly fair weather. Not too hot so you could stay out literally all day and just cool enough to throw a light jacket on and be comfortable.

Delicious food. Agreeable weather. The freedom to roam. The positive energy was catching. It was a good place to be.

I walked the length of the entire fair repeatedly throughout the day, thankful for the comfort of my reliable Chucks II. Everyone I met was in a good mood and it truly felt like the entire town was present. I handed fliers to all the young people I met, happily explaining the fundamentals when they asked questions. I don't know how many excited teenage girls I sent Brieann's way. I lost count.

Near the end of the afternoon, I took another cold tea and I sat at the edge of one of the stone benches off the path. I put down what was left of my stack of fliers and leaned back. The sweet tea was very good. It was easy to daydream. In the ambiance of the carnival, this world adopted a surreal tone.

I saw a few couples walking arm in arm or holding hands. They were enjoying the moment.

My good mood faltered.

They took for granted their reality. Each of them in a stage of their relationship that was dependable. It seemed unfair that it was idealistic and easy for them. It was almost impossible to feel happy for them considering how complicated things were for me.

The ultimate distant relationship. If only it was the kind that Brieann thought it was. How simple that would be. Texting here, video there, and a jump on a plane. Nothing to cry about.

But no, it had to be undefined. Questionable and evasive.

I took a deep breath and tried to be rational about this. Pooled together all my courage to try to analyze it in a non-emotional light.

Could he exist in the world outside my imagination? I've heard of actors who immerse themselves deeply into a role that they take on traits of their fictional characters. Is that all he is? A product of my active imagination? If so, then why is it beyond my control? Why can't I dream about him in my world? Why is he always so hard to decipher?

If he was nothing but a vision I created, a fictional character with no real-world basis, then how is it I know so little about him? And what I do know is new and unrelated to anything I've ever experienced? Why is every contact with him a new experience for me? A new memory. A deeply real memory.

Why do I feel so strongly for him?

I chewed thoughtfully on the straw of my drink long after I was done with it. My attempt at impartiality had failed once again under the strength of my passion.

He had to exist. If not in this reality, then somewhere else. But he was real.

I tossed my empty cup into the bin more forcefully than was necessary. Once again, thinking about him resulted in a conflict of emotions. I spent the past two weeks staying up late trying to force myself to dream about him. Instead, I dreamt about friends I hadn't seen in months, my brothers, school, and even the sneering face of Amanda. He continued to elude me.

It was incredibly unfair. Why mock me with such a person and strong emotions then tell me, oh, maybe it isn't real? I should hate the clarity of these dreams. I should despise what he does to me. Yet the memory of his touch and depth of his eyes served to comfort even as they taunted.

Even the little I could share with him was grace enough. Consolation and blessing. The allure that brings me closer to the absolute insanity that I would willingly embrace to be with him.

What am I doing to myself?

I plastered a large, fake smile on my face, and I handed out a flier to one of the young couples I was secretly envying. I refused to think any more.

I tucked the remaining fliers under my arm when the fair was coming to a close. We had two days to go, and I didn't want to run out. When I got to the booth, there was still a line of impatient teenagers waiting their turn for a makeover. The girls working the booth all looked tired and frustrated. I found Brieann putting blush on a little girl that could be no older than 8.

"I'd offer to help but I'm no good at this sort of thing," I apologized with a shrug. Sorry. Not sorry.

"You can handle the tickets, and send Tasha over," she suggested.

We finally had to start turning people away and promised that we'd be back in the morning. We turned in all our collected tickets for the end of the day count with administration and awaited the official tally. By the time we left the grounds, it was almost 11p.m. I didn't get home until near midnight.

Strangely, I didn't feel as tired as I thought I should be. I had enough in me to grab a snack and take a lingering hot shower. The ache in my legs from all that walking came full force when I lay down in bed. The day caught up with me all at once. I didn't feel sleepy exactly. I was light headed.

First Date

I blinked. Or else I thought that I did.

I was standing on the grass by a large overly filled metal garbage can.

People walked around me, smiling and laughing excitedly. Little kids weaved through the legs of adults. I looked around and saw wooden booths with brightly colored peeling paint and people milling about. Music I didn't recognize played in the air. The sounds of grinding metal and rickety wheels of the amusement rides were drowned out by squealing passengers. I was in the middle of a fair. The booths were familiar. Oktoberfest.

I had on my Chucks but interesting enough, not my jeans. I was in a casual pull-over summer dress over a tank top. I remember the dress. It was hanging in my closet, having been worn once. It was certainly not something I would ever wear to a fair in real life.

That was how I knew that I was dreaming.

I strolled aimlessly, seeing if my dream would take me to

old friends. Maybe in this one, I've got mutant abilities. I was expecting the scene to change at any moment. The cotton candy and pretzel booth distracted me momentarily and I decided to linger. I could use some mental sugar for my mental fatigue.

"In line for lolly. I shouldn't be surprised."

I looked toward the voice I know so well that I hear it even when I'm awake. "Ethan!" A few people turned to look my way. I had on a huge idiotic smile that would not be contained. I was bursting with excitement. Here he was after all!

He was shaking his head in obvious amusement and glanced at the people who had turned our way. He was standing as he often did, with his arms crossed. He stood a little to the left of the line to the booth. No longer in his Paradigm issued uniform, he had on a collared shirt and his old jacket on top, as if trying to hide that he was neatly dressed. An old baseball cap with mismatched colors covered most of his head.

He stepped toward me so I didn't have to leave the line. "You scrub up well. Nice dress," he said.

"Nice cap." He pressed his lips together. Was that a palpable level of unease? He wouldn't look at me. "Wait. Are you blushing?" I said in surprise. Closing his eyes as if he was in pain, he pulled the cap off.

He ran his fingers through his hair. His very short hair. Military short. It was spiked upfront but flattened everywhere else, whether by design or because of the cap, I didn't know. It was flattering. It made him look neater, and I loved that I could see more of his face. He had his head down, his eyes still squeezed shut and cheeks aflame. His embarrassment was palpable. I bit my lip to stop from laughing.

He opened one eye and winced at my expression.

"No! No --" I tried to say before he thought the worst but

opening my mouth was a bad idea. I started to laugh. He groaned again and hastily moved to put the cap back on. I tried again, "No. No … don't!" I grabbed at his arm. He gave me a pained look but stopped. It made it even more difficult for me. I was trying to restrain myself so hard that I had tears in my eyes. He waited for me to control myself, trying not to look at me. I blinked the tears away.

"Really, it's not bad," I was able to say. I didn't sound convincing. He scowled.

"Yeah," he mumbled. "Hysterical laughter is always a brilliant sign, ow."

I wrapped both my arms around his to keep him from putting the cap on again. "I'm only laughing because you look absolutely mortified." He looked away and mumbled something that sounded like he was glad his humiliation could be a source of delight for me. "Stop," I said. I didn't let go of him. I waited until he looked at me. His jaw was set and his cheeks still burned. "I think it looks good," I insisted. "I think you look good." There was no way he could doubt the sincerity in my voice now. He raised an eyebrow. It had no place to hide. "I like being able to see your eyes," I offered.

A pause. He had such difficulty with this.

"Even when hazel isn't your favorite color?" he asked, finally relaxing a little; the burn in his cheeks slowly going away.

"Well, if you keep your hair away from your eyes like this, maybe it will be." I released him.

By this time, we got to the front of the line. I was about to order when I realized that while I wanted something sweet, I didn't have pockets and thus no money. He noticed my hesitation and guessed the reason behind it. He pulled out cash from his back pocket and I looked away, embarrassed that he had to save me like this. "Floss," he said to the haggard looking teenager behind the counter.

She plucked one of the ready-made ones in a bag, hanging around the stall and handed it to him with his change. "Thanks."

We walked away, and he handed the candy to me with a smirk. "Sorry," I said, taking it gratefully from him. I fumbled with the knot. It was my turn to blush. He laughed softly. "She'll be 'right. My shout."

We found an empty bench by another overfilled trash bin. Part of it looked a bit sticky from spilled pop so I claimed one end while he sat without hesitation on the ground beside me. I offered him some candy as I had before and just as before, he declined. He watched me as I ate, his expression growing more and more somber.

"I didn't blink," he said abruptly.

I looked at him questioningly. "I didn't blink," he said again. "But you disappeared anyway."

The candy was suddenly too sweet and I didn't want it anymore. "It's not like I can control it," I almost whispered. *Whatever it is.* "It sucks because I don't know when it's over and I don't know when I get to see you again." *If I get to see you again.*

"Where do you … go?" He wasn't looking at me.

I go to a world that is nowhere near as interesting as the one you are a part of, I wanted to say. *I go to everyone's reality, where people don't know me. I go to a place that has become almost intolerable if it weren't for the hope that when I close my eyes, I may see you again.*

I wake up.

I sighed. "I don't know, Ethan." I hesitated. "To be honest, I'm beginning to question what's real and what isn't. That doesn't make for a stable mind."

He seemed to silently agree. His face fretted in deep thought and worry. I saw his hands itching for his blade but I could see that he was well aware that this was not a good venue to be spinning sharp objects. Instead, he balled them into tight fists.

We sat there contemplating the unpleasant aspects of our unusual relationship. I swung the cotton candy idly. "Considering how uncertain and limited our time is together," I pondered. "You'd think we'd use more of it enjoying what we do have …"

"You would think," he repeated. He finally looked at me and smiled. It was a form of surrender.

The road to insanity …

"Let's go," he said. "Jump into this madness with me." He got up and offered me his hand. Smiling, I took it and we walked, hand in hand, toward the game booths. He smelled of freshly laundered clothes. I leaned a little more against him and the cotton candy was appealing again. I saw him look down at me, awakening a warmth that generated throughout my body.

I realized that this wasn't the Oktoberfest fairgrounds. Though the booths looked strikingly similar, this place lacked the variety of food and rides that made Oktoberfest the biggest event in town. The colors on the banners and the sounds that filled the air were different. It made the atmosphere even more surreal.

"Why a fair?" I asked him as we walked.

He laughed softly. "Because I'm quite mad."

I wished he would make more sense.

He squeezed my hand and slowed his pace. "This sounds even more mental when I have to admit it out loud," he mumbled. "When you … disappeared the second time," he began, "I wanted to … find you." He swallowed hard and hesitated. He was looking down at our intertwined hands, not meeting my gaze. "I didn't know where to look. I stayed in the mall until it closed then

I spent hours at the park, just walking and waiting. I was hoping to find any sign that you came back. Or that you were even there. I almost convinced myself that you never existed."

This was familiar.

"I considered all kinds of outrageousness. Are you a figment of my imagination? Some sort of manifestation of my damaged psyche? You're like no one I've met before. You can't possibly be real."

He searched my eyes, holding my hand with his left and he brought his right to touch my face lightly. I held my breath. "You're real," he whispered with intensity. "I can't explain how or why but you are.

"I did everything that you had suggested I do, hoping that it would somehow, I don't know, win your approval, I suppose. So that you'd show up again. When you didn't, I ..." he looked away. "I was angry. I thought that you were just another form of persecution."

My heart ached, and I wanted to reassure him but I also didn't know what to say. "You showed up again in the forest when I had given up looking for you," he continued. "Seeing you again was ... what I needed. You are everything positive that I've ever believed in. When you disappeared, there was no question in my mind. I knew that I had to find you.

"I went back to the mall. You weren't there either. And I was running out of time." His voice took on a desperate tone. "I leave on the waka in the morning. I don't know where I'll be going. I don't know ..." he stopped. I knew exactly what he was thinking because it's the same worry that's been haunting me.

Will I see you again?

He took a deep breath and smiled. It was not without effort. "I came here," he said slowly, "because they have heaps of lolly here."

What?

He bit his lip to stop his smile. "London, I'm certain that you're real but …" he hesitated.

"But?" I prompted.

"I don't know if you're … human." He looked apologetic.

"What?!" I froze in disbelief. He didn't let go of my hand. Instead, he held my one hand in both of his, holding on as if I would run away. "Look," he said hastily, his words ran into each other. "I don't care. I know nothing about you except this … this hold you have on me. I saw you eat floss and you admitted you liked all sorts of lolly. For all I know, that's all you eat."

I looked at him in confusion. It was such a leap. What did he think I was if I wasn't human? He thought I was an alien?

Was I?

"I thought I'd look into places that had high lolly content," he continued, still apologetic.

I nodded, a bit numb. "Logical."

Convinced I wasn't going to bolt, he pulled me along and we started to walk again. "After the mall, I went to lolly stores. I checked out the local circus. This was one of my last stops." He smiled. "I was going to head to the bowling alley after …"

"You think I'm … not human?" I wasn't listening to him anymore. I was trying to wrap my head around it.

He shrugged. "I don't care," he repeated. "I am chuffed that your fondness for floss was strong enough to lure you here." I pondered this for a moment. I was caught between feeling affronted that he thought I wasn't even the same species as he was and feeling elated that he wanted to be with me regardless. Finally, under the stress of the two emotions, I just laughed.

He believed in me. I believed in him. Believed in him

beyond reason.

There was no help for me now. I've gone too far and have all too willingly let go of the rope. There was no point denying it.

"Great," I said sarcastically but with a smile on my face. "I thought it was bad enough that I was questioning my own sanity. Now you have me questioning my humanity." He didn't mirror my smile. He looked concerned.

"No, not like that," he said. I laughed again.

"I know." My mind had finally reached its limit and I had to laugh it off or I'd lose it. "My brothers always did tell me I was adopted." He frowned.

"Well," I began, feeling reckless, "since we're coming out of our psychosis closets I suppose it's only fair I declare myself out loud as well." I suddenly understood how hard it was for him to admit this vocally and realized that I could only because he had the courage to do so first. We stopped walking. I held his hand tightly and assured him, "I don't want to disappear but if I do, it's nothing you did." He nodded silently. I took a deep breath. "I'm dreaming."

I thought those were the words that would bring all this crashing down. It was the admission of reality; surely that was the antithesis of this fantasy world. I did not look away from him. I wanted to memorize everything about him just the way he was now. In case I never see him again.

Nothing happened.

It was a positive sign and continued. "I was doped up on drugs the first time I dreamt of you."

His expression was legitimately troubled. "You're on drugs?" I could see all the provisions he was planning in his head to compensate for this revelation.

"No, no ..." I amended right away. "I mean, not like the way you think. Not illegal drugs."

"Prescription, then?" He looked even more worried. His eyebrows almost fused together into a single anxious line. I laughed. I was doing the worst job explaining things.

"Will you let me finish?" He pressed his lips together. I waited until I was sure he wasn't going to interrupt. "The night Dad and I arrived in town, I caught some sort of nasty virus and ended up in the emergency room. I had an incredibly high fever that triggered some kind of seizure. You're not supposed to be aware of it when you're experiencing it but I did. I was trying to reach out … to wake up but I ended up somewhere else." I remembered the paralyzing fear and shuddered involuntarily. He pulled me closer to him.

"That was the first time I dreamt of you. I thought it was a fluke … some vivid dream brought about by the drugs or the virus but at the same time, you were crazy real to me. Everything I experienced … the emotions, the sensations … I thought the reason I was in the hospital was because the truck had hit me.

"When I realized that it was all a dream, I was crushed. I never expected to see you again. I tried," I admitted. "I couldn't wait to go to sleep. I was impatient most of the day. I went to bed thinking about you, hoping that I could force myself to dream about you but it didn't work. I ended up staying up a lot. Then one night, without willing it, I dreamt of you again. Just like before. And this time, without the fever and without the drugs.

"What does that mean? How is it possible to feel this strongly?" I looked up at him, wondering if my questions would be the downfall of this dream. "And should I continue to dream about you? Should I want this? How healthy can it possibly be to want to be unconscious? How can I know that you're real? That you aren't some unconscious materialization of my sick mind?"

His lips were pressed together and his expression somber.

There was a war going on in his head, and the conflict was evident in his eyes. "I'm not the person to ask," he finally said. His expression softened ruefully. "I'm your bloody fictional construct!"

I sighed. "Well, it's not as if I'm taking steps to avoid this." It was more accurate to say the opposite.

We stopped in between two amusement rides and he turned his body to face me. "Right now you're dreaming? You're asleep?" I could see he was trying to make sense out of this.

"I don't know if I'm in any position to really know but, yes, I think I'm dreaming." He looked doubtful. "That said," I continued, "You should know that I am much more awake now than I am when I'm not sleeping." That made perfect sense to me and I somehow knew that he would understand what I meant.

"I don't think I live in the same world that you do."

He processed that theory. "How do you get here?"

"I don't know. I can't control it. It's just stupid random!" I was frustrated. These were the same questions that have been hounding me endlessly for the past two months. I smiled at him. "I don't think I'm here for the cotton candy, though."

I was becoming more confident, convinced that if he did want this as much as I did, there were no worlds to keep us apart. "I'll find you over and over again." He gave me his signature half-smile. "Technically, I found you, eh? You were more interested in floss than finding me." That wasn't true and he knew it. I didn't bother to restrain myself. I stuck my tongue out at him. He grinned, we walked on.

Our collective mood was better when we arrived at the game booths. We walked past the flying rubber chickens, the darts, the ring toss, and even pellet guns. We stopped in front of the knife throwing booth. "You're not serious," I said to him and rolled my eyes. He grinned. He was in his element. I already knew that he would be able to hit any target that was up there, and it wouldn't even be a challenge to him.

"Try your skill to win something for your little lady?" the greasy haired man behind the counter pitched to him. It was an obvious sales tactic but a tingle of pleasure ran up my spine at being called his 'little lady'. It was irrational and I refused to acknowledge it outwardly.

The man offered Ethan the hilt of one of their plain throwing knives and winked at me. "Who doesn't want one of these big stuffed toys, eh? You want one, doncha, darlin'? Eh? eh?" I bit my lip to keep from laughing. The stuffed toys in question were cheaply made fake replicas of one popular cartoon character or another. Off colors and oversized features. None of them were cute.

Ethan paid the man and took the three knives. "If ya hits the yellow circle, ya wins a small prize," He indicated a tray of generic candies. On the shelf above were small notebooks with neon print on the covers. "The orange circle wins ya a medium prize and the bull's eye wins ya a large prize." I rolled my eyes again when Ethan hefted the knife in his hands. He grinned at me. The look on his face was devious. I laughed out loud. It was the delight of being in on a secret.

It should have been easy for someone with his talent but his first throw was wild. It didn't even get close to the target. The man snickered, and Ethan gritted his teeth. I laughed at his expense. He gave me a withering look that made me laugh even harder. "You can do it!" I cheered mockingly, waving what was left of my cotton candy in the air. There's a cheerleader in me yet! He flipped the second knife, holding it by the blade and not the hilt. Bringing it up to his face to aim, he narrowed his eyes.

I watched him throw it forward with a little more tension this time and heard the thud it made on the board at the far end of the booth. The greasy haired man exclaimed in surprise. It was dead center. Ethan turned to me triumphantly.

Testosterone.

He laid the remaining knife on the counter. "Which one did you want?" he asked me, pointing at the grotesque looking stuffed toys adorning the top of the booth. "Hang on there," the man stepped forward with a tray. "Thems the gigantic prizes, eh? These are the large prizes." He offered us a tray of colorful beaded bracelets.

Ethan looked at him in frustration. "Gigantic prizes? How do you win those?"

The man grinned. "Ya gotsta hit that bull's eye three times in a row, sonny boy."

Ethan's eyes narrowed at the challenge, and I saw him reach for his back pocket. "No thank you," I interjected. They both looked at me. "I'd like one of these," I said, pointing at one of the cheap bracelets. "And I don't need three." I pushed myself between the two of them and took one of the less ostentatious ones. There was no clasp. Of course not. That would be fancy.

I pulled Ethan away from the booth before he could waste more money. "It's not a problem, you know," he insisted. "I can win you something bigger." I rolled my eyes.

"No thank you," I said again. He frowned at me. I could see that he still considered going back.

"Here," I said to distract him. "Will you help me put it on?" I offered him the bracelet and my left wrist. He grinned at me, a spark of mischief in his eyes. "I wonder," he said as he tied it to my wrist, "if this means that you belong to me." I laughed gamely.

"Like your slave?" I said, pretending to be aghast. He shook his head and just continued to work on the elusive knot. The strings

131

were short and he was having a hard time with it. "Property?" I suggested. He shook his head again, his smile soft.

"No. Like … mine." He finally got the knot and he let it hang on my wrist. "My London. My girl."

I looked down at what has to be the ugliest thing I've ever worn. His knots weren't perfect and the little strings stuck up and about. It wasn't exactly a quality piece to begin with. Emerald green and royal blue plastic beads were strung together and braided by cheap, plastic, black string. It didn't even look like it would last the rest of the afternoon.

It was absolutely the most beautiful thing I've seen.

I looked up at him in wonder. "Whether or not I wear this, Ethan, I am your London."

He took my left hand in both of his and brought it up to his lips. "I don't know how I'm going to stand it when you disappear again," he whispered. The pain in his eyes was heartbreaking. I know it was mirrored on my own. "Just hold on to the belief that wherever you go, I'll find you." Please believe it, I thought. "You believe me, don't you?"

He smiled again, a different kind of determination in his eyes. He lowered his chin and looked at me through his lashes. "I'll steal all the lolly in the world to light your way to me." I laughed and tried to shove him, he stepped out of the way. "It is not the candy, OK?!" But I still had a little bit of the incriminating candy in my other hand. He smirked. I looked at him haughtily and stalked to the nearest garbage bin. I made a big show of tossing the rolled up paper into it. I put my hands on my hips and faced him. "See?"

"You look like such a child when you do that, do you know?"

I crossed my arms in front of my chest and frowned at him. He snickered. "That doesn't help your case." My eyes narrowed. He closed the distance between as in two steps. "I don't mean that it isn't adorable ..."

"Oh, shut up!" I rolled my eyes. He put his arm over my shoulder. His touch was instantly comforting. "I've been trying but I don't think it's possible when I'm with you. I don't know how you do it.

"I have said more to you in the short amount of time we've been together than I have to any one person in all my life." He shook his head, marveling at the idea.

"Maybe nobody just knows you well enough."

He blinked, surprised. I was proud of myself. With a grin of his own, he gathered me up in his arms. My back to his front, his chin in my hair. He rocked gently side to side and I sank into him, trying to squeeze out any space that would come between us. It was only a few seconds but the seconds stretched to allow us a shared moment where we danced to music playing only for us.

I smiled, floating on the surface of deep happiness. I played with the bracelet he had won for me, appreciating that I can feel the beads between my fingers. He took notice of it. "Regrets already?" His voice was teasing but I sensed the serious uncertainty beneath them.

"I'm just wondering if I get to keep it, you know? When I wake up. It would be really nice to have something from you." Some tangible proof that this relationship isn't all in my head.

"I didn't think of that," he admitted, letting go of me. The space between us expanded. I turned around to see the sadness reflected in his eyes like a dark cloud. This won't do at all.

"If I do get to keep it," I said teasingly to pull him out of his mood. "How come you get some fancy silver chain and I get this thing of thread?"

He looked at me earnestly. There was a slight hesitation. He frowned. I didn't know if I had stepped over another of his many invisible lines. I was about to apologize when he finally said, "Did you want it? It's yours." He started to remove it.

"No, no!" I put my hand over his and he frowned. "I like mine!"

He gave me a look of disbelief. "You're joking. It's a trinket."

I laughed. "Mine was hard won. You can't buy this kind of quality."

"Well, that's for certain." He rolled his eyes but the darkness in them was lifted. "I want to give you something," he insisted. "I don't have much but if you want this," he held up his wrist, "I want to give it to you."

I looked at it closely for the first time. It was a silver ID bracelet with simple links. It was tight around his wrist, not how one would traditionally wear it. The links weren't enough to go around his wrist so that the clasp did not connect. Instead, two end links were held together with a rubber band. It was a child's bracelet. Engraved on the face of it was his name, Ethan Robert.

"Ethan Robert?"

He lifted an eyebrow. "What's wrong with Robert? Robert is a good name. It's not something silly like, oh I don't know, London or something."

"Ha. Ha. You just don't look like a 'Robert'."

The very edges of his lips curled up. "Oh, really? What exactly does a 'Robert' look like?"

I shrugged. "It's such a proper name. Like 'William' or 'Alexander'. I feel like a 'Robert' should be having tea with me."

"What about Robert De Niro? Robert De Niro doesn't look like he'd have tea."

"You want to be like Robert De Niro?" I asked speculatively.

"I didn't say I wanted to be like Robert De Niro. I just said

Robert De Niro doesn't fit the let's-have-tea version of Robert that you're profiling in your head." He was teasing me.

"De Niro can have his own category," I said. "He's more of a 'De Niro' than a 'Robert' anyhow. No one refers to him as 'Robert'. They call him 'De Niro'." I crossed my arms. "I doubt you're Ethan Robert De Niro, are you?"

"Ethan Robert Mattis at your service." He bowed as if introducing himself. I laughed and offered my hand like a lady-in-waiting.

"London Anne Evans." He took my hand and pressed it to his lips. I shivered.

"It's a pleasure to meet you, Ms. Evans," he said in a low voice, sweet velvet tempering the huskiness. He pulled me to him, sporting that trademark half-smile. I looked up and I couldn't see past his face. At that moment, he was all there was in the world. The unrecognizable music, the loud grinding machines, and all the many voices that filled the air were gone. It was silent but for the sound of his voice. It was hard to breathe. There was a twinkle in his eyes. He leaned down, his lips closer to my ear.

"So," he said in a whisper. I held my breath in anticipation.

"Did your parents name you on an average?"

Wait. What?

Those were not exactly words of sweet nothingness I was expecting. The rest of the world came rushing back to focus. It was as if someone had turned up the volume. I pulled away and looked at him in confusion. His lips were pressed tightly together to repress a smile.

"Did they figure a strange name like London and a common name like Anne averaged to an acceptable name?"

He is frustrating. Charming. Mysterious. Intoxicating. So goddamn frustrating! My brain was trying to catch up to all my mixed up emotions. My mouth opened and closed like a gaping fish but nothing was coming out. "What," he said innocently. "You made fun of my name!

Aaaaaaaaaaaaaaaaaaarrrrghhhhh!

I took a swing at him. I took several swings at him, as a matter of fact. He blocked my assault with ease, laughing the entire time. He grabbed me by my wrists, pulled me to him again. "I thought your brothers taught you self defense," he taunted. I tried to kick him in the groin and he dodged me effortlessly. After he had had enough of my pathetic attempt at physical violence, he wrapped me into a tight hug, still laughing. I glared up at him but stopped struggling. I really didn't want to struggle.

He met my glower with an open look. His eyes, dancing and honest.

"London Anne Evans," he said simply. "I love you."

Represent

I opened my eyes to darkness.

The very descriptive and vile swear word in my head almost left my lips in a scream. I threw my face into my pillow to muffle the frustration.

Why did I have to wake up now? Why? Why? Why?

I was decidedly awake. I was neither tired nor sleepy. My heart was pounding in my ribcage almost painfully. The physical reaction to him was undeniable.

He was not just a dream. I refused to believe that he could easily be categorized. That there was nothing more to him than this.

It was a connection. A connection only within a dream. The dream was just a medium in which we could both exist and interact.

He was real.

My body hadn't yet forgotten the feel of his hand in mine or his lips on my fingers. The shadow of his arms around me was still fresh in my head. I looked down at my wrist, hoping to find tangible evidence of his reality. The light filtering through my window was enough for me to see that it was bare.

The injustice. I pressed the palms of my hands to my eyes until they hurt. I wanted to feel it. Remind myself that I was still alive in my unstable world.

I took intentionally measured deep breaths to calm myself. It would not do to have a nervous breakdown. I would not be able to appreciate him fully if I did.

He loves me.

I lifted my hands off my eyes and dropped them over my head. I lay there on my back, staring up at the ceiling.

Ethan Robert Mattis.

I rolled out of bed and flicked the lights on. The clock said it was past 4 a.m. Sleep was out of the question. I pulled out my laptop. I found a lollipop in my desk drawer and unwrapped it thoughtfully as I waited for my computer to boot.

If he was here in this world, I would find him.

It seemed to take longer than usual for my browser to pull up. I knew it was more because of my impatience. I bit into the lollipop to release some of my tension. By the time I was connected to the internet, I was chewing on an empty stick.

I typed his name up on the search window, my stomach in knots. The search button revealed 311,000 results. Everything from politicians to artwork to street signs appeared. I tried again adding the words Paradigm, in an attempt to narrow the search field but it didn't help.

I tried different search engines, different combinations and different words. I tried and tried again, unwilling to give up.

When I was down to 300 sites, I clicked on the ones that were the most likely candidates.

Not what I was searching for. Not even close.

By the time the dawn light filled my room, I wanted to throw my laptop out the window.

I was angrier at myself, of course. I should've paid more attention to my surroundings. I should've been able to find one clue that could tell me where he was. The problem is I'm never in the right state of mind when I am with him. No matter where we are or how many people are around us, it's always just the two of us.

Yet if he really couldn't be found, it wouldn't make him any less valid. There were other possibilities. As crazy as it was to contemplate time travel or alternate universes, It was still better than admitting he didn't exist. That it was the more plausible explanation.

It didn't matter if he wasn't a part of this world. He was part of my world.

I shut the laptop harder than what was probably factory-recommended.

There was a knock on my door and Dad popped his head in. "I knew I heard something. You're up early, Sweetheart."

Dad called me "sweetheart" as long as I could remember. Even in the middle of an argument. I wondered if he actually even remembered my name. I smiled fondly at him.

"I woke up around four and couldn't get back to sleep."

He stepped in and sat on the edge of my bed. "Everything OK?" He was genuinely concerned.

The really great thing about Dad was he wasn't ever judgmental about the things that bothered me. Even when I was as young as 8, he'd listen intently to my concerns and then address them in an adult manner. He always took the effort to consider my feelings whether we were dealing with identity issues or why it was important for me to have privacy in the bathroom. I was actually closer to him than I was to any of my brothers.

This, however, may have been more than he could handle as a father.

"I'll survive," I said as kindly as I could. Then sounding more like Ethan than I ever thought I could, I added, "She'll be 'right." My smile was genuine. Not because of the words I said but because of who I thought about while I said them.

"OK," he said as he got up. "But if you need to talk." He held out both hands to me in open invitation.

"I know, Dad. Thanks."

"What time are you going to be at the fairgrounds?"

I sighed. "Soon?"

He laughed. "I'll give you a ride."

The second day of Oktoberfest didn't seem as exciting as the day before. Maybe I was still exhausted from my sleepless night or the novelty has worn off. I avoided people I knew for the most part, knowing that the group would have more than enough business today, judging from yesterday's turnout even if I didn't pass out any fliers today. I had a stack with me purely for show. I had a different purpose today.

The first thing I bought, at 10 a.m. was cotton candy, hoping that he would show up before I got to the front of the line. Even though I met him in a place other than this fair, mimicking my actions was a silent kind of tribute to him. To us.

I paid more attention to the game booths. The Oktoberfest didn't offer a knife-throwing booth. It wouldn't matter because, without him, there was no way I could win anything there anyway. Not one of them, and I checked every one, had cheap bracelets as a prize.

What was I expecting, really?

It was late in the afternoon when a trinket at the Girl Scout booth caught my eye. Besides the stacks of Thin Mints and Gluten-free Toffee-tastics was a small assortment of friendship bracelets. They were, by far, made better than what I chose from with him. No beads. Just made with colorful thread. I picked up one made with a light turquoise blue and a bit of mint green. I smiled, thinking about what he said as he tied his gaudy version around my wrist.

"Good afternoon! Proceeds go to our program initiatives," a 7 year-old little girl in full Girl Scout uniform and braids began her pitch. "Our programs encourage increased skill-building and responsibility. They also promote the development of ..."

"How much?" I interrupted. I was already sold on buying it before she started talking anyway. I gave her the appropriate amount of tickets and pocketed the bracelet.

I found an empty bench where I spent 20 minutes trying to tie the bracelet on to myself. If he wasn't around to do it himself, I would not let anyone else take his place. The results still looked better than the sloppy knots he ended up with. I smiled.

I shook my wrist and felt a comfortable weight settle on it. It felt the way it should. Made me feel less of the London of this world and more like his London. The version of myself I'd much rather be.

The rest of the night was a repeat of the one before except we were smart enough to end the line earlier. That meant that we could pack up at a more reasonable time. There was still one more day of this. I was grateful that I had hitched a ride with Dad in the morning and I didn't have to bike back home. The ache was gone from my legs and though I didn't feel as worn, my bed was ever welcoming. My body was eager for a good night's rest though my heart was hoping for another sleepless night. If it meant being with him again, I wouldn't mind at all.

I got my sleep.

In The Spirit Of Things

Brieann hounded me the week leading up to Halloween. She was throwing a costume party at her house. Of course. As her 'best friend' (When did this happen? *How* did this happen?), I was required to be there. I've failed dramatically in my intent to stay far away from social events. It was a lost cause to begin with anyway. Not when you're friends with the most popular girl in school.

I had to admire her. She did what she wanted and still maintained her social status. Not the easiest thing to navigate in high school. Even as gorgeous and well connected as Amanda was, she couldn't go toe to toe with Brieann. And it was no secret that she wanted to. It was like being on the set of a badly scripted teen TV series.

New on Netflix… Selfish Little Bitches.

With invitations in the hands of the majority of juniors and select seniors, I sat in the cafeteria trying to tread the social waters of this predator-filled high school soap opera.

"Do you have your costume yet? The party is, like, three days away!"

"I got my costume today but I look like a cow! I need a new one!"

"Chris is going to be there! He's so freakin' hot!"

This wasn't even prom they were talking about. It was Halloween. It happens literally every. Single. Year. It was a long week.

I went along with the crowd largely because I didn't want to hurt Brieann's feelings. Events like these are designed for people who want an excuse to hook up with other people, a prerequisite I certainly do not meet. It's not as if he would be there.

I was at Brieann's house two hours before the party started. As early as I was, the decorations were all up and the house was pristine. Her mother, a slim executive Realtor who didn't look old enough to have children Brieann's age, intentionally stayed out of the way. She was there to provide the least amount of parental supervision necessary.

Brieann was dressed in a stunning Hollywoodesque-Red-Carpet-Oscars gown with enough sequins to blind you. Her blonde hair was done up in a Marilyn Monroe way. She even sported a mole on her upper lip. Absolutely gorgeous, of course.

I grabbed a seat on the couch, dressed in my newly painted old jeans, tie-dye flower power shirt and a 60's bandana over a wig of waist-length straight hair. I pulled down colored glasses way too big for my face and answered her disapproving look with a peace sign. I had a lollipop in my mouth and Tootsie Rolls in my back pocket.

"Exactly what are you supposed to be?" she asked me with her hands on her hips.

I gave her an innocent look. "I'm a hippie protester from Berkeley in the 70's!"

It was easy to see that I exasperated her. "Well, it was either that or take clothes from Dad's closet," I said in defense. "I decided not to go as a nerdy Math professor."

She rolled her eyes. "It could have been worse, I suppose."

I smiled when she turned her back on me to attend to the candy bowl that I already had pillaged. She would be off my back for the rest of the night. I'm just going to have to endure until I could leave as soon as it would be considered appropriate.

The hour did not come quickly enough. The house was filled with people and the party spilled outdoors. Her 65-inch flat screen TV was playing some outrageous horror flick in unnecessary high definition. It was really just more excuses for flirty girls to throw themselves shamelessly at their dates. It really wasn't my scene. I finally left Brieann's company and headed for the front of the house.

I sat on the curb, a few steps outside her front door, playing with the stick of the fourth pumpkin shaped lollipop I had that night. Beyond the sounds of the party was a three-foot-tall vampire going door to door for treats. A tired-looking mom was pulling a wagon, where an even smaller vampire sat, sucking on a pacifier that resembled fangs. Classic treat or treating.

Dad wasn't one to be excited about candy giving. He left out a large bowl of candy on the steps of our front door with a sign that read: Please take only one. He claimed it was the "honor system". I call it being lazy.

The family avoided Brieann's house, where the party was obviously made by and for unruly teenagers. I smiled at the little ones that made eye contact with me as they passed.

"I hope you aren't planning on mugging kids for their candy," a deep voice said behind me.

I looked up and saw a boy I didn't recognize grinning at me. A plain white shirt with faded black print boldly declared: THIS IS MY HALLOWEEN COSTUME. He wore an open green flannel over it. This was clearly an ensemble that had seen many Halloween days.

"Well, now that you've called me out on it ..." I trailed off. I thought about going back inside to avoid him and glanced behind me. Another scream followed by rowdy laughter emanated from the open doors, reminding me why I was outside in the first place. Lesser of evils.

He put his hands on his hips, chest out, and looked off into the distance. "Yet another crime I've managed to prevent," he announced to no one in particular. He brushed a mess of reddish hair off his face and tossed his chin up. "You're welcome, citizens." He paused for a moment, in all his superhero glory, to take in the gratitude of his imaginary admirers before sitting his lean frame down on the curb next to me.

"They have no idea what you've just done for them," I said sarcastically.

"Heroes don't do it for the glory," he winked.

"Oh? Why, then?"

"Cookies."

"Cookies," I repeated in disbelief.

"Sure. They tally up all your good work at the end of the month. and then award you with cookies."

I laughed. "And here I thought that altruism was the driving force." He pointed at me gamely, "That's what we want you to think. That way you don't join in and try to take our share of cookies."

"I can see how that could be a problem." He tapped his finger to his brow in knowing agreement. "You've given up the secret, though," I pointed out. "What's to stop me from taking a stab at your cookie share?" He scoffed, completely unthreatened. "It's not that easy," he said. "You have to be a hero."

"Doesn't seem like there's a strict acceptance policy," I countered, watching another family walk by. This time, the baby was in a pumpkin outfit. There was an overflowing bucket of choking hazard candy that she wouldn't be allowed to eat in front of her. I slid a sideways glance at the boy next to me. "After all, they let you in."

"Ooooh!" He lifted his hand up to his eyes and squinted. "Shade!" I laughed. "First of all," he said, counting off with his fingers, "You'll need a hero name. Second, you'll need a snazzy outfit, preferably in basic Pantone approved colors." He looked me up and down and said, "I see you in 871C and 15-0332 TCX. No cape."

I looked up at him sharply. I've been recently made familiar with those colors. "Commonly known as gold and green," I supplied, speaking slowly.

"Ah!" He clasped his hands together in theatrical delight. "You do speak my language!" He leaned forward, tightening the distance between us. "What's your medium? Acrylics? Oil? Adobe?" When I didn't answer right away, he continued dubiously, "Chewed up betel nuts?"

"That's oddly specific," I conceded, putting the chewed up lollipop stick back in my mouth. He shrugged, his shoulders coming up almost all the way up to his chin face and his hands palms up in the air. "To each his own. Maybe it's not my cup of latte but I don't judge." He let his shoulders fall. "OK," he added, "Maybe I judge but I just won't admit it."

"Same," I nodded knowingly. "As it should be. Silently judging." He put a finger up to his lips and winked. I let the conversation pause to allow another bout of exaggerated screaming from the open door to die down.

"I mostly sketch," I admitted. "I tried watercolor but found the flow to be a little too unpredictable."

"What you're telling me is that you have issues giving up control," he said, acting like he was a therapist writing on an imaginary pad. "What about you, hero," I challenged. "What's your medium?"

"Ballet," he said without expression. I narrowed my eyes at him in obvious distrust. "What?" he asked defensively. "A dude can't be in ballet?"

"A dude most certainly can," I countered. "You are not that dude." He threw a hand to his chest in mock incredulity, amused. "You do not have the build of a ballet dancer," I added.

"You're judging me," he accused. "And not silently!" I put a finger to my lips and winked. He laughed. "Go on then," he waved the hand that he had used to demonstrate defensiveness. "Let's hear it. What do you think I dabble in?"

I looked at him closely and noticed a few smears of paint on his flannel. The lighter colors of soft gray and eggshell. I leaned closer for a better look and could detect the faint smell of supposedly odorless mineral spirits. The aftershave of oil painters.

"Oil," I guessed. His grin confirmed that I guessed correctly. "But more Magritte and less Renoir," I added as a wild shot in the dark. He stopped, his mouth half-open in surprise. "I'm right," I declared delightedly, in spite of myself. He nodded slowly and seemed to look at me in a different light.

"What you're telling me," I said, adopting the same stance he had earlier with an imaginary pen in hand. "Is that you enjoy confusing others in order to maintain the upper hand."

"You do have super powers," he said in a stage whisper. "Can you make things float with your mind too?" I held the empty lollipop stick out to him, "I can make candy disappear."

"I hate to tell you but that's more like a villain's manifesto." I shrugged. "I guess I'm your nemesis now." His eyes widened. and he jumped back up to his superhero stance. "So it shall be!" Fat pause. "But the plot twist in this story," he continued, "Is that we're actually really good friends in our mild mannered civilian lives." He held out his hand at me, "I'm Drew."

I took his hand and shook it, "I'm London." He nodded. "Yes, I know. You're in my History class."

Oops.

He sat back down. "You always sit with Bree and never talk to anyone. You just doodle all throughout class." I grimaced, embarrassed that he called me out on both my anti-social behavior and inattentiveness in class. "How come you haven't joined the Art Society? Do you have an aversion to organized authority?"

Deja vu. I was playing a different role in a familiar conversation. I searched him, not really sure what I was looking for. I did not find it.

I shrugged. "Still settling into the whole 'new kid' role, you know?"

"I've lived here my entire life. I guess I wouldn't know." He leaned back on his hands. "On the other hand, you've got the advantage of still being mysterious and interesting."

"You find me mysterious and interesting?" These were words

never used to describe me before. It was surprisingly flattering to hear.

He nodded. "If you think about it, I think it's my responsibility to get to know you."

"Your responsibility," I repeated.

"As a protector of the general public's Halloween candy. I feel like I have a duty to know all there is to know about my nemesis." I laughed. Well played. "It's just research," he added.

"Then wouldn't it be in my best interest to remain mysterious and interesting? So you don't thwart my well-laid plans?" He nodded. "It's a good thing that the hero always wins in the end." He handed me a chocolate Tootsie pop. "I also come bearing gifts."

"That helps," I conceded, taking the lollipop from him. It was a weakness. "Are you here with anyone?" I asked, unwrapping the Tootsie pop and enjoying the sweet taste in my mouth. He smiled. "Is that your forward way of asking if I have a girlfriend?"

I almost choked.

I pulled the lollipop out of my mouth, coughing uncontrollably. The steady thumping on my back was Drew's open hand helping me breathe. I held up a hand to show him that I didn't need the assistance, gulped air, and the coughing quickly subsided. I had the hint of tears in my eyes. My cheeks burned. His hand lingered on my upper back. He looked concerned. "Do you need water?"

I nodded. "Yeah, that would be great," I said in a raspy voice. His hand left my back as he scrambled to his feet and ran inside. I watched him go. I was just caught by surprise. I didn't actually really need the water but I did need time to sort out what just happened and how to redeem myself.

What just happened here?

He was back almost too quickly, an unopened bottle of mineral water in his hands. "Are you OK?" he asked while I took a sip. I let the mouth of the bottle linger on my lips to avoid answering. I just nodded. He watched me closely. I took more sips, taking my time. His eyes didn't waver and I was profoundly conscious of how many seconds were going by much slower than they should. The quiet was interrupted by hollering and applause. The movie had come to an end. Drew looked away and I closed my eyes, relieved that the moment was broken.

By the time he looked back at me, I was finally composed. "Well," I finally declared, "I think I'm done with candy for the rest of the night." He looked apologetic as if the fault were his. "I can take you home if you'd like," he offered.

"I took my bike," I shrugged in response.

"I can walk with you if you don't mind the company." Then added with a grin, "I wouldn't forgive myself if I find out tomorrow that you mugged Batman Jr. for his pixie stix."

We made our way through the bodies to find Brieann in the backyard, innocent-looking red solo cup in her hand. She looked at me, looked at Drew, then looked back at me with a meaningfully raised eyebrow that was full of implication. I narrowed my eyes at her, not certain how I was feeling about all this.

"Hi, Drew," she greeted him, totally glossing over my presence. "Hey, great party," he responded casually. "Where have the two of you been?" she asked, not exerting much effort into hiding her intentions. He shrugged, "I saved her from literally killing herself over candy."

The second eyebrow joined the first high on her head atop questions that she already answered without my participation. "That sounds exciting."

"Which is why," I interjected before I was completely unable to follow all the subtext floating in the air, "I'm going to call it quits and just head home." I thought that would annoy her, but it just gave her more ammunition.

"Taking her home then, Drew?" She intentionally ignored me to speak to Drew. "You never know what damage she can do when left to her own devices." Brieann tipped her cup in agreement, the liquid inside expertly staying in. I rolled my eyes at her and just spun on my heel and left. Drew followed me. Behind us, Brieann called, "Goodnight you twooooo ..."

Drew waited patiently, his hands in his jeans pockets, while I fished my bike from Brieann's garage. I hung my helmet on to the handle bars as I weaved it between cars, making sure it wouldn't swing against either vehicle. Brieann warned me against possibly marring the paint on her mom's bright red Tesla. The blinking light visible from the dash was a reminder to be careful with my helmet.

Instead, one of the pedals hooked on the jet black Jeep that sat next to it. I caught the bike before the whole thing went crashing down. It wasn't a flattering position to be found in when Drew peeked his head through the garage door in response to my swearing.

"Need a hand?" he offered.

"If you start clapping, I swear I will injure you." He grinned then took the bike from me. I could straighten up and collect my dignity. "That's twice I've saved your life in one night," he commented, walking my bike for me. I would take it from him but he was accomplishing it with significantly more ease than I.

"But who's counting, right?" I responded. He held up two fingers, demonstrating that he, in fact, was keeping count. "It's how I collect my cookies, remember?"

The noise from Bree's party faded as we walked away. Even the kids have stopped trick or treating. The neighborhood settled into a familiar quiet night. Street lights on every corner made it comfortable to walk through, and we found ourselves straying from the sidewalk. Before long, we were walking, without care, right down the middle of the street.

"Does it suck?" Drew asked. "Moving?" His question was generic but there was a sincerity that I had not picked up from anyone who had asked me before. It seemed appropriate to be honest.

"Not really." I looked up at the dark sky, enjoying how different it looked from what I had grown up with. "For one thing, the weather is better."

"Seriously? The weather? That's worth moving for?"

"Clearly, you've never had to deal with a polar vortex."

He was right, though. I was projecting my father in an attempt to delay really responding. "It's nice," I added. "Being able to start over."

"Sounds like there's some questionable history there," he said but in the form of a question. Like he didn't believe it himself. "No, not at all. It was great," I assured him. "I had friends I've known all my life. Safe. Familiar. I'm sure you get it." He was studying me now, not just looking at me. "Did you not like who you were when you were there?"

That was a good question.

I shrugged. "Hard to tell," I said, avoiding his eyes. "When I'm not sure who I really am." I was suddenly vulnerable. Like I had admitted too much, too quickly. He was quiet. I risked looking at him from the side of my eye. He wasn't looking at me anymore. He had followed my gaze up at the stars.

"Somewhere between who you want to be and who everyone expects you to be." His tone was whimsical. He caught me looking at him. "That's who you are," he said more strongly. "The person between who you want to be and who everyone expects you to be."

"You've given this thought," I accused, equally impressed and surprised. "Too bad I don't know who I want to be either."

He laughed in agreement. "Isn't that the truth!"

"Do you know who you want to be?" I asked him. He did a half shrug, more reflexive than anything, "I figure that I'd approach life in the same way I would my lunch …"

"Hungry?"

"Well, yeah … but I mean, sometimes I'm in line at the cafeteria and I'm not sure what I want to eat, you know?" I nodded. I can appreciate that. "But," he added. "I know what I don't want. Like, sure as hell, I'm not eating that bologna sandwich that's been sitting on the shelf for three days." I laughed. I knew that sandwich. "So, in life, I know I don't want to end up in jail. That eliminates all illegal activity."

"Jail is a bologna sandwich?"

"That particular bologna sandwich anyway."

We walked a few steps in silence. Together in thought.

"What are you having for the lunch of life?" I asked. He tilted his head side to side, "Not sure yet. I've at least got until graduation before I get to the end of the line and have to make a decision."

I considered what he said. It was strangely comforting.

He walked me up to the steps of the front entrance, where he left my bike leaning on the side of the wall. "Thanks for walking me home," I said sincerely, in spite of myself. "Are you heading home now?"

He stepped back down to the sidewalk, hands back in his pockets. "Nah, I'll head back to Bree's to pick up my car."

I blinked at him. "You have a car?"

"I did offer to take you home. It would be awkward if I didn't actually have a means to do so?"

Well, yeah. That makes sense. I just felt badly that he had walked all this way when he didn't have to. "Oh, sorry about that," I said just because I didn't know what else I was supposed to say. He tilted his head, "Don't be. It was a nice walk, and it's good to finally meet you."

"It was good meeting you too." I meant it.

I unlocked the door and stepped in. When I turned around to shut it, he was still standing on the sidewalk, smiling at me. He waved once. I smiled back and shut the door. I peeked out the window and he was walking down the middle of the street, his hands behind his head and looking up at the stars.

Paparazzi

After Brieann threw a party like the night before, you would think that she would take full advantage of Sunday to catch up on some sleep. On the contrary, bright and early the next morning, Brieann was ringing the doorbell with a desperate sense of urgency.

I ran down the stairs with my toothbrush in hand. Dad was still sleeping.

"All right already!" I threw open the door, my mouth full of toothpaste. Her face was alight with excitement. Completely ignoring the state I was in, she launched into full interrogation mode.

"So?" She threw her purse on the couch and followed me up the stairs to the bathroom.

"Keep it down, will you? Dad is still in bed!"

She obediently lowered her voice but did not temper the excitement. "So? So? So? What happened?"

I gave her a long-suffering look through her reflection in the mirror as I rinsed my mouth of bubbles. I deliberately took my time drying my face, taking vindictive pleasure in seeing her pace outside the open bathroom door.

Two steps. Turn. Two steps. Turn. Not taking her eyes off me the entire time.

"Nothing happened," I seethed to this predator in ankle boots.

She followed me to my room. I closed the door while she threw herself, cross-legged, on my bed.

"He took you home." Her words were heavy with implication. She was bouncing on the bed.

"We walked home together," I corrected, halfway in my closet, looking for a suitable shirt. What goes well with your-best-friend-might-just-make-you-throw-up?

"That's even more romantic," she gushed.

Correction: I need a shirt that says I-had-no-choice-but-to-slap-her-your-honor.

"Not cool."

She let herself fall back on my bed, whining. I could now appreciate my father's aversion to the sound.

I decided on a weekend staple: Keep Calm and Make it Yourself. Keep Calm … keep calm … keep calm …

Good advice.

"Oh, come on, London! Really? I can't believe I didn't see it earlier! Of course, Drew Clark! Of course! You guys are way too cute together."

She wasn't wrong. Drew was surprisingly easy to talk to. We had more in common than I've ever had with anyone. Especially someone I just met. He was interesting and funny and cute. There was a connection there that I couldn't ignore. Like Ethan but also very much not like Ethan.

I didn't want to think about it. It felt like disloyalty.

"He's not my type." It's not really lying if you don't give yourself a chance to think about it, is it?

"You're crazy."

I laughed. "I told you I was," I pointed out. I grabbed the pair of jeans I had tossed on my chair the other day. Still clean. Ish.

Brieann stayed on her back, on my bed, her arm over her face. Best Dramatic Performance goes to Brieann Hendrixson for her role as frustrated matchmaker. I changed out of my pajamas.

"Why are you fighting this?"

How was I supposed to answer that? I decided to just not answer.

"Are you going to join the Art Society now?" she asked, fluffing up a pillow.

I sighed, my hands fumbling on the button fly. I hate button fly. Why do I even own button fly jeans? "I dunno. Maybe."

"I knew it! You like him!" She yelled loud enough that I heard Dad stir in the other room.

"Shut up! Dad!" She had both hands over her mouth but she didn't look the slightest bit apologetic. I hadn't yet fully exhaled before there was a knock on the door. Dad poked his head in.

"Is this positive cheering or negative yelling? Oh, hello, Brieann."

"Good morning, Dr. Evans," her melodic voice, the polar opposite of all her yelling. "That was my fault. Sorry. I'm just excited 'cause this guy we know brought London home last night ..."

"Brieann!" I threw my jammies to her, only because nothing more damaging was within reach. This was a total breach of the friendship code.

Dad's eyebrows both shot up. "Is that so? Who is this mystery boy?"

"Nobody," I answered but Brieann spoke over me.

"Drew Clark, Dr. Evans."

"Oh really?" Dad had stepped inside and sat on my desk, deeply interested in what Brieann had to say. I may as well not have been in the room.

"He's a really good guy!" Suddenly, she's an expert on this one guy whom I've never seen her once speak to prior to last night. "He's an artist, just like London. Like, he's the vice president of the National Art Honor Society."

National Art Honor Society. That's actually impressive.

"He's in band and theater too. His mom and my mom are friends at Rotary" she added with a side look at me. "I've known him since we were 6." He came with personal references too, apparently.

"Then you should totally date him, Bree," I said with thinly veiled sarcasm.

Despite Brieann's glowing recommendation, the expression on Dad's face was far from pleased. "Hmm. When do I get to meet this fantastic boy you're going out with?" he finally addressed me.

"I'm not going out with anybody, Dad! You can relax!"

"He brought you home last night," they both said together, comically. I would've laughed … but no. Not laughing.

"I walked home, OK?" I was defensive and I didn't like that I was. "He just happened to be walking next to me." It was transparently lame.

Dad looked confused. Brieann was exasperated.

"Both of you are making a big deal out of nothing. There is nothing going on. He's a nice guy and all but frankly, I am not interested." I stressed the last part with a look that dared them to argue. Dad pursed his lips, considered my expression then relaxed.

"OK. What's for breakfast?"

Brieann wasn't as easily swayed. She sat there, fuming in silence while I spoke with Dad. When he left, she opened her mouth to say something and I held up a hand. "Just stop! If you really want me to give him a chance, then seriously chill with the Drew propaganda."

She narrowed her eyes at me. "Fine," she said in a tone that meant the opposite.

"Good," I said with finality as I pulled my Chucks on. "Let's go downstairs and make my dad his pancakes."

Victim

I thought that would be the end of it but it was only the appetizer to the seriously blown-out-of-proportion meal.

Rumors about Drew and I had already circulated around the school even before I made it to my locker on Monday morning. Everyone at Brieann's party had seen us leave together. It was the universal unspoken sign that we have "hooked up". I don't understand why anyone would even care.

Few people spoke to me directly about it, making it difficult to defend myself. Brieann didn't help. If anything, I'm pretty sure she was responsible for half the rumors. Good God, what has Drew been hearing about me?

I saw him in fifth period, during lunch. He was standing five people ahead of me in line but caught my eye while he stood in front of the display. He pointed at the bologna sandwich on the shelf and pretended he was throwing up. I laughed.

Brieann nudged me. That's when I realized that three of the

five people between us were exchanging knowing looks just as Drew had turned away. Brieann's smug smile was louder than the cafeteria noises. "You've already got inside jokes," she said in a high-pitched whisper, insufferably pleased with herself. "You guys are sooooo cute together." I closed my eyes. It's going to be a long day.

"He's right there, London," Brieann pointed out indiscreetly. "Yes, I know," but I didn't look in his direction. She went out of her way to stand right in front of me. "You have a shot at an actual relationship here," she scolded. "Not some long-distance thing with Ethan."

I seethed when she said his name. Not just because she said it in that manner but also because she equated him with "some long-distance thing". It was insulting. It wasn't her fault that she didn't understand what this meant, but I was still offended that she had brushed him aside like he was ... a figment of my imagination? I was indignant and deflated at the same time.

I watched Drew sitting with a few friends at another table, being normal. Being real.

I was downright sulky by the time school was out.

I went straight home, justifiably throwing a private tantrum. I slammed the front door with such force that the mail Dad had left on the entrance table slid off. I refused to pick it up. It was a matter of pride. I threw my pack on the floor and watched it slide until it hit the bottom of the stairs. Had it been a bowling ball, that would've been a strike.

Or a gutter ball.

Probably a gutter ball.

I sank into the couch and grabbed the remote. I refused to think about dinner, and I sure as hell didn't want to do any homework.

After sorting through the Netflix menu (How many movies did Nicholas Cage actually make?), I shut off the TV and threw the offending remote on the other side of the couch, as if it were the cause of all my grievances. I stared at it for a full minute before I finally admitted that there were better distractions.

I didn't even bother taking out my sketch pad. I was not in the mood to focus emotionally. It wasn't the kind of emotion I wanted immortalized on paper anyway. I needed to do something both productive but mindless.

I had to do it soon or I'd end up ripping my hair out and spinning in circles on our living room rug.

I was struck with inspiration sitting on the toilet, of all places. The white walls and the white bathroom cabinets were screaming at me. My bathroom was as much my domain as was my bedroom, seeing as how Dad had his own connected door to the master bedroom anyway. It desperately needed color.

Slapping some paint on the wall was a perfect solution. It didn't take much concentration, and it would be good to release pent up frustration that threatened to consume me.

It wasn't late in the afternoon, and my bathroom wasn't particularly big. If I wasn't too picky, I could get the job done tonight. I emptied my pack on to the floor. An assortment of folders, papers, pouches, and Tootsie Rolls tumbled out. I put on the near-empty pack and got on my bike, grateful that I didn't have to walk.

I was almost half done with the bathroom when Dad got home.

"Are we doing this again?" He regarded my painter overalls and splattered with paint with a theatrical sigh. He didn't really mind. He was just being difficult. I grinned at him. I was already feeling better. There was a different kind of physical exertion involved in painting a room versus painting on paper. It was just the kind of distraction I needed. And I got to use my overalls again.

"It was therapy. I was having a bad day at school."

I would guess that had my mother been alive, she would've picked up on my tone and encouraged me to talk things through with her over something home-baked and sweet. She'd give me consoling pats on the back and maybe impart timeless wisdom to help me face the next day with courage and grace.

My father was more concerned about what was going on in the bathroom than the driving force behind it. "Going for the whole aquatic look? That's not very creative," he admonished, eyeing the ocean blue paint I picked out. I wasn't doing anything outrageous. Just plain blue paint.

"Actually, I wasn't really in a very creative state of mind. I picked blue just because it matched the toilet water," I admitted. I was grateful for Dad. I didn't really feel like analyzing anything.

He laughed. "You aren't hungry yet, are you?" I asked. "I didn't make any dinner." Now that I got most of my frustration out, I was feeling guilty.

"Take your time. There were donuts in the faculty room today," he said over his shoulder as he escaped into his room.

Donuts. Great.

This adult man was incapable of making proper food choices. I criticized him unforgivingly in my head while I unwrapped another Tootsie Roll.

My estimations were wrong. It took me much longer than I anticipated to finish. Dinner didn't take long but the clean-up after always took more time. It was late before I was able to start again and another couple of hours before I pulled off all the masking tape and put away the equipment.

I was showering in my freshly painted bathroom when it occurred to me that I hadn't done any of the homework for tomorrow. I cursed silently. Time to pay the price for idiocy.

I fell asleep on my desk, my laptop still on beside me.

Fair Compensation

My back was hurting from leaning over the desk that had mysteriously disappeared. I was lying face down in yellow dust. How dignified of me. I stood up to dust myself off and leaned against a chain link fence for support. Instead of my plaid pajamas, I was in yesterday's jeans and a shirt proudly celebrating Taco Tuesdays with two happy cartoon tacos. I tapped my Chucks against each other to loosen stray pebbles.

I was optimistic. I didn't recognize where I was. Anything that was unfamiliar was a good chance of finding the person I was very familiar with. The one person that could brighten the prospect of facing another torturous day in school.

Off to the side was the back of large almost identical prefabricated buildings. Echoes of overlapping chatter and loud noises percolated the air. The volume spiked whenever the door was opened. Men and women in varying layers of green camouflage attire entered and exited.

I ducked behind random steel barrels, out of sight while I considered my options. Should I take a soldier aside to ask him privately if he knew my Ethan or should I go for the grand entrance and just walk in and see what happens? The latter didn't sound like a good idea.

I decided it was probably smarter to be discreet. I would ask the next soldier who stepped out of the building. I waited, palms sweating.

The next soldier that stepped out of the building was almost a full head taller than me. Metal dog tags swung freely from his neck. He wore boots and a cap that hid his light brown hair. His hazel eyes met mine. He was the most attractive boy I've ever met.

Ethan.

I grinned wildly. His eyes widened when he realized who I was and his lips parted in a smile. He glanced quickly behind him, shut the door, and crossed the steps to me as if they were a mere suggestion. Before I could say anything, he grabbed me by my upper arm and tugged me toward the smaller building. When we turned the corner, out of sight from the door, he pushed me toward the wall and stood close as if to shield me. I was out of breath by the time we stopped.

He turned to face me, his eyes brilliant. Without a word, he pulled me into a tight hug. I voluntarily melted into him.

There was urgent desperation in how he held me. It was coupled with relief. I understood. It mirrored my own.

When he finally let me go, he asked me in a low voice, "Has anyone seen you?" I shook my head. His smile was contagious. He cupped my face gently in his hands. "My God, London, it is wonderful to see you again." Then he placed a finger to his lips in the classic request for silence. I nodded. He held my left hand with his right and pulled me behind him. His eyes darted side to side. When he determined it was prudent, we ran. I giggled in spite of myself but after a playfully stern warning look from him, I kept it together.

We snuck up a tower near the edge of the woods. It was a utilitarian look-out made out of lumber. He motioned for me to hide beneath it. I ducked under the rafters. His eyes alight with mischief, he hoisted himself up to the platform with ease. "Malcolm!" It was a stage whisper. I couldn't see who he was calling.

An automatic weapon appeared instantly at the edge of the platform pointed right at Ethan, inches away from his face. I gasped in alarm. He didn't seem worried. On the contrary, he had a big grin. I heard Malcolm swear. "Bullocks," he hissed in angry frustration. "One of these days, I will blow your brains out. Then what, you effing drongo?!" The gun disappeared and Malcolm swore again. Ethan didn't move, still dangling over the edge of the platform, still grinning.

"Language, eh?" He grinned at me. "There's a lady present." There was a pause. Then I saw Malcolm for the first time when he leaned over the edge of the platform. His standard issue military cap hid most of his hair but I could see his dark eyes and long lashes to match. He looked like he was in his early 20s. His eyes were wide in surprise. "You muppet! You didn't!"

"Chill," Ethan said, there was assurance in his tone. "She'll be 'right. She can get out. I just need a few minutes. Cover me?" Malcolm balked. "Come on, mate, I never ask." Ethan executed a masterful puppy dog look, but Malcolm hesitated. "I'll owe you," Ethan offered. Malcolm swore again but grinned. "Owe me? Mattis, I'll own you!" Ethan nodded. "One day. I'll cover duties." It was the start of negotiations.

"A week."

"Two days," Ethan countered.

"Three."

"Done." They pounded fists, a sign that the deal was made. "You have one hour," Malcolm warned. Ethan checked his wrist and nodded. "Don't need that long. I've got less than half an hour before I've got my own to deal with." Acknowledging the information with a nod, Malcolm touched the bill of his cap and said to me, "Ma'am". He disappeared back to his post. Ethan dropped down and joined me under the rafters.

"You're here," he said, grinning openly. I smiled. "I'm here."

He pulled me into another hug and kissed my hair. "I can't believe it," he whispered.

"I told you I'd find you," I said triumphantly. He laughed quietly, like a low rumbling in his chest. A comforting sound.

"It's the least you could do," he mumbled.

I pulled away and gave him a face. "The least I can do? Excuse me?" He laughed again. "I leave myself vulnerable, bare my soul, tell you I love you and you disappear. It's enough to give a guy a complex."

I frowned. "You know I can't control it!"

He hugged me again. "I know. I'm just giving you a hard time. It doesn't matter. You're here now."

I allowed myself to drown in his embrace. I filled my lungs with the scent of him. There was little left of the freshly laundered scent I've come to associate with him. It made him seem less like a boy and more a man.

Beneath the smell of the mess hall lingering on his clothes, I could detect that light musk that belonged solely to him. That belongs to me. His breath was in my hair. His embrace was tight, and I could feel the tautness of his muscles under his long-sleeved uniform. Basic training suited him well.

"You've changed." It was an observation.

He chuckled. "Astute."

He let go of all but my hand. He leaned on one of the rafters and I sat beside him. "You cannot begin to imagine, London." There was awe in his voice. "I mean, I couldn't have imagined this myself. I couldn't have imagined me this way and it's all because of you." He was giddy with excitement. I was confused.

"When you disappeared I had expected to feel lost again, but I wasn't. You'd given me hope … and confidence. It was powerful enough that I just knew we'd find each other again. I didn't know how long … but it also doesn't really matter. I'd wait forever because I knew. I had to be with you."

He brought our intertwined hands to his lips and kissed my fingers gently. "On the way here, I thought this would be the absolute worst. I'd avoided and dreaded it this entire time. I was preparing for alienation, isolation and physical exhaustion. Everything I feared and hated in one place. I should have been apprehensive. I should have been worried." He laughed lightly. "London, I couldn't get you out of my mind. It was near impossible to sulk when I just felt … love.

"You make me look at the world differently."

His smile was free of the haunting sadness that had always followed him before. "Sometimes that's all it takes. It's like you said … maybe I can't change the end. I have a say on how it happens.

"I've actually made mates, London. People who I like. People who I know have my back just the same way I would protect theirs. There's a sense of camaraderie that I've never experienced before. It's incredible! I feel like I belong here. This was the family I've been looking for."

He seemed genuinely happy. It was contagious. "What? No

never-ending hikes? No push-ups for disobedience? What happened to the grueling physical torture that the military is famous for?" I teased.

He laughed. "You sound like you want me to be tortured."

"Well, not like you don't deserve it for being so mean to me!" I crossed my arms in mock anger.

"What?" He looked too innocent that it was completely unbelievable. "I told you I loved you! That's being mean? What do you want from me?" The smile continued to play in his eyes.

"Oh, no you don't! You are not the victim here!"

"Of course I am," he insisted. "I'm being unjustly accused!"

"I am very much justified!" I narrowed my eyes to glare at him. It didn't intimidate him the slightest.

"What? What did I do that was terrible?" When I didn't answer right away, he took advantage of my hesitation. "See? You can't come up with anything because I did nothing!"

I couldn't take it anymore. "You made fun of me!" My accusation came out like a whine. Not at all impressive.

"But, London," he almost broke into laughter before he finished. "You make it too easy."

I heard a distant snort of suppressed laughter from somewhere above us. I flushed in embarrassment. I had forgotten about our unseen audience. Since I could not yell at Ethan without it being reflected back to me, I redirected my anger at the poor soldier I just met instead. "Shut up, soldier," I called loudly. "This does not concern you!"

I heard a cough and a crisp, "Yes, ma'am".

Ethan laughed. I glared at him and he held his hands up in mock surrender. "Thanks a lot," he said. "Malcolm is going to give me a hiding for that."

I raised my chin in defiance. "Good! I hope he makes you clean toilets or something!"

"I don't care. It's worth it." He took me into his arms.

I leaned my head on his chest and sighed. "I am glad you're happy."

He laughed as he put his chin on my head. "You have no idea," he mumbled again. "A decade of unnecessary anger and heartbreak. Literally years of useless therapy and wasted effort. You come into my life like wildfire and suddenly everything works. You *must* be magic." He pulled his head back to look at me. "Now if only you would stay."

I sighed. "I know. This whole thing sucks."

He laughed lightly but shook his head. "Well, not everything about it sucks." He lifted my chin gently with his right hand. There was undisguised adoration in his eyes. He smiled.

I was light-headed. He was even better than I remembered. Better than any dream I could come up with on my own.

"You are the best dream ever." I hadn't even realized that I said it aloud.

His lips parted. "I want to kiss you," he breathed.

I was sure my knees buckled but I was still standing. I swallowed hard.

"Maybe you should."

Still smiling, he bit his bottom lip and shook his head. There was solemnity in his words. "No, not here. Not like this." He grazed my lips with his thumb and leaned in even closer. I couldn't move. "When I kiss you," he promised. "It won't be a dream." I thought that I would be disappointed but the confidence in which he said that was enough to sweep me off my feet. It was more than a declaration. It was an oath. This is more than just a dream. At the very least, it will be someday.

I could feel his breath on my lips. He smiled in wan surrender then spun me around. I leaned back to him. Less of a temptation that way, I assumed. He nuzzled my hair. I leaned back into his chest, enjoying the sensation. I looked down at our intertwined arms and noticed the absence of the ever present band on my left wrist. How strange that I didn't have the bracelet. It made me feel off balance. "What happened to the bracelet you won for me?"

"I found it on the ground when you disappeared."

Figures.

"I wonder why it is that your clothes don't fall to the ground when you disappear," he teased.

"Oh, stop it," I admonished, my fist bouncing off his arm with little give. He smirked unapologetically. I didn't really want him to apologize. I didn't recognize all the different emotions that were simultaneously stumbling around inside me like a classroom of uncoordinated penguins. I had an immediate understanding why horror movies and ridiculous parties were enticing. There was something here that I couldn't get enough of. I blushed and looked away so he wouldn't see my smile.

He was in such high spirits. He wasn't the same Ethan I met when I was lost in the forest. It seemed to be such a long time ago. The difference was apparent. I would have never equated the brooding, rebellious teen with this easy-going, lighthearted man with me now. And yet, without question, he was the same Ethan I'd hopelessly fallen for.

"At this moment, your hard-earned trinket is tied around my knife under my bunk."

"You know," I said casually, "I bought a similar bracelet back … home." The word sounded wrong in that sentence. His voice was muffled in my hair. "You wasted money on something that bad?" I laughed.

"Why?"

"I don't know. I wanted to have something that reminded me of you." I twisted around in his arms. He never let me go. "For the record, it was prettier and I did a better job tying it on my own hand than you did tying it on mine," I said with relish. I waited a long time to say that. He snorted, acknowledging the ribbing.

I leaned up against him again, feeling his heartbeat through his uniform. It was strong and steady. "I found you," I mumbled into his chest. "You didn't even need candy." He grinned but looked away. I knew instantly that he was hiding something.

"What?"

He reached into his pocket and pulled out an unopened roll of hard candy. It wasn't in the best condition, as if it had been in his pocket through a number of cycles in the washing machine. I looked up at him quizzically.

"I bought it at the waka depot. I've had it with me since. You know, just in case you need incentive."

I opened my mouth to speak when we heard Malcolm swear.

"Incoming!"

Ethan's head snapped up and he let me go, tucking away the candy as he would've his knife. "Who?"

Malcolm swore again. "Strickland. Visual on you in five ... maybe three."

Ethan checked his watch, controlled panic on his face. He swore. "Stay here. I'm sorry our time is short. You will come back to me?" I searched his eyes, the gold even with his green.

"Always." He grabbed my hands and brought them to his lips. "I love you."

Before I could say anything else, he was gone running.

"What's going on?" I asked Malcolm. He hadn't popped his head over the side. "Must've missed call time. Staff Sergeant sent the biggest prick …

"Sorry," he added belatedly.

Language was really the last thing one needed to worry about around me. "What are they going to do to him?" My anxiety dominated. He was in trouble because of me. "He'll have a mare time of it, won't he, eh? Push-ups. Laps. Duty. It's not the brig but yeah, he'll be hurting for sure.

"Your wish that he be physically tortured is about to come true." He said it with the barest of accusations. My mouth went dry. I felt like I was going to be sick. There was no point in trying to defend myself. It was my fault. All my fault.

Issues

It was the first time I had awoken feeling incredibly miserable after dreaming of Ethan. Stiff shoulders reminded me that I had fallen asleep in the most awkward of positions. The discomfort contributed to my unhappiness. My laptop had gone into hibernation and there was an unattractive puddle of drool under my chin. I couldn't be more of a loser if I tried.

My muscles protested as I stretched, a sad attempt to alleviate the ache. I let out a long indulgent groan and instantly felt guilty. Here I was groaning over this while Ethan would be suffering for days because of me.

I lay back in bed wishing that I could bear a little of it on myself. I won't even be there for him when it's all over. God only knows when I'll be able to see him again. Another two weeks? Three? A month?

A lifetime?

My stomach dropped.

Where was that certainty I had in his arms? It disappeared the moment we were apart.

Six in the morning. I still had another hour of available sleep time. I was tired but feared closing my eyes. Would I see him? Would I not?

And if I saw him, would it only make it worse for him?

I've never dreamed about him twice in one night. Not even two consecutive nights. But then again, nothing was ever predictable when it came to him.

I closed my eyes knowing that I was not going to sleep. Not if I could help it. I was selfish enough to want to see him no matter the cost. I did not want to give myself that option.

Frightened to be with him. Terrified to be without him.

I can't win.

That revelation fresh in my head, I got up and headed for my newly painted bathroom.

My mood continued to get worse as the week went on. I used every excuse not to eat lunch in the cafeteria or stay in school any longer than was required. I avoided any chance I'd bump into Drew. I started my days early to avoid breakfast conversation with my father. I then wasted time riding my bike in lazy circles around the park. I made it to the school parking lot right as the bell rang. I slept little.

I was feeling a bit sick.

I kept it up for three days. Come Friday, I decided that I had to find another way to deal with things when Brieann confronted me between classes.

"Stop it," she said. "You're ignoring me and you're ignoring

Drew. Don't think you're being slick. You're being stupid."

Our conversation was cut short by the proverbial bell. She ran off to her next class, throwing back a concerned look my way. I waved at her, feigning a smile. She answered with a deeper frown.

I was at the door of my French class. The weariness hit me as I was about to swing the door open. I haven't slept well in the past three days. I was just exhausted. My head was pounding. The fluorescents made me see double. There was no way I'd sit in another class without passing out.

I didn't know if I could sell it to the teacher or the nurse. I've heard that it's easier to ask for forgiveness than for permission. Words of wisdom that conveniently suited my current situation. I ducked down the hall for the red and white exit sign.

By the time I was out of the building, I was almost doubled over in pain. I belatedly identified symptoms the doctor had enumerated when I was at the hospital. I even had the right meds for this exact situation. Hurrah for modern medicine! My hands were shaking when I reached for the migraine pill that I should have taken hours ago. I sat on the walk under some shade, leaned my head back on the dirty bricks and swallowed two large pills without water.

I shut my eyes and concentrated on not throwing up.

Painful Development

Everything was dark when I opened my eyes.

Night.

It took me a moment to realize that I was standing. I wasn't on the sidewalk. I wasn't in school. I waited for my eyes to adjust and found myself between two prefabricated one-story buildings.

The slight breeze carried unfamiliar smells and sounds of random insects. The only familiar thing was a whispered voice above me. "Stay where you are." I looked up to see Ethan's head leaning over the edge of the building's low roof. The darkness could not hide the sparkle in his hazel eyes. He was happy to see me.

He got up to a crouch and silently jumped to the ground beside me. He landed with a soft thud, his knees bent, low on the ground. Dust settled around his non-regulation sneakers. In the next second, I was in his arms.

"Can you get up there with me?" he whispered in my hair.

Probably not but I nodded anyway.

He took a step back and launched himself up and forward, grabbing the edge of the roof securely. I don't know how he managed that so quietly. Then he pulled himself up and disappeared. When he came back into view, his stomach was flat on the roof and he was reaching down for me with both arms. "Jump as high as you can and I'll catch you."

It took me two pathetic tries, but he finally caught me by the wrists. With much more strength than I thought he had, he pulled me up to join him. I wasn't remotely as fluid as he had been. I didn't really have the energy. Mostly because I possess less elegance than a drunk orangutan on stilts. My bare arm found a jagged edge of the metal roof that was bent outward and out of place. The metal dug into my arm and I felt a sharp pain. I bit my lip to stop myself from crying out and felt the tears spring to my eyes. I swung my leg over the edge as soon as I was able and scrambled up to the roof with considerably more noise. He cringed and motioned for me to stop moving and lay low. I rolled to my back while he lay frozen in position listening carefully around him. My free hand grabbed the arm that was still protesting.

He hadn't noticed that I was hurt. When he was satisfied, he exhaled deeply and rolled over so that he was on his back beside me. His grin evaporated when he saw the look on my face. Realizing what had happened; he sat up and gingerly took my arm to take a look. There was an ugly looking gash that ran from my lower left arm and up over my elbow. I have a low tolerance for pain. Looking at it made it seem doubly painful to me. It did, however, help me forget about the pain in my head. He swore.

Being without a tourniquet, he took off his shirt and applied pressure to the wound. It hurt considerably less when he did that. I looked away and toward him. His face was crumpled in an expression of concern. Shirtless, I could see just how much more defined he was. My scruffy rebel boy was … not so scruffy … and much more than just a boy. He was an excellent diversion from the pain.

"I'm sorry," he mumbled. He kept his voice low. I followed suit.

"Wasn't your fault. I'm just not graceful." I was braver than I was just five minutes earlier. He made me braver.

"Dad tried to enroll me in ballet classes when I was younger," I prattled on to maintain the distraction. "Not because I wanted to but because his friends' daughters were into it."

The lift I saw at the very edge of his lips encouraged me to continue. "I did way better with the running away part. After blowing money on a summer's worth of lessons, he just gave up and let me do my own thing." No response this time. I lapsed into silence and his brow continued to furrow.

The sharp pain withdrew to a more tolerable throb. "I think the bleeding has stopped."

He lifted the shirt a little and peeked underneath. "We need to clean that off," he said almost to himself. "The medic station is a few buildings away. Maybe we can get you something …." I was shaking my head. I was not about to get him into more trouble than I already had. I sat up.

"It's OK." He looked at me disapprovingly. "No, really," I insisted. "I'm asleep, remember? I'll be fine when I wake up. It's no big deal." He wasn't entirely convinced.

"It's a bad cut, London. You'll probably even need a shot."

"Why would I need a shot for a cut?" It sounded ridiculous to me. "I'm already opened up. What do they need to pierce my skin for?"

He shrugged. "I don't know. I got one."

"When did you need a shot?" He continued to hold his shirt over my arm. He wasn't looking at me. Already I knew he was trying to hide something. "Last year. Got cut up on some old barbed wire."

He says things like that and expects me to leave it. Yeah. No.

"Were you sneaking out or sneaking in?"

He made a show of refolding his shirt to hide the stain. He put a cleaner side back on my arm. "Neither." That only confused me more. "In any case," he continued. "It's not relevant at the moment. Only one of us is bleeding right now, and it isn't me." This commanding presence must also be another product of his training.

"If I need it when I wake up, I'll get it, OK?" He was not convinced. "I promise," I added.

I pulled the shirt away to show him that I wasn't in a lot of pain anymore. The air was soothing. I handed it back to him. It wasn't in the best of conditions. "I'm sorry your shirt is all messed up now."

"You worry about all the wrong things," he said. "Keep it on. You need pressure on it to help it clot." I accepted it from him. "I'm sorry," he said again.

"Did you get into a lot of trouble?" I asked over his apology. The wave of guilt made me sick. I've been anxious to ask him.

He looked at me quizzically. "What are you going on about?"

"The last time I was here? For being late," I prompted.

Understanding dawned in his eyes. "Not even, ow. She'll be 'right."

It was assuredly not right. "I didn't really mean it when I said I wanted to see you tortured."

He grinned at me. I could see he considered teasing me but

decided against it. His expression softened. "It's nothing. I've had worse."

"Were your squad mates really mad at you?"

He scoffed at me. "Who cares even? It was well worth it." He held my hand and squeezed.

I chewed on my bottom lip uncertainty. "I care."

"Look," he assured me. "It's fine. It happens. It happens all the time."

"Not to you," I insisted. He stifled a laugh. "Have you met me? It happens especially to me, London. It's always me. What I'm telling you now is it's not a big deal." I cringed.

He frowned at my expression. "You know this. All the heavy classes ... harassment, ridicule, abuse." He counted them out in his fingers.

"I have a master's degree in all three subjects," he said sarcastically. "No, the squad was great. Mates being mates and all that. It's not like it was some kind of dark, life-threatening torture. They're my mates. It's just a bit of rough-housing. The transgression is a misdemeanor. It's not like it's going to go on my record or anything."

"That's what you're worried about? Your record?"

He looked away, embarrassed. He lay back on the roof and I did the same beside him. He didn't let go of my hand. "My record is clean now. I actually get a do-over. How many people can say that? I'm actually doing right." I heard the smile in his voice.

"I've beat out older cadets in war games," he said with pride. "They've even allowed me to lead a team during scenarios. London, we actually won. I could see every soldier in DPMs."

I frowned at the unfamiliar abbreviation. He caught on to my civilian ignorance and elaborated.

"Disruptive Pattern Material. Fatigues."

"Oh. Yeah?"

He shrugged. "The kick in the arse is that something about me being color blind makes it easier to see them. I can spot them in a glance. It's a wicked advantage. No one's been able to ambush us that way.

"And, really? A firearm is much less subtle than a blade. I'm killing it in artillery target training."

"That's impressive."

"Something I'm actually good at," he mused. He looked relaxed. Healthy. Happy. "It's a new kind of life," he marveled. "I'd really like to make this happen properly."

"It sounds like you've really found your place here." I should not risk it. After everything he had lost, I will not be the reason that they take this away from him too.

"All because you led me here." He brought my hand to his lips. It was a guilty pleasure.

I watched him as he spoke and just marveled at how incredible he looked. The soft light of the moon filtered over his face like a caress and I was jealous of it. I wished I could touch him with that same elegance. He was lean and agile even in stillness. There was no way someone like him could be meant for me.

"Your hair is shorter."

You're glorious, was what I really wanted to say.

He ran his fingers self-consciously through his standard military crew cut. "I kept getting called on it because it was close to deviating from regulation. It just wasn't worth it. I've never had my hair this short. Is it awful?"

"I like it." That's all he needed to hear.

There was a pause.

"What are you doing here?" We said together, stopped abruptly then giggled quietly. He gestured for me to answer first. "I'm obviously here for you," I said. "I can get Sweet Tarts elsewhere if I wanted." He snorted.

"No, I mean, at night? This is different or have you been doing this while I slept?"

"Yeah, that's not creepy at all," I laughed. He shurgged. "No. Never happened before. Strange, huh?"

What was different? I wondered.

"Well," he said thoughtfully. "This is actually better for me. If you can keep the noise to a minimum, I'd probably have more of a chance to spend time with you this way without getting into trouble."

"Because it's night time?"

"Early morning. And, yeah, I'm supposed to be in my bunk. Everyone is. If you make too much noise, we're bound to get caught up here."

"What are you doing up here anyway? Isn't it too much of a risk to your record?"

"I come up here after lights out if I'm mates with the man on watch. It's a non-issue unless an officer catches me." He looked up into the clear night sky. "I like being up here. It's soothing." He gazed up at the dim glimmer of lights, deep in thought. "Doesn't it look like the universe just goes on and on forever? In forever, there are infinite possibilities. No matter how unlikely; there's always hope."

I followed his gaze up into the stars. It was a beautiful night.

"Yeah," I agreed lamely. I was not as poetic.

Somewhere out there was the universe that I had belonged to. Far, far away from this one.

And yet, by some fate, we found each other anyway. Destiny.

My best destiny. With him.

How can I possibly reconcile my desperate desire to be with him and keep from destroying his newfound peace? And if I can't, can I live with myself for wanting the former life more?

The unlikeliest of scenarios in a universe of infinite possibilities.

We lay there side by side for a few moments. I couldn't understand how the air could feel both charged and comforting at the same time. It was just like him to be this confusing. There was a little sweat between our hands.

"It's a warm night," I said, feeling a little embarrassed.

"It's summer," he said matter-of-factly.

I sighed. "It figures," I mumbled. I felt his unasked question. "I like summer," I said absentmindedly. "Dreaming about you in the summer is just what I need with winter coming up fast." He said nothing.

"Then again," I added in afterthought, "I've never had a summer in California. It may just be torture."

He let go of my hand at once and sat up, leaning over me. There was a multitude of unsaid emotions in his expression, shouting in silence. I didn't understand. Before he could say anything, we both heard the sound of a door opening. He turned sharply to the sound and ducked low. His face was less than an inch away from mine. My lips were almost grazing his cheek. The pounding in my heart was louder than a hundred slamming doors.

When enough time had passed to move safely, he turned to me. He met my eyes for two heartbeats then ever slowly, pulled back. The air swirled around him like unseen waves of missed opportunity. He rolled over to his back beside me, his head next to mine. I didn't know how long it was before I was finally able to breathe again.

"Are you in trouble?" I finally asked.

He closed his eyes and sighed heavily into the night before answering in a strained whisper. "Yes. What am I going to do?"

Exhibit A

One second, I was watching Ethan under the magic light of night. The next, the sun was blinding my eyes. Ethan was gone. A different guy was leaning over me, blocking most of the sun.

I knew him.

"Drew?"

"What are you doing here?" I managed to croak out, trying to right myself from the uncomfortable slouched position I was in.

"Easy," he cautioned, holding my arm gently. His hands were warm but lacking. There was no spark there. No electricity in his touch. The contrast was impossible to ignore. I fought back frustrated tears.

"Ow." A sharper pain I did not expect ran up my arm. It made me inhale sharply.

"What happened to you," he demanded.

I looked at the offending arm and saw the gash I received

from being on the roof with Ethan. I couldn't understand it. I was dreaming. I shouldn't feel this.

What I did feel was a powerful surge of justified satisfaction.

Everything. Everything was real.

I had physical evidence to prove it.

I didn't care that Drew looked at me as if I had lost my mind. I was grinning. It was a fierce grin. This was my victory.

"London?"

My triumph was sobered by the memory of Ethan's face right before I left him. I had gotten him into trouble again. And this time, he didn't look confident in the outcome. The sinking feeling in the pit of my stomach temporarily won over the pain everywhere else.

I was a danger to his future. Now that he finally had everything going his way, I was going to ruin it for him because of my selfishness.

"I think I need to get to the clinic," I said, still shaken by the whole incident. Drew nodded, then pulled me up, a hand under my arms to keep me balanced.

"You think?" His sarcasm was justified. "Can you walk?" I nodded even before I was sure. I wanted to get away from the building.

The first step almost made me hurl. My head hurt so badly that the gash on my arm was almost refreshing. Drew held me to him to keep me steady. I was in no condition to protest. He smelled of light cologne and pencil shavings.

"What are you doing here?" I asked again. The universe was laughing at me. I just knew it.

He held up a small notebook. "Sketching." He half-lifted me up a few steps. "I have a free period. I like being outside.

What happened to you?"

"I have a killer migraine," I groaned, avoiding his question. He looked pointedly at my arm. I followed his gaze, trying to come up with some explanation. "I, um, think I snagged my arm on, um, something."

"You sure this isn't evidence of a zombie attack?" His question was unexpected and almost made me laugh. "Because you know you're instantly infected once there's an open wound, right?"

"You'll have to shoot me in the head," I suggested, smiling.

"Amateur," he chided. "Axe. A gun is too noisy." He pushed the door to the nurse's office with his shoulder and smiled down at me. I grinned through the pain.

The nurse was unfazed and surprisingly efficient for her age. She cleaned out the wound with an antiseptic that didn't hurt too badly. She applied a large bandage and confirmed Ethan's suspicions. I was going to need stitches as soon as possible … and a booster shot. She had my complete records on file. She recommended a trip to the Acute Care.

"I can take her," Drew offered.

"While that's both a generous and logical solution," she responded without glancing up, "It doesn't satisfy regulations. It's not severe enough for an ambulance. Her legal guardian should come get her."

She handed me a slip to excuse me from my classes and went into her office to call Dad. It was humiliating but I didn't think whining about the unfairness of the situation would help my cause.

The better my arm felt, the worse my head hurt. The nurse could do nothing for my migraine since I already took pills for it. She suggested I lay down in a darkened room until it went away. Drew waited with me until Dad arrived.

"How's the head?" he asked gently. "Would the axe be more of a relief?" With the blinds drawn and the lights off, the room was as dark as possible. A glass of cold water sat on the desk I was leaning over with my eyes tightly shut. Despite the darkness, it was like I could still see flares of light.

"Is it normal to see sound?"

"That depends … do you have synesthesia?"

"I don't know what that is but it sounds like a red and purple word … with orange spots." He laughed.

"Well, then I'd say you don't have it. Historically, people with synesthesia only see the world in shades of green."

I didn't remove my head from the desk but I smiled. He rubbed my back gently and I found that I didn't mind so much.

I grimaced when the door cracked open. I was assaulted by the sudden stream of light. Drew's axe to the brain sounded more and more welcoming

"Sweetheart, what happened?"

"A migraine." I heard the scraping of his Drew's chair as he stood to meet Dad.

"They said you needed stitches!"

I sighed. It was hard to talk. I had to swallow a couple of times and tried hard not to throw up. When I didn't answer right away, Drew chimed in.

"She has a pretty bad cut on her arm …"

There was silence and I knew Dad was caught between his concern for my immediate medical needs and his concern for who this guy was that was sitting in a dark room with his daughter. Certainly not the best way for them to meet.

"Dad," I said, knowing I owed it to Drew to at least bail him out of this one. "This is Drew. He helped me to the nurse's station after the migraine hit." Drew held his hand out and my father shook it, still filled with suspicion.

"Thanks again, Drew," I said as I stood up.

He handed me my pack. "Just don't turn into a zombie on me."

I snaked an arm on to Dad and dragged him out the door. "Come on, Dad," I said, not wanting to stand around and talk any longer than what was necessary. "Let's get this over with. I want to get back to lying in the dark."

I ended up having to endure two shots, including an anesthetic. I left the hospital with nine stitches and a temporary bandage that made it look worse than it was. I was stuffing discharge papers in my pack with one hand while Brieann blew up my phone. Apparently, I wasn't texting fast enough because she actually called.

"Were you trying to kill yourself," she yelled into the speaker. I jerked the phone away from my face so quickly that it flew out of my hand. It bounced off the gray leather dashboard and slid under my seat. I fumbled for Breiann's frantic 'hello's. I saw Dad sneak a sidelong look to me from the driver's seat. I found my phone.

"If I wanted to commit suicide, Bree, I would slit my wrist. Not my arm." I raised my eyebrows at Dad in challenge. He kept his eyes on the road.

"Good thing Drew was there, huh?" Just like that we went from concerned friend to enthusiastic matchmaker. "Were you cutting class together? Were you waiting outside for him?"

"The answer is 'no' to all of the above. I'm going home now, and I'm going to rest. My head is killing me. I'll call you when I'm feeling better."

Translation: Please stop harassing me.

"Fine, fine!" I could almost see her pouting as she admitted defeat. "Maybe I'll call Drew," she threatened.

I honestly didn't care. "Yeah," I said. "You do that."

I put the phone down, leaned my head back unto the headrest and closed my eyes.

In truth, my head wasn't as bad anymore. My arm was still numb from the anesthesia. My body was slow but it was healing.

"Are you hungry?" Dad asked.

"Not really. I feel a bit dehydrated, though. I'll just have some orange juice, take a shower and head for bed." I didn't feel as tired anymore but getting some more sleep wouldn't hurt.

"Are you sure?" I heard the doubt in his voice. I opened my eyes. He needed to see that I wasn't faking it. "Yeah, I'm OK. I don't want to eat a lot. I might throw up. The migraine caught me by surprise, that's all. It's Saturday tomorrow. I'll be able to get enough rest."

I saw that he wasn't happy with my assessment but went along with it anyway. "Watch out for your stitches. Does it say you can take a shower? Don't you have to keep it dry or something? Locke had stitches on his chin when he was younger. I can't remember what the rules were then."

"He had stitches when he was 3, Dad. One or two things might be a little different. I'll read the material before I attempt it. I'm pretty sure it should be fine. If not, I'll compensate."

"I have to work until late tomorrow but I'll have my phone on me. Call me if you need anything, OK?" Dad isn't one to overreact but I've noticed that when it comes to things like this, he loses perspective.

I've learned that the best way to deal with him is to just pacify him without sounding condescending. I hoped the forced sincerity in my voice would be convincing enough.

"You know I will, Dad."

It helped that his eyes were still on the road and not on me. He nodded to himself, satisfied.

I didn't even feel guilty.

Pattern

I got a full night's rest.

How disappointing.

Lying in bed, I poked the bandage covering my arm and smiled masochistically. I took greater comfort in this injury than I had in all my renderings of Ethan's face. It was a permanent verification of his existence. It was like a tattoo.

Still here. Still true.

It was late in the morning. Almost noon. Brieann had kept her promise not to harass me. I went downstairs still in the oversized Dr Who T-shirt and pajama pants that I wore to bed. Dad left a note on the kitchen counter reminding me to call him if I needed anything. When I opened the fridge, I noticed that he had stacked it with three jugs of orange juice last night, after I had gone to sleep.

Overkill but appreciated.

I took a swig of some juice and decided I would need something more substantial. I had gone almost 24 hours without anything solid to eat. The pantry was slim pickings. My decision lay between instant ramen or canned corned beef. The doorbell rang just as I reached for the can opener.

I expected that Brieann couldn't keep herself away much longer. I swung open the door, ready to berate her when I saw Drew standing there.

"Just checking to see if you're still human."

He took me by surprise. I ran my fingers self-consciously through my hair. I hadn't even brushed my teeth yet. He looked me right in the eyes, not diverting his gaze.

"What if I wasn't human to begin with," I offered.

"Then you're immune and all is well." I stood there half a minute before I came to my senses. "Oh, sorry, come in?" I stepped aside.

"You know, that's three times I've saved your life." He held up three fingers for emphasis. "You're making my cookie collection this month real easy for me."

"It's part of my long-term plan."

He stopped mid-stride. "Wait. You're going to jump me on collection day and take my reward for yourself, aren't you?" I tapped the side of my forehead.

"You are diabolical," he said in a whisper. I laughed. "I'm your nemesis, remember?" He put two fingers to his eyes and then pointed them to me. He mouthed out the words: I'm watching you.

He sat on one of the breakfast stools and leaned on the counter. I ran my fingers through my hair again, trying to make myself more presentable. "Your head still hurt?"

I shook it. "No. Sleep helps with the migraine."

"Good. Did you want to go get something to eat?"

I looked at the can of corned beef. I was hungry and I did not want that. "Yeah, let me get dressed."

Drew's car was parked in the driveway. It was a candy red classic BMW, freshly washed but with worn paint and dirty wheels. He walked around the other side and gallantly pulled the passenger door open with some effort. The little car was clean and almost empty except for a flannel shirt in the backseat and his sketchbook. It smelled like leather and painter's oil. Not entirely unpleasant.

"Is this a 3 series?" I asked when he got into the driver's seat. He paused with his hand on the gear shift, looking impressed. "You speak car?"

I was pleased with myself. "Not fluently. Three brothers who do, though." He nodded and tried to start the car. It turned over twice before catching. "Yes, she's a 3 series. 1979," he added with pride.

"1979?? Are you serious? How is it still running?" He patted the steering wheel affectionately. "Sporadically." The engine revved and the car jerked forward.

"Sporadically," I repeated. "Are we even going to make it to Caden's?" He shrugged. "We're about to find out."

We made it without incident. I had to wait until he opened the door for me because the door handle from the inside wasn't working. "This is the first time I've ever been child-locked in the front seat," I said, stepping out. He smiled apologetically. "I don't often have other people in my car."

It was not a Phad Thai moment at Caden's this time around when Cindy took our order. I was still in the mood for breakfast and a hot breakfast skillet sounded just right. He ordered the chicken fried steak.

"Have you been avoiding me?" he asked bluntly after Cindy walked away. The question may have been off-putting to others but I appreciated the candor.

"Sort of," I answered honestly, not meeting his eyes.

"Did I do something wrong?" I sighed heavily. "No …" I trailed off awkwardly. He cut me off. "I gotta say, I've never been a recipient of the whole 'it's not you, it's me,' speech before."

I laughed. "That sounds lame," I admitted.

"So it's really me, not you?" I laughed again. It was easy to laugh with him. "That's not what I meant!" He grinned. "I'm confused."

I didn't answer. How can I explain Ethan without sounding like a liar or a mental case? I've been able to get away with generalizations when Brieann asked, but Drew was more direct.

If I tell Drew that I am in a relationship, no doubt the entire school will soon know about it when he tells them why I shot him down. What then? Anyone looking into this will find no real evidence of Ethan. I'd end up looking like a liar.

At the same time, not mentioning Ethan was just wrong. It would be denying his existence. It would feel like cheating on what has become the most important relationship to me. I didn't even need the ache in my arm to remind me.

I was his London. I was his girl.

I looked back at Drew, not knowing what to say. He held my gaze and I knew that he could see the affirmation in my eyes. The strong inevitability that Ethan had talked about.

"It's hard to explain."

"You've got a boyfriend." There was no uncertainty in his voice. I didn't respond. "He's in Illinois?" That was really more of a question. I didn't respond. "He's not in Illinois?" I covered my face in my hands. *Why was this so hard?*

"Does he know he's your boyfriend?" I looked up at him sharply, offended. He was grinning at me, clearly teasing. I covered my face again. He laughed.

"London, talk to me." I peeked at him through my fingers and saw him looking earnestly at me. There was something. I don't know if it was dreaming about Ethan in the middle of the day. I don't know if it was the gash on my arm. I don't know if it was because Drew was just really easy to talk to. There was something. I wanted to tell him. I let my hands fall.

"How do you know when something is real?" It's a question I was posing to the world but momentarily to just Drew. He let it sit out for a minute before responding.

"Like if you're in a real relationship or if it's just fun and games?" he asked.

"No," I said, finally looking him in the eye. "Like how do you know when something is real and not a figment of your imagination? Not a hallucination? Or just wishful thinking?" He weighed the seriousness of the question against escaping with humor.

"That's a loaded question. Exactly what are we talking about here?" He was handling this rather well, all things considered. So far, so good.

"This is going to sound crazy," I cautioned him.

"Not gonna lie," he said with a shrug, "You're already sounding pretty crazy now." I put my head back in my hands and groaned. "I didn't say you should stop," he encouraged. He spread his hands open and leaned back on his chair. "After all, *ma chérie*, we are all mad here."

"There's ... this ... guy," I began hesitantly. I thought of Ethan as just this guy and I couldn't continue. Drew jumped in. "Is he an axe murderer? Does he own a windowless, white van? Does he sport a mustache?"

I threw my napkin at him. "Shut up," I admonished, laughing. He dodged unapologetically. "Well, hurry up then. The suspense is killing me."

"Stop interrupting then!" He threw my napkin back at me. "OK, there's this guy," I started again. "He's not from around here and he's just different. Not at all what you expect." Drew's impish expression required me to respond with mandatory eye rolling. "No, not an axe murderer. No white van. No mustache." Drew gave me a thumbs up. I stuck my tongue out at him and continued.

"He's someone I connect with, you know? I … I … like him a lot. I think I even love him." Drew wasn't smiling anymore. He wasn't just hearing my words. He was really listening to what I was saying.

"What's the problem, then?" he asked. I've had this conversation before. It wasn't any easier explaining it to him than it was to Brieann. I looked up at the ceiling, unable to meet his eyes.

"The problem is I only see him when I'm sleeping."

Silence. I still couldn't look at him.

Cindy brought out our order. I picked half-heartedly at the food I was starving for just minutes ago. There was a clenching in my stomach that wouldn't relax. He wasn't touching his food. This was such a bad idea.

"He's … a dream?"

I risked looking at him. His expression was thoughtful. He wasn't looking at me like I was a freak. He wasn't making fun of me. He was trying to make sense of the senselessness I was offering him.

"Like a recurring thing? Do you see him every night?"

"No. Not every night. Sometimes I go weeks without seeing him and then when I … when I dream about him again, weeks have gone by too. Things have changed." Drew nodded, as if this was all logical.

"Like a massive multiplayer online role playing game," he suggested. "The game keeps going even when you log off." There's a game playing in my head. I hadn't considered that.

"At first, I thought, oh, I had a nice dream, you know? One I actually remembered. That's fun. Everyone has a dream or two that they remember, right?" I looked at him pleadingly and he nodded in assurance. "It wasn't too weird. He was like some random fantasy guy." Drew smirked but didn't say anything. I barreled on. "But then every time I dreamt about him, there was a … connection. I got to know him. He was a totally separate person. It was just as real as you and I sitting here right now."

Drew finally started to dig into his meal and I relaxed. I started to as well. "Then yesterday, I passed out and dreamt about him again. This time, in my dream, I caught my arm on something and when I woke up …" I lifted my bandaged arm. Drew had his fork halfway to his mouth when he stopped.

"No way."

I nodded. He put down his fork. "No way," he said again. "Maybe you were flailing when you passed out or something?" I shook my head. I was certain of this.

"Did you see anything I could've hurt myself on? Blood anywhere else other than what was on me?" I took a mouthful of skillet. It tasted good. Really good. It may very well be the best skillet I've ever had in my life. That's how good it was to finally be able to tell somebody about this. Drew tapped his fork to the side of his dish, deep in thought.

"It's like a parallel universe," he mumbled more to himself than to me. His eyes lost focus.

"Think I'm crazy?" I asked in a small voice.

"Huh?" He snapped out of whatever he was thinking, and looked at me as if I just materialized out of thin air. "Oh, yeah," he said, grinning. "Certifiably, but what does that have to do with anything?"

"You're such a douche," I laughed. He tipped me a two-finger salute. I buttered my side of toast.

"Two summers ago," he said around a mouthful of chicken fried steak, "I met someone on one of my online games. Now, my momma raised me to never talk to strangers; so even though Player 2 was good enough to kick my ass, I wasn't going to offer up any personal information and I wasn't going to ask, you know? Don't ask. Don't tell, right?" I nodded instead of pointing out that he had gone out of his way to talk to me when I was still a stranger. "She did tell me she was 15 and lived in Virginia." He shrugged. "For all I knew, I was actually really chatting with Patrick from PreCal. Whatever."

"The thing is," he continued between mouthfuls, "while we didn't talk about what school we went to or even what our real names were, we had solid conversations. Not just trash talk. She talked about how she hated to hear her parents arguing. I talked about how I hated being the "artistic one" in a family of athletes. Deep stuff. Real stuff. We'd sometimes chat for hours.

"I was able to talk to her about things that I couldn't talk to my friends about. Definitely things I wouldn't talk to my family about. It was just easier." He took a swig of his drink. I didn't interrupt.

"Then when school started again," he hesitated. "Um … let's just say I had no time to be online anymore." He looked guilty and I couldn't understand why. I just looked at him blankly while he fidgeted. It took me a second to put two and two together.

I laughed.

"OMG, You were grounded, weren't you?" I called him out on it. He laughed, accepting the accusation. "What did you do?"

"Irrelevant," he insisted. I kept laughing. He talked over me. "Any-waaaay, when I did get back online, she wasn't there anymore." It was an expected outcome, but it made me sad anyway. I could see that it had affected him … that it still did.

"My point is this," he concluded. "I never met her. What if, all this time, she wasn't even real? What if the conversations were all made up and some creepy old guy with a mustache AND a white van was actually just messing with me?" He shrugged. "It doesn't matter. What matters is that she was real to me. What matters is that what I offered was real."

His insight was the validation I had needed but also afraid to ask for. It was exactly this and he understood it. This blessing of a boy.

"Are you crazy?" he asked. "Sure, why not? Is he real? Maybe not. What you really should be asking yourself is, does it matter?" He took another bite and grinned at me.

He just became my second favorite person in the world.

My mood was infinitely lighter when we stepped outside of Caden's. I hadn't expected lunch to go the way that it did. I was able to talk about Ethan, and it didn't end with me strapped in a straightjacket. Also, getting lunch didn't hurt. This was the best I felt in a really long time.

I gave Drew a tight hug. "Thank you," I said into his shoulder. He wrapped his arms around me in a light response and he patted me gently on the back.

"Hero, remember?" he whispered with a smile. This time, I had to agree.

He dropped me back home, struggling again with the front door of his car before letting me out. I acted like I was suffocating inside until he got it open. He acted like he was pulling the door off a moving train. It was all stupid, and it was all fun.

"Glad you're feeling better," he said when I got inside.

"For real."

"Hey, try not to die before Monday, OK? I'm off duty until then."

"No promises," I yelled, waving as I shut the front door. I leaned against the door and smiled. Things were finally starting to fall into place.

It wasn't as confusing anymore. I had that certainty that Ethan spoke of. It was like Quantum Entanglement. It existed long before we were born into this world and it would continue to be that way long after.

The only problem was finding him. Finding him and not destroying his world in the process.

I was doing a second load of laundry, near the end of the afternoon, when I remembered that my bike was still locked to the rack at the school parking lot. I didn't feel like it was fair to call Drew. He wasn't an Uber. Calling Brieann for a ride would've been my next choice but the price for it would be a complete cross-examination about my lunch with Drew. And not in the way I wanted to talk about. It was a type of toll that I was unwilling to pay. Finally, I decided to hoof it. The school really wasn't that far away.

Yeah, no. The school was really far.

I dropped down unceremoniously unto the sidewalk beside my bike when I finally made it to the parking lot. As healing as lunch was, I wasn't recovered. Aching everywhere and short of breath, I hadn't thought to pack water. I just didn't consider how far the school was. It seemed infinitely closer by bike. Even more so by car. This must be what Einstein's law of relativity was all about.

I eyed the water fountain in the playground. I remember the water being lukewarm and tasting like the tears of dodgeball victims. It might be worth dying of thirst than to have to taste that again.

I wasn't sweating, but I was thirsty. I lay on my back, feeling the pounding in my temples. It wasn't a headache. Just the rush of blood. Star athlete of the 11th grade, I was not.

Why do I do this to myself?

The sun was setting when I decided that I couldn't procrastinate any longer. It would be dinner time soon anyway.

I eyed the water fountain again but decided that it was just against my religion. It will go faster by bike anyway.

It was yet another in a series of bad decisions. In my defense, I was already dehydrated and not thinking properly. It's actually a testament of my improved bike riding abilities that I didn't fall over even once on the way home. Take the win.

By the time I got home, I was parched and feeling feverish. My breathing was labored. There was a tightening in my chest. Dad wasn't home yet.

The blood flowing in my temples was threatening to turn into a full-blown migraine. I stopped at the kitchen and chugged down two cold glasses of water. It went down quickly. I had a brain freeze and started to see double. The kitchen was tilting again. Why was the kitchen always tilting? It's a California thing, right? Like earthquakes.

I found my pack on the floor near the front door where I dropped it the day before. I rummaged through it to find the pills I needed.

I hesitated when I had them in my hand.

Through the haze I was in, I had a flash of awareness. There was a pattern in all of this. An obvious pattern that I had not recognized until this moment.

The first time I had a seizure, I had dreamt of him so clearly that I believed I had been killed by a truck.

Every time I've dreamt about him since was when I was too exhausted to think, or too sick to be lucid.

I put the pills down on the kitchen counter, staring at them with conscious decision.

That's what it took to find him. All I had to do was let go.

There was a sense of anticipation mixed with odd accomplishment as I fell to the floor and catapulted into familiar darkness.

Debate

The pain was not as bad this time around. There was the transient environment moving in and out of focus just as before. The light was frequently interrupted. There were no voices this time. No silent screaming. I was bound in place, tied to myself. I was convulsing uncontrollably.

Yet, the panic that had once been overwhelming was absent.

This was the path I chose. I was certain where it would lead. The pounding on my head was still there. The discomfort was real but now that I knew what was at the end of this, I was patient. I waited for the trashing to subside and the surroundings to settle.

I found myself among familiar oversaturated green trees. The light of the sun filtered between the leaves and branches. I was right. This was the pattern. I must have found Ethan again. I peeked carefully toward the clearing and saw that I was at the edge of the forest closest to the lookout where I had first met Malcolm. There was no way I could step out without being seen.

Potentially problematic.

While I solved the first dilemma of how to find him, I still had yet to resolve how to find him without getting him into trouble. What were my alternatives? If being seen would cause him to be the center of more chastisement, then it wasn't an option. I really could not do that to him again no matter how tempting it was. I would not. I should not. No matter how badly I wanted to see him again. Just to hear his voice. Feel his arms around me.

I bemoaned inwardly. Thinking of him did not help my resolve.

I sat down and prepared myself to be bored. I had to wait it out. While I discovered how to get here, I wasn't clear on what it took to get back. The increasing migraine and the itch in my arm were reminders that physical pain was not the answer.

Sitting down with nothing to do left me with all the time to debate with myself and chip away at my determination. I involuntarily considered compromises.

What if, let's say, his friend, Malcolm, was on duty maybe there was still a way to see Ethan. The risk was minimal. That was acceptable, wasn't it? I rose to my feet. I was hiding behind the bigger tree again before I hit the first snag to this desperate plan. How to check who was on the tower. The insistent thrum in my head would not help my vision. I doubt that I would recognize the guard from this distance. I only met Malcolm once and it was a quick glimpse.

No, this just wasn't going to happen. I have to resign myself to my situation. I peeked tentatively, foolishly, around the tree to the tower before I turned around.

The guard on duty noticed me right away and had his gun raised in my direction. I froze. He raised his head suddenly. The eyes that met mine across the distance were recognizable. I'd know them a mile away. Not Malcolm but Ethan.

He lowered his weapon immediately. He glanced over his shoulder then motioned for me to come to the tower.

I ran to him.

He didn't leave his post but followed my progress. When I got to the rafters, I caught a glimpse of camouflage green above me. Tiny binoculars swung freely around his neck. He looked over the platform, his gun still at a ready position in his hands but his face alight. "Can you work a ladder without ripping yourself in half?" I stuck my tongue out at him and began to climb. I was on the third rung when I hesitated. My conscience was winning over my delight. "Will my being up there get you into trouble?"

He looked uneasily across the field over my head. "No, but hanging on the ladder in plain sight will." There was the absolution that I was looking for.

When I got up to the platform, I scrambled to the corner, next to an olive drab plastic canteen. I sat with my legs bent and my arms around it. I kept my head shorter than the waist high walls of the tower. I giggled. This whole cloak-and-dagger can be fun if only the consequences weren't dire. He hadn't moved from his position but smiled at me. I could see the welcome in his eyes.

"I'm sorry I can't give you a better reception but I am on duty."

I leaned back. The pain in my head was causing my vision to blur but the adrenalin rush made it tolerable. The excitement of being with him temporarily overrode the persistent sensation. "I don't mind. It'll be interesting to see you work." He continued to sweep the area with his eyes as he spoke. "It's monotonous. Guard duty is one of the most tedious things."

"This actually works out best for us. I get to see you, you don't even have to get into trouble, and I can help alleviate your boredom."

"Leave it to you to find the perfect compromise."

"Yeah, because I totally planned it this way," I said sarcastically.

"How's your arm?" The slight crease between his eyebrows reflected his concern. It was then that I noticed he wasn't the carefree Ethan that recently found solace in his new home. He was deeply troubled again. I wondered if my actions had caused this to happen. I swallowed the guilt.

"I'm totally fine." I assured him. "I needed nine stitches and yes, you were right, I did have to get a shot." Instead of placating him, it seemed to disquiet him even more.

"I don't understand how you could have gotten hurt."

I shrugged. "It was dark. I'm not quite up to your level on the whole bootcamp work out routine."

He snorted. "No, I meant if you're dreaming shouldn't you be, I don't know, impervious to pain or something?"

I considered that. "Maybe it's a trade-off. I mean, I get to feel you so maybe it's only fair that I feel the unfun things. But isn't it great?! It's still a connection to you. Something tangible that I get to take back with me," I blushed, grateful that he wasn't looking directly at me. He wasn't listening to me anymore. I could see that his attention was already occupied by something else.

"London, you got hit by a truck when I first met you."

"No, I *almost* got hit by a truck," I corrected. "I woke up before I felt anything."

His eyes met mine. "If you can get physically hurt even here, then you could also easily have been killed." That dampened my enthusiasm. I hadn't considered that.

"Good thing I woke up." He held my gaze for another moment before going back to work. "All these things could've happened to me even while awake." I insisted. "It's not like I'm juggling knives when I'm here."

"Not funny," he rebuked.

"Very funny," I corrected, laughing. He spared me a despairing look. It made me laugh harder. The corners of his mouth curved slightly up.

He looked at me critically. "You look tired. You sick?"

I must look like crap for him to call me out on it. "I am tired but I think that's it, though." I closed my eyes, smiled widely, and continued. "I think I've figured it out. Remember how I told you I was on drugs when I first met you?" That sounded wrong. I didn't wait for him to answer. "Every other time I've found you, I've been super tired or sick. I think physical exhaustion has a lot to do with it. Maybe my mind enters some kind of alternate state to recover. Maybe it lowers my mental barriers or something."

I waited for him to share my excitement. When I opened my eyes, he was frowning. "You intentionally make yourself sick?"

"Well, I didn't before. Everyone gets sick at some point. I just noticed the pattern now."

"What? *Now* you'll intentionally get yourself sick?"

It didn't seem like such a bad thing. I shrugged. "It doesn't have to be exactly sick I think. Just, you know, really, really tired." I brightened up. "Maybe all it takes is an aggressive gym period. Who knows? The takeaway here is now I know how to control it!"

He frowned at me. "That's just not right, London."

"What? You want me to stop coming around?" I said it like a joke but my stomach dropped at the idea and I almost choked.

"Well, no ..." he said carefully.

His denial didn't come out convincingly enough. I stopped laughing abruptly and bit my lip. He glanced at my face and quickly averted his eyes. "Of course I want to be with you, London. Of course. That's not the problem."

"I know what the problem is."

He looked at me in surprise. "Oh?"

My eyes started to water. "I'm going to screw up everything that you finally made right by coming here." I was trying to be mature but that fortitude had abandoned me. I was queasy and it wasn't entirely because of the migraine. He heard the break in my voice and looked at me in alarm.

"What? No!" He had raised his voice but quickly lowered it. He glanced about to see if his gaffe was noticed. He started speaking rather quickly, stumbling over his words. "London, what are you going on about? No. I wouldn't even care to begin with if it weren't for you. This isn't more important to me, no. I would rather ..." He stopped, closed his eyes and took a breath. "Bloody hell."

I didn't understand. I was caught in the jaws of impending rejection.

When he opened his eyes again, he was looking at me in earnest. The distance between us didn't matter. I might as well have been locked in his embrace, and it was just the two of us in the world. I held my arms tighter around my legs.

"London, I love you." His words were comforting even as my heart steeled for the blow of disappointment that was sure to accompany them. "I love you deeper each moment I spend with you, I can't even explain it. Without even trying, you can reach me like no one else can. You bring out the best in me." He looked away. I wasn't sure if he was really seeing the landscape in front of him anymore. "I'm just not certain if my best is anything worth offering to you. What kind of future can you even have with me? Is it even possible?

"Consider what you have to do ... what you have to give up for me. This isn't healthy for you ... mentally or physically. I can't give you anything in return." He sounded broken. "I've got nothing to show for. Nothing. I'm mounted. I can't take you on a date. I can't buy you anything. I can't call you on the phone. I can't even talk to you without you having to give up something for me. How is that fair? How can that be right?" He held his gun tightly, his knuckles turning white.

"You should be with someone who can be there for you. Someone who can treat you right. Treat you the way that you deserve to be treated. Better than I can offer. What gives me the audacity to believe that someone like you should be with someone like me?" When his eyes met mine, they were pleading. "And yet, I want you. I want to ask you to stay. Beg you to keep seeing me. It's fully selfish. Why would you even want to be with me if I wanted that?"

I ached to hold him but if I moved, I would end up stumbling into his arms. He still wanted me. "What makes you think that my world is better than this? Better than you? I really don't care what I have to give up to be here." I wanted him to fully realize that it was impossible for me to not want him. "Being with you is the only time I even feel like I'm really awake."

Please don't ask me to leave.

He opened his mouth to argue but looked away when something on the field caught his eye. He narrowed his eyes first, then jerked his head to another direction before I heard the distant sound of approaching cars. The radio attached to his upper arm came alive with chatter. He raised his weapon a fraction. He took the small binoculars that were hanging around his neck and brought them to his eyes.

He swore. "You need to go."

Please don't ask me.

"To the forest?"

Please. Don't.

"No." He emphasized every word. "You. Need. To. Go."

Please.

"I can't control this, Ethan," I reminded him. "I'm stuck here until I wake up, and I don't know when that's going to happen." I had difficulty keeping my voice steady. The platform beneath me had started to get hot. Burning. If I left now, will he want me back?

His eyes were narrowed. He was deep in thought.

"What's going on?" I asked in a small voice. I hadn't moved.

"We have a surprise visitor."

"A commander?"

It would be. He's in deeper trouble because of me. Again. Maybe he's right. I shouldn't be here. I'm not good for him.

"Not exactly." His lips were tight. "Royalty."

War Zone

"Royalty?"

He nodded tersely, looking into his binoculars again. "Looks like the Queen's grandson. There were rumors that he might visit."

"Does, um, royalty visit often?" I was convinced that Ethan was definitely not of my world. I half expected to see dragons fly above us.

"No, not really. Honestly, I didn't think they were serious."

"Great."

He nodded in agreement, putting the glasses down. He turned away from the convoy that was approaching the camp and back to what had originally caught his eye. I couldn't see who he was looking at from where I sat. He gestured oddly then waited a beat. He angled the radio to his face and adjusted the frequency. He spoke quickly and quietly into it before adjusting it again.

"We need to get you out of here. With Royalty on the premises, we're automatically on amber alert. Unauthorized visitors will be considered threats. It's not safe for you." As he was speaking, I heard someone coming up the ladder. I jumped at the sound but he didn't seem worried. I recognized Malcolm. He took one look at me, set his jaw disapprovingly but didn't say anything. I cringed. He went to stand by Ethan and make room for someone else coming up.

I didn't recognize the young man that joined us. He had a darker complexion and equally dark eyes. I couldn't tell what color his hair was under his cap. He stopped half way up the ladder and his eyes widened when he saw me. He looked at Ethan, agitated. "Balls …" he swore.

Ethan held up a hand. "Save it, Nikau. I've got it. I just need your help." The young man looked uncertain.

"Please." There was a tinge of desperation in his tone and I wondered if I was the only one that detected it. Nikau groaned but nodded. "What do you need?" Ethan looked at Malcolm. Malcolm's expression didn't change but he nodded as well.

Ethan exhaled in relief. "Mate." He handed the gun to Malcolm and turned to me, determination written all over his face. "London," he went down on one knee to meet my eye to eye. At that same moment, a shot was fired.

Even as Malcolm crumpled to the ground, I didn't register what happened. I didn't have enough time to scream. As Malcolm fell, Ethan kicked the legs out from underneath Nikau. Another shot was fired but it didn't hit its intended target. Nikau was on his back beside Ethan, unhurt. Ethan grabbed the gun from Malcolm's lifeless hands and threw himself over me. He swore.

"Security Breach! Security Breach!" Ethan was yelling into his radio repeatedly. "OP3! Zero, zero, zero! Contact! Perimeter dropshots! 10-24!" In two seconds, alarms were ringing all over the base. The noise reverberated in my skull, amplifying the pain. I couldn't see clearly.

He grabbed Nikau by the front of his shirt and pulled him toward us. He spoke to him with an expression of such controlled fury that I was frightened. "Nikau, London is priority. Take her to the west dummy. I'm right behind you." He pulled him even closer that he was only inches away. "She means everything. Her safety is your responsibility. Understand?" Nikau nodded. "I'll cover you."

He turned quickly to me. The alarms continued to ring. I was staring at Malcolm's fallen body. I couldn't see his face. I couldn't distinguish where the pain in my head began and where it ended. Ethan grabbed the back of my neck with his free hand and pulled me to his face so that our foreheads were touching. I saw nothing but his strong, hazel eyes. "When I say go, I need you to run as fast as you possibly can with Nikau. He'll keep you as safe until I join you. I will be right behind you."

I nodded numbly. I believed him. He kissed me quickly on the forehead. "I love you," he mumbled.

He directed me to Nikau and together we moved toward the ladder while Ethan positioned himself on the wall furthest from us. Nikau grabbed my upper arm. "You'll have to jump," he warned. I nodded again. It was almost laughable that I could. The last time I did something this physical, I ended up with stitches. And shots. I just knew that I was a liability and had to be as minimal of one as possible.

Nikau was barking instructions over the sound of the alarms. His voice was a hollow echo in my ears. "Jump feet first and when you land, you need to roll forward then get up as soon as you can, yeah? Make sure you bend your knees or you're going to break something. We're going to make a run for it." My mouth was dry. I nodded again, at a loss for words.

Ethan took a deep breath, set his jaw then nodded. With a yell, he got to his feet and started shooting at the general direction of where the sniper was.

I jumped.

My sneakers scraped the ground. I rolled forward to break the fall, tucking in my knees. The pain of impact on my shoulder travelled up my neck and down my side like electricity, almost paralyzing. I scrambled to my feet. Nikau grabbed my arm and pulled me another direction. I stumbled again but followed his lead. Blasts and explosions punctuated the sound of the blaring sirens. The wind around me whipping violently, carrying with it dust and distorting my view.

We made it to one of the buildings closer to the camp, where more soldiers were running to their posts. Nikau didn't slow his pace and continued to run. I almost fell forward a couple of more times. I looked back and saw Ethan hit the ground rolling. He pivoted on his feet and took cover in the opposite direction of our escape. I lost sight of him.

Nikau threw me into one of the smaller buildings. The acidic smell of urine received us. It was empty. My eyes welcomed the dark. The concrete walls muffled the alarms. He pushed me toward one of the walls and motioned for me to get down.

I slid to the ground, my back to the wall. The tile was damp but it offered no reprieve. It only made me feel hotter. My mouth was dry. There was a constant ringing in my ears.

Nikau stayed at the entrance, he would glance back at me once or twice but would not say anything. I kept my silence.

I closed my eyes to stop the tears. My migraine was full blown. My heart hammered in my chest. I could hardly breathe. What the hell was going on?

I lost track of time but soon I heard slight movement from

Nikau. I opened my eyes a fraction to see Ethan slide into the room. He was breathing hard. He knelt toward me. "London?"

I smiled. I was blacking out and wondered, almost idly, where I would go if I had a seizure while I was already in a dream. The blaze in my head exploded in a blinding light.

Everything went dark.

Fate

I was trapped. I couldn't move. For an immeasurable amount of time, I floated in the deep black, deprived of my senses. It was unnerving. Then from nothingness, there was a loud hammering in my head and I didn't know how to get it to stop. I expected to feel an onslaught of pain but I wasn't in pain anymore. It was a dull ache.

Ice cold water was hitting me on the face and neck. It pelleted my exposed arms. My clothes were utterly soaked through. It should've been uncomfortable but it wasn't. It was refreshing. All I could hear was the rain.

I opened my eyes.

I was greeted by the beautiful combination of green and gold. His anxious face hovered closely over mine. I was lying in Ethan's arms, looking up at him. I smiled.

"London?"

His voice sounded like it was coming from far away. I reached up and touched his face gently. Just to be sure he was there. He was close. So close to me.

"Ethan." My voice sounded weak and, again, it hurt to talk. I swallowed painfully.

He hugged me tightly to him and mumbled into my hair, "Thank God." I looked past him up to the sky but instead I saw dirty tiles and a shower head spraying us both in cold water. There was no sound other than its steady beat. The alarms had stopped.

"What happened?"

He pulled back to look at me. He stroked my hair away from my face, water streaming down his back. We were both fully clothed. "You were burning up a right fever," he whispered. He searched my face, relief all over his. "You passed out. I didn't know what else to do. It was the best way I knew to lower your body temperature."

I tried to get up and the vertigo knocked me back down. He caught me.

"Slowly."

I turned to the side and saw Nikau in the shadows, still standing guard by the door. Ethan's discarded gun in his hands. I blinked the water away from my eyes and tried more slowly this time. I managed to sit up without falling over.

"You're all wet."

He smiled. "You too." He knelt in front of me, our eyes level. "Why didn't you just disappear?"

Why didn't I? "I don't know."

"You scared me."

"Sorry."

"How are you feeling?" He put a hand gently on my cheek and

I leaned my face toward it.

"Like crap."

He smiled. "At least it looks like your fever broke." I didn't feel hot anymore. I didn't feel cold either. Just damp. He reached over and shut the shower.

"How long was I out?"

He checked his watch. "Not long."

I looked toward Nikau. "Malcolm …?"

Ethan angled his face away from me and closed his eyes.

Everything happened just the way I remembered it. I've never seen someone die before. I've never seen someone shot. I thought I should have more of a reaction but I was oddly detached. Maybe that's just how it is when you're dreaming.

"What's going on now?"

"They've taken hostages. Including the prince. They've already taken down our entire command staff and executed two soldiers." He wiped his face with his hand in frustration. "I don't know what I was thinking bringing you here. We aren't far from where they're being held. We're caught between hostiles and the squad. There's no way I can get you out safely.

"I caught a glimpse of two soldiers trying to get close west of us. I don't know what the plan is but they're pretty far off to take any kind of immediate action. They're maintaining radio silence for obvious reasons."

I watched him carefully and saw that he was holding back. "What's *your* plan?"

He set his jaw.

"We're going in."

Cold fear gripped my heart. Suddenly, all the emotions that were absent when I saw Malcolm die were present at once.

I stumbled forward and he caught me. "No." Shaking my head I grabbed at his shirt. "No. No. No." I was almost hysterical.

I saw Ethan in Malcolm's place. It just as easily could've been him. Then I realized that it would've been Ethan shot down. Had he not been distracted, it would've been Ethan. He was the guard on duty. He was the target.

What if it had been? What happens to him then?

"No. You can't go out there." I would hold him here. Right here with me until it was over.

He shook me gently by the shoulders, "London. London, stop."

I didn't. I was completely consumed. I knew, I just knew that if he stepped out there, he would be gunned down just as quickly. Would die just as easily. If he did, I knew I would never see him again.

He put both hands on either side of my face and forced me to look at him. His eyes burned with a ferocity I have never seen. "London, listen to me. I have to help. They're going to take out another hostage in 10 minutes when they don't get what they want. We don't negotiate with terrorists. We aren't giving them shit.

"Every soldier in that room is as good as dead if we do nothing. They are the closest thing I have to a family and I will not stand by and watch them get slaughtered."

"No!" I allowed myself to be selfish. This isn't right. This isn't fair. I did not get this far only to lose him. "I am the closest thing you have to family. ME!"

He looked earnestly into my eyes. "What would my life be worth if I didn't even try and save theirs?"

I shook my head, unconvinced. "Why should I care about their lives if it means yours?"

"London," he said again, more commanding. "If any one of them even has a shadow of what I have with you, then their lives are equally worthy. Equally worth saving."

"Let someone else do it," I begged weakly, knowing then that I could not win the battle. "Not you."

"Nikau and I are the only ones close enough to make any kind of difference, London. It has to be us." I knew he was right. I was sinking in lost hope, weakly pounding on his chest. "Now you want to be a hero? Now?"

"No," he said quietly. "I'm just not a coward anymore."

Tears came unbidden. Why is this happening? Why now?

"Will you come back to me?"

He hugged me. I couldn't see his face. "I don't know what's going to happen. I just know that we have to try."

"I don't know what I'm going to do if something happened to you."

"London," he whispered into my hair. "You need to stay safe." He stroked my wet hair gently. "No matter what happens out there, it would make it worth it to know that you were safe." He laid a hand lightly on the side of my face. "I need to know that my life made a difference to you."

"How can you doubt that?"

"Stay safe for me," he insisted. "Please."

I couldn't do it. I couldn't say no to him even as my soul screamed. I followed his lead from the first day I met him. I will always follow. I nodded. He took my hand and brought it to his lips, as he always did to comfort me. It did and it didn't. Tears were streaming down my face.

"Stay here," he commanded, taking me to the far corner of the showers. "If live fire breaks out, I want you to stay in the corner and lie flat down." He knelt and pulled up his damp pant leg. Belted to his leg was his knife. Tied around it was a cheap-looking beaded bracelet. He smiled resignedly, undid the bracelet and handed it to me. He wiped my tears gently. "I'd put it on you but I think it'd fall apart."

"I thought it was in your bunk." I said lamely.

"Good thing I'm not one to follow the rules," he said ruefully. He looked at the only gun between him and Nikau. "The automatic would be too noisy anyway." He frowned deep in thought.

"London," he said carefully as if he was making a decision then and there. As if anything else mattered. "When this is all over, I don't care what it's going to take. I'll do it. I'll find you. I'll be that guy you deserve. I swear it. I won't ever make you regret loving me."

I possessed neither the knowledge nor talent to put into words the profound feelings I had for him. Every sappy prose written, that I had once thought to be exaggerated and over-dramatic, made absolute sense to me. Whether he existed in my world mattered very little. This was love. It has the power that gives you the strength to transcend the obstacles that it has made in the way of itself. I loved him deeply. It was indefinable. It was lunacy. It was impossible.

It was real.

In this dream turned nightmare, I found the one magical truth that people kill for. That people die for.

"Ethan Robert Mattis, I love you. I will never regret loving you."

With only the determination in his eyes to serve as a warning, he pulled me close and pressed his lips to mine in a kiss he had promised not to make in this world. It was a broken promise, we both knew, but also an opportunity we did not have the luxury to miss. In that kiss, I understood the conviction of his feelings. I saw the promises that he had fully intended on keeping but may be all in vain. I shared his desires. I witnessed his fears.

In that kiss, I felt all the things he couldn't say.

When he pulled back, his eyes were brimming with unshed tears and uncontrolled emotion. "I'm sorry." The apology was not for the kiss. It was for all the things that had to happen after, over which he had no control. It was for the broken promises. It was for the worst that could happen.

He stood up and walked to where Nikau was standing, his hand gripped tightly on his knife. Just as tightly as I held that piece of flimsy thread in my hands. With a last look at me, they both slipped quietly out of the door.

I was alone. It was cold.

World End

I strained to hear any indication that the fighting had started. I heard nothing but water dripping in the showers. I started counting the beat of the drops just so I had something else to do than just be scared. I don't ever remember being this scared in my life. I'm a kid. Really just a kid … I don't even drive! That mundane world was far away.

I wondered how long it would be before I woke up. Would I know the outcome of this suicide ploy? Would I ever be able to see Ethan again? I sobbed quietly. This whole dismal affair was beyond reason. I had done it. Gone willingly over the edge of sanity and jumped with arms wide open, free of fear. I had no grasp on what was rational. Somewhere in the normal world, I'm probably rocking in a fetal position similar to how I am now. Except I would be in a room with pure white walls and they would be padded. Doctors would see me now and again, do some tests, shake their heads. Nobody would be able to understand.

And, yet, there was no argument strong enough to convince me that this wasn't right. That this wasn't worth it.

In this short time, I have loved far deeper than most people who have lived their entire lives. Love not confined by the boundaries of space. Against all odds, against even reality itself, we found each other.

Please, God. Please don't take him away from me now.

I jumped at the sound of weapons fire. Despite my promise to Ethan that I would stay at the corner, I couldn't help myself. I had to know what was going on. I had to see him.

This was my own personal horror movie. I was no better than every fated idiot that went toward the danger instead of away from it. They all ended up dead, and yet here I was following in their example.

I crawled slowly toward the door. The opening near the showers was across the room. My stomach was weak and my limbs weaker still but I continued on. Pulling myself beside the door, I lay flat against the wall. The sounds were louder. That meant they were also closer.

Before I could reach the handle of the door, it flew open, almost hitting me. I pulled back. The angry, wild-eyed man that entered the door swung to face me, his gun right at my face. I let out a strangled cry. That was all I could do before someone shot him in the back and he fell forward, never even pulling the trigger. I didn't move.

Ethan came through the doorway the next second. He was furious. "I told you to get down," he practically yelled at me. I was both happy to see him and taken aback by his tone of voice. I was torn. I didn't know what to do. I just stood there.

"Get down!" He threw his arm over my shoulder and pushed me down with more force than I thought was necessary. Weapons fire exploded around us. I was down on the floor with Ethan's arm around me. The sound of his automatic was deafening. It reverberated in my head, muting everything else. I closed my eyes, trying not to scream.

He pulled me up. It was time to move. I opened my eyes again and saw that someone else had joined us. A good looking man with a regal bearing, lighter hair and bright eyes that showed no fear was on Ethan's other side. He was dressed in a suit that was obviously the best that money could buy, still flattering despite being covered in dust and grime. He met my eyes in surprise but didn't say anything.

Ethan was backing us into the showers. "Please stay here and stay down," he said to the man, who could only be the prince. Part of me wondered how he could be extremely polite in this situation. He turned to me and I saw his eyes flash in anger. "Are you trying to get yourself killed?! I said stay down! How hard is that to understand?!"

Before I could answer, two more people were at the door. Ethan leveled his gun toward them then realized that they were soldiers. Lowering his weapon, he barked orders as if he had been expecting them right at that moment. "Nikau, the package is yours. Ari, take point." The one he called Ari turned toward the door. Nikau bent down to take the gun from the man that was on the ground. As he straightened up, six shots in succession slammed right into Ari. He fell back and hit the wall.

The enemy came barreling through. He fired first at Nikau, who dropped the gun and dove for cover. Ethan was able to release a round that caught the man in the chest. The man fired at us as he fell. I threw myself against the wall, knowing I wasn't fast enough to dodge bullets. When I hit the ground, I realized that I was still alive only because I had not been the target.

The prince was on the other side and Ethan had thrown himself in the line of fire to protect him.

No!

I watched in horror as the last of the bullets found its mark with a sickening thud. Ethan first stepped back under their impact before falling forward on his knees. His grip faltered on his gun and he leaned forward on it. His left hand was clutched to his shoulder. Blood spilled forward from the wound, staining his uniform a dark color. It ran deep red down his arm.

NO!

I scrambled to my knees, my own blood cold in my veins. My heart lurched forward, an invisible force ripped it out of my chest. My own body betrayed me as it wouldn't even give me tears to blur the clear, tormenting vision of him dying an arm's length away from me.

NO! NO! NO! NO!

The last thing I saw before I was completely engulfed in the madness of my mind was Ethan's lifeless body falling forward to the ground.

Wrong World

The scream ripped from my lips before I opened my eyes.

I struggled against invisible bonds that held me in place and continued to scream. My reality ripped completely in half. There were two worlds in sharp focus but a darkness in between that I couldn't navigate. The pain was intangible, impossible to identify, and infinitely more agonizing.

NO!

It was not Ethan I saw over me but the panicked face of my father. I was strapped down to the hospital bed, an IV in my arm. The abrupt change made it even more bewildering and only added to my distress and terror.

While I knew I should attempt some sort of restraint on his behalf, my mind and my heart were not communicating properly.

I need to go back! Please! Please!

The screaming did not stop. Tears obscured my vision, causing the one in my head to be stronger. The memory playing and replaying in cruel clarity. I was dying every single time.

Send me back! Please! I need to go back!

Even as I heard Dad yell for help. Even as I saw the nurse add a sedative to my IV. Even as the drugs started to work.

I need to go back.

ETHAN!

I could not reunite the two worlds. The distance was too great and I was trapped in the indefinable space between. My own purgatory. My own hell.

I did not dream of him again. The darkness won.

There was nothing.

"London?"

My eyes fluttered at the sound of my name.

"Sweetheart?"

Not Ethan. I didn't open my eyes.

A cool hand on my forehead. Again on my wrist.

No warmth. No electricity.

Not Ethan.

I smelled something floral.

Artificial.

The beeping was insistent.

I ignored it. Ignored everyone. Ignored the world.

The voices around me were garbled and muffled. The beeping continued. Not so annoying. More like a steady rhythm to help you stay grounded. The light was brighter than it should be. I was parched and my eyes were swollen, crusted around the edges. I was tired. Drained.

Numb.

I opened my eyes.

"Dad?"

I hadn't used my voice in a long time. It was weak, gruff, and almost unrecognizable. I coughed; tried again.

"Dad?"

He was at my side in an instant. A gentle hand over mine. My eyes had difficulty focusing.

"I'm here, Sweetheart."

"My head feels like it's full of cotton," I complained, not attempting to get up.

"You've been asleep for a long time," he said gently. I swallowed, unwilling to think. Unwilling to remember. Not now.

"Can I have some water?"

"Of course."

He found the button that would incline the bed. I felt vertigo despite the slow progress. It took a moment for me to breathe evenly again. I took the small cup from him and sipped gingerly. My stomach hurt.

"Are you hungry?" he asked. I nodded. "Yeah, actually."

"I'll go ask the nurse what you can have. I'll get you something. I won't be long."

He looked like he was afraid to leave me. I tried to smile encouragingly. "Sure."

He hesitated before he stood up. I could tell that he was trying to restrain himself but could not. I steeled myself. "What happened?"

I opened my mouth to answer but nothing came out. There was a lot I couldn't say. A lot of things I didn't want to say. I looked at him helplessly.

He stroked my hair. "It's OK. Whatever it is, Sweetheart, I promise, we'll take care of it."

I didn't have it in me to tell him that it was beyond even the powers of a father.

"I'll be right back. Get you something to eat."

And he was gone.

I was alone with my flimsy cup of water, trying my best not to lose it again.

A nurse came in minutes after Dad left. Now that I was awake, she wanted to check my vitals. She spoke in a soothing, steady voice. I didn't hear what she said. I was slipping between the cracks. The soft hum of the machines was getting increasingly louder. Louder and louder until it drowned out the nurse's voice. Until it was all I could hear vibrating in my skull. I started to shake and the water inside the plastic cup splashed over the side. I tried to stop the shaking in my hands and accidentally crushed the cup I was holding. Water spilled on the sheets.

I stuttered an apology. The nurse quickly cleaned up the mess. It was only water, she assured me. Nothing to be concerned about. Nothing to apologize for.

I couldn't stop the shaking.

I closed my eyes tightly and held my arms to my chest, fighting for control. Tears were streaming down my cheeks from the effort but it made no difference.

The nurse was speaking again.

"Don't worry," she was saying. "It's normal."

Nothing about me was normal.

I nodded anyway. She put an arm around my shoulder, speaking to me softly. She stayed with me until the shaking stopped.

Dad was back. He pulled the tray over the bed with a handful of saltines. "Just crackers and water for now, OK? You've had an empty stomach for a few days. You need to start slow."

"A few days," I repeated. "How long have I been here?"

He looked concerned. I didn't miss the significant look he traded with the nurse. "Three days, Sweetheart. It's Tuesday."

Three days.

I was sick for three days. Unconscious. Pumped with drugs. Perfect conditions in which I could find him and still, I saw nothing.

He was gone.

I didn't have to fight the tears. They didn't come. I was all dried out. Empty inside.

"I'm sorry," I said weakly. Not quite sure what I was apologizing for. I didn't even know who I was apologizing to. Everything wrong was all my fault.

Dad stroked my hair, trying to reassure me. "It's OK, Sweetheart. It's OK." He didn't know what to say either.

"We'll get you back home soon."

It took longer. The doctors did more tests. We waited for more results. I went through a similar battery of diagnostics that I had gone through the first time around. I was slowly permitted to eat more than just crackers and water. I was weaned off certain medications and prescribed others. Not just migraine pills. Not just anticonvulsants.

Antidepressants.

I was sent home with an appointment to see a therapist.

Dad treated me like a soap bubble; speaking to me in a soothing voice as if I were a 2-year-old about to throw a tantrum. I should've felt guilty but I didn't feel much of anything. I was on medication that they hoped would somehow chemically prevent me from falling apart. I didn't fight it. I didn't want to feel much anyway.

In truth, it wasn't any of the drugs or even the combination of them that held me at bay. It was the last promise I could keep in memory of him.

Stay safe.

Thanksgiving break was coming up. It was determined that I should stay home from school at least until after. I was not in any great rush to return to the world that never even knew him. I agreed. My brothers would all be flying in for the holiday. I'd been able to avoid meaningful conversations with them over the phone, but I knew they would be making attempts in person. I almost didn't want them to come. I didn't really want to see them.

My family used to be my rock. The foundation on which I could always fall back. I don't know exactly when that had shifted, but it had. The person that held that designation now was gone. I was lost. There was little of myself left in me. The person I had become had died when he did. The person that I was no longer existed.

I was nobody now.

If I couldn't see him, I didn't want to see anyone.

I didn't go into my room. I set up residence on the couch in the meantime. I barely got dressed in the morning or moved from my spot during the day. I ignored phone calls and messages. Dad didn't question me. I binged entire seasons of bad mystery shows on Netflix and ate takeout.

I didn't cry.

It was another week before I had the strength to set foot into my own room.

I waited until Dad was out of the house, running errands. I didn't want him to be home when I did this.

I knew it would be difficult. I didn't feel particularly stronger or braver but necessity made it unavoidable. This three-bedroom house was going to have to host four adult men and me for four days. Something had to give.

I took a deep breath and stepped inside.

I almost fell to my knees. I was assaulted by the kaleidoscope of colors that mirrored eyes I would never see again. I couldn't breathe.

I saw every moment I had with him in flashes. It swirled around me with the life of its own, Everywhere I looked, I saw him. Every touch. Every breath. Random clips of non-sequential events. Sitting by the brook. His hair so long that it veiled the windows of his soul. Brooding. Walking through the carnival. Laughing. His awkwardness. Him in his uniform. Self-assured. Certain. Happy.

The visions slowed when I saw him bent low over me, his uniform still damp. I welcomed the ghost of the broken kiss we shared. I relived the pleading in his eyes. The courage behind his decision. The sacrifice he was willing to make. What that sacrifice cost us both.

The discharge of bullets that was deafening at the time was louder in my heart now. The minutes that had determined our fate blew by too quickly for me to hold.

Then in even more detail, I saw the pain in his face. I saw the realization in his eyes. On his knees.

On mine.

I saw everything slip away.

I balled my hands into fists, focusing on the pain of my nails digging into the inside of my palms. My heart beating erratically in my chest.

Breathe.

With trembling hands, I picked up the rough sketches I had drawn. Different angles. Different expressions. Different emotions.

All one man. I will not forget. I cannot forget.

I no longer have a choice. No longer days. No longer weeks. No longer months. A lifetime.

My lifetime.

I forced myself to be methodical. I found the sketches, drawings, and likeness of him. I collected every physical link I constructed to stay connected to him. I emptied a box and laid them all inside. Then I sealed it. In doing so, closing my life to any kind of redeemable future.

I spent a long time sitting on my bed, tracing the scar on my arm with my finger. I idled in the pain of my perfect reverie. Feeling resentment from far away whispering on the edges of my ravaged heart, I was both removed and unable to move. My tears were silent. I wasn't even aware that I was crying until I realized I couldn't see my hands in front of me. I was petrified, staring down the brink of what was to come.

The hollowness of a lifetime without him.

Sleepwalking

Drew was the first person I talked to. Really talked to. He came by the following day. He didn't ask any questions. He didn't make light of the situation. He didn't give me advice. He just sat with me. In between the silence, I cried and he hugged me. It was what I needed.

He came by every day the next few days until I cried less and less. By the fourth day, we were sitting in silence, drawing together or talking about the schoolwork I was receiving online. Dad started talking to me like I was sane again. He went back to work full time.

Life was starting to mirror how it had been before. At least to everyone else. I already knew it would never be right for me again. Back to normal.

"Did you want to go back to Illinois?" Dad asked me seriously over dinner.

"What do you mean? For Thanksgiving?" I was puzzled, my

pasta filled fork paused halfway to my mouth. Hadn't it already been decided that the boys were coming here?

"For good."

I put down the fork and frowned. "Did you get fired?"

"No. I was just wondering … if you'd be happier going back."

"To Illinois?"

He nodded, watching my reaction carefully.

I sighed. What difference would it make to me? He wouldn't be there either.

"You can stay in Chicago. I spoke with your brothers. Both Chase and Liam can make room for you. You can stay with either of them." Belatedly, I realized that he wasn't planning to move with me.

I had been inexcusably selfish. I had made things too difficult for him to handle. He had work and I was only getting in his way.

Getting in everyone's way.

What was the whole point of me now that he was gone? I'm done contributing. There was nothing left for me but to get in everyone's way. People I cared about.

Staying safe.

"I'll be 18 in June," I reminded him. "That's just a few months from now. I'll be legally an adult. I can move out. I won't be in your way anymore."

Get my own apartment. Get out of the way. Stay safe.

He frowned. "That's not what I meant, Sweetheart. You're not in my way. You're my daughter, not some kind of obstacle."

"Why are you trying to get rid of me then?"

He looked aghast. "I'm not trying to get rid of you!"

I started to raise my voice, not in anger but in frustration.

"You just wanted to send me off to Liam and Chase!"

"I don't want to send you anywhere!" He was exasperated. So was I.

"But ..."

He raised a hand to stop me. I lapsed into silence. He started again. "We've been in California, what? Three, four months? Already you've been admitted in the hospital twice and in the ER three times. Clearly, this move was a bad idea."

I was about to disagree but then he added in a soft voice, "In the hospital ... you'd wake up screaming." I saw the haunted look in his eyes. I felt a deep shame. I had not considered my father's feelings and had hurt him far worse than I could imagine.

He looked away.

"You kept saying that you wanted to go back."

The memory kept me from speaking. He had misunderstood my desire. Not that it was at all surprising. How could he understand? How could he even envisage? How can I explain?

"You said a name."

My blood ran cold, freezing me in my chair. I forgot to breathe.

Dad looked right at me. My face was blank but drained of blood. "Who's Ethan?"

My heart tightened at the sound of his name. I couldn't answer.

"Your friend, Brieann said it was a friend of yours from your old school. I had Locke ask around," he admitted. "No one knew who you were talking about."

"He's not from there," I was finally able to say. The words came out in a rush of one breath but devoid of emotion.

He waited. Considering all that I had put him through, I knew I owed him an explanation. At the same time, I didn't know if he could handle it. Or even if I could.

"I can't explain, Dad. Please don't ask me to."

I could see the conflict on his face. He wanted to make me happy. He wanted to give me everything I could ask for. He also wanted to find the person responsible for the pain I was in. His restraint was remarkable.

"OK," he conceded. "But whatever happened wasn't right."

"No." I was sure he could hear the bitterness in my voice. It was ill-concealed. "It wasn't."

"Sweetheart, I don't know what to do anymore."

Neither do I.

"Just … give me time?" I tried to keep my breathing steady.

He nodded slowly. Reluctantly.

"Thanks, Dad."

I was at Caden's next afternoon with Brieann and Drew. We found a small table beside a window that faced the street. Though nothing like the weather I was used to, it had cooled enough to want a hot beverage. I nursed a mug of spicy hot chocolate while we talked, welcoming the bite on my tongue. Little things that reminded me that I was alive.

The conversation was light despite the unspoken questions I knew Brieann burned to ask. I wanted to tell her everything but also didn't want to say anything. She sat beside me, occasionally leaning against me to offer her wordless sisterly support. To my surprise, I welcomed it. Drew shared a look and an encouraging smile.

It was bizarre. Everything that happened since Ethan felt scripted and staged. It was like watching my life, Rated G, on stage with bad lighting and canned laughter. It was oddly comforting.

Almost as if the universe was feeding me just the right amount of predictability that my damaged mind can handle. I drifted in and out of the conversation.

"I'm crazy stressed over finals," Brieann was saying. Drew nodded in agreement. "I think I can pretty much handle it all except for Economics and that massive paper in English." I'd be going back to school in time for exams and although I was barely making the grade, I wasn't at all concerned.

We were interrupted by a convoy of three heavily window-tinted, black government cars flying down the street. "The hell --?!"

"Oh, look, someone who drives just as crazy as you," Brieann noted.

Drew was unapologetic, "You said you didn't want to be late. Were you late? No."

There was a story here. I looked at Brieann questioningly but her eyes still followed the cars as they disappeared from view. "What is that all about?"

Drew shrugged. "It's election year next year. I'm guessing it's some senator doing a campaign up at the college." He leaned toward me on the table, "Did you know Schwarzenegger himself was at the college a few years ago?"

"I'll be back," Brieann quoted in the worst Schwarzenegger impersonation ever. Her failing effort made me smile. Drew shook his head. "Lame."

The conversation continued to old movies, new releases, and pop culture. Nothing deep. Nothing serious. Exactly what I needed.

We chatted until it was close to dinner. I ordered an extra meal to take home for Dad.

"Double bag it," Drew demanded.

"I don't want that spilling in my car."

"Not a fan of Loaded Baked Potatoes?" I asked.

"Happy in my tummy, not on my floor mats."

"I'm surprised he's even letting you bring it in his car," Brieann said as she pulled on her coat.

"You wanted to bring ice cream, Bree! In a cone! My mom left a gallon of milk in the back of my car once. It exploded. Never again will dairy be allowed." He stood tall and dramatic. "The line must be drawn here! This far, no further," he quoted some obscure line from a film that I did not recognize. Brieann rolled her eyes.

"I'm not even talking about the ice cream!"

"What are you talking about then? The sardine sandwich? The dripping blue cheese burger?"

"You are such a liar! I've never ever eaten those things!"

He allowed me to take my food with us. Double bagged.

Brieann got into the back of Drew's car while I rode shotgun. We headed to my house first. The conversation fell to the background. I cradled the double secured dinner on my lap and consented to be distracted by the dictates of social niceties. It prevented me from thinking. It stopped me from feeling.

I welcomed the numbness. It was better than the pain.

From The Ashes

The road to the house was blocked by the convoy we had spotted earlier. Government service agents in suits and earpieces stood outside the vehicles. "Oh, this can't be good," Brieann muttered with a sideways glance to Drew. He pointedly ignored her, slowing the car down to a crawl.

We were flagged down as we got closer. Drew rolled down his window.

"This road is temporarily blocked," the agent said to him. "You'll have to take the detour around."

I released my seatbelt and leaned past Drew to the open window. "I live here," I said.

He looked sharply at me. "This is your place of residence, ma'am?"

"What's going on?" Brieann asked from behind.

"Yes, I live right over there." I pointed to where the front of the convoy had stopped. "Should I just get down and walk it, then?" I opted to forgo the sarcasm. I've watched enough BlackList to worry about an undisclosed location where they could take rude minors to be never heard from again.

"Do you have identification?"

"What's going on?" Drew asked while I rummaged through my pack for school I.D.

"I'm not at liberty to say." Their businesslike manner made me nervous.

"Would you know if Dad is OK?" I asked in a shaky voice as I handed him my ID. He took it from me and studied it. He looked back at me but didn't answer my question. "London Anne Evans?"

My stomach turned. "Yes?" How much more bad news can I take? First Ethan ... now my father? From the corner of my eye, I saw the look of concern that Brieann exchanged with Drew.

The agent stood up so that we couldn't see his face anymore and spoke into his radio. Then he bent down to Drew's window again.

"Ma'am, if you'll come with me please?"

I was about to explain that I couldn't get out when Drew stopped me. "Hang on a minute, London." He turned back to the agent. I've never seen him this decisive. "You haven't shown us a badge or told us what this is about."

The agent dutifully showed us his badge and allowed Drew to study it. The gold and blue metal identified him as Secret Service. "Wait. Is the president actually here?" Breiann asked over Drew's shoulder. "Like, actually here??" I could see that the agent was getting impatient. "This business does not concern you directly, I'm not at liberty to discuss anything."

"It concerns me, though, right?" I asked in the smallest, non-threatening voice I could muster. "I'd like to know what this is about." Let Dad be a spy. Let him be a government resource for some super-secret military project. Let him be part of the goddamn witness protection program. Please, please, please just let him be fine. "Is Dad OK?" I asked again.

"This does not concern your father, ma'am," he said, probably deciding that it was safe enough to say. "This is about you." The relief was like a rush of cold water that left my legs weak. I closed my eyes.

"What about her?" Brieann insisted. He ignored her. She threw herself back on her seat with the dramatic flair of an undiscovered center stage thespian. I heard growling from the back seat.

"What about me?" I asked solely to prevent Brieann from launching herself at an armed government agent. The said agent opened his mouth to answer but it was a different voice I heard.

"She won't get out of the car, eh?"

I froze, my heart in my throat.

Impossible.

A second person joined the agent. Unlike the black suits the agents were wearing, he was dressed in an olive colored army dress uniform. His right arm was in a sling. A medal hung on the left side of his chest. He bent down, his face in view. The grin on his face matched the teasing in his voice.

"She has issues with following simple instructions," he continued.

The setting sun made his eyes more gold than green. Beautiful hazel eyes alight with triumph. Eyes I never thought I would see in this life again.

"Ethan," I whispered in disbelief.

His grin softened into a warm smile. The mischief in his eyes melted into affection. "My London."

I felt, rather than saw, both Brieann and Drew look first at me then at him. I understood their wordless surprise and confusion. I would console them but I couldn't move. I was afraid that any motion on my part would dispel the illusion.

An agent opened the door. The disruption jolted me into action and suddenly, I couldn't get out fast enough. The dinner I purchased at the café, carefully double bagged, fell to the floor, forgotten. I fumbled around the front of the car and threw myself at Ethan, afraid that if I let him out of my sight, he would just as easily disappear. He caught me with one arm and absorbed the rest of the impact with his body. His breath once again in my hair.

I had both arms wrapped tight around him as I looked up to meet his eyes. He held me to him one-handed. Despite the awkwardness of his sling and the medal on his chest digging into my shoulder, I was comfortable. Whole.

Was I dreaming again? Was this real?

And if not, do I care?

"Aren't you dead?" I asked him in a shaken voice. "You aren't that lucky," he quipped, reminding me of the very words I said to him not three months ago.

I thought that I would be laughing but I wasn't. I was crying. I've never experienced such an intense feeling of reprieve and elation. It was impossible to contain. I buried my face into his chest, taking in his scent. Allowing myself to delve into his physical presence. Allowing myself to melt into him.

He said my name again, his voice shaking with emotion.

I was aware that we were standing in the middle of the street surrounded by the secret service. The most unimaginable of reunions. I should have been embarrassed. Maybe I should've even been suspicious. I just didn't care.

I stood there in the warmth of his embrace, feeling the life I lost return to me. It was my first real breath of air.

"How?" It was all I could manage to ask. He tilted his head to the side and gave me that half-smile that had the power to stop and start my heart. He was about to answer me when another agent interrupted us.

"Ethan," he said. "I'm sure you can appreciate that this is a security risk. We'd all be better off if you take it inside. We've swept the area."

"Don't you think you're being slightly fanatical?" Ethan asked patiently, disentangling himself but holding on to my hand. "I'm not a target for assassination."

The agent wasn't easily persuaded. "With all due respect, it's my job to assume that you are."

"You went inside my house?" Like that's what really mattered here.

"Yes, ma'am," he said, daring me to argue. I stepped behind Ethan, wiping my tears and trying to not look like a drowned raccoon. He held my hand and encouraged me forward. As always, I followed his lead.

"London, this is Agent Roger Davis. He's the head of this operation."

"Ma'am," he said, inclining his head. I shrank further behind Ethan.

"All right then," Ethan said, resigned. He turned back to me with a soft smile. "Do your friends want to come with or would they feel better escaping this nonsense?"

Oh, right. My friends.

By this time, Brieann had found her way out of Drew's car and was standing next to the open door. Drew kept his hands on the wheel. "Ethan, this is Drew and Brieann." I gestured at them.

"Guys, this is Ethan."

Ethan stood at attention and inclined his head in their direction. "Sir," he said politely. "Ma'am." Brieann's wide eyes were filled with awe. She gave a small, slightly awkward wave.

"Um ..." I didn't really want them to join us. I needed this time alone with him.

Drew, ever-dependable, did not miss my hesitation.

"If you're OK, London, I'll be taking Bree home now." Brieann was about to object but stopped when she saw the look on Drew's face. I saw her protest die before it left her lips. She slid back into the seat next to him, deflated. I mouthed the words 'thank you' to him. He cracked a smile, pointed to himself, and mouthed out the word: hero. There would be no argument from me. Drew was worth his weight in platinum. Brieann waved again.

"Nice to meet you," she called as Drew shifted the car to reverse. She held her pinky and thumb to her face in the universal sign for "call me later". I shook my head a fraction. She gave a frustrated look. I smiled at her as they drove away.

"Let's go inside," I whispered to Ethan. "I want to talk to you."

The agents waited outside to give us a semblance of privacy. We stood there, in each other's embrace, for a long time. Just inside the entrance. Neither of us spoke. I concentrated on breathing. Every breath I took was loaded with his presence. It was only for the promise of permanence that I released him.

"How?" I asked again in a quiet voice. "I saw you get shot. I saw you bleed. I saw you fall."

I saw you die.

"I caught three bullets," he declared softly, almost with pride. "Two in the arm. One in the shoulder."

How does one even survive that?

"I lost a lot of blood, didn't I? It really could've been much worse." He walked me to the couch. We sat side by side but angled to face each other, our knees touching. I needed the physical contact to get me through this. "It turns out, earlier that week, the government had led a raid over some suspected terrorists. One of them was some big shot leader that was scheduled to be extradited to England.

"Prince James's visit was unconventional. It also made him the perfect target. They were going to use him for leverage, him for their bloke and all, eh?"

I tried hard not to show my impatience. "Ethan ... I'm not really following ...". I don't really care ...

He smiled. "Patience, right? I want you to understand something. Extremists, who are well-trained and well-armed, studied our routines. They studied our schedule and our practices. They were planning this for ages. They were prepared for every possible scenario."

The gold in his hazel eyes glistened. "But they were not prepared for the impossible, were they? They were not prepared for you."

I was confused and he was enjoying it.

"You showed up just the right time. Because of you, there were three men in the outpost tower and not just one when the prince arrived. Because of you, Nikau and I didn't head toward the armory. We avoided the ambush that seized our men. Instead, we ended up in the dummy, of all places. No one goes to the dummy when we're under attack. Because of you, Nikau and I were close enough to make a difference."

What he said wasn't entirely all true. It was because of him that Nikau survived the sniper at the outpost. It was because of him that they were able to catch the enemy by surprise. It was because of him that his prince survived.

I shook my head, a useless gesture to make sense of it all.

He continued. "When we got Prince James out of their hands, it gave the rescue team freedom to descend," his eyes glazed over. "We lost more ... we had casualties," he was talking about men who had fast become family. It was a difficult thing for him to remember.

"But the results," he continued, "were far more favorable than any other scenario we could have hoped for.

"The balance of power shifted quickly. I was in surgery within the quarter hour."

As he spoke, I could see the blood running down his arm. The memory threatened to pull my fragile existence apart. The warmth of his hand around mine was the steel thread that kept my heart together. The nightmare wasn't any less haunting but I was made braver by his presence.

"You disappeared. I knew you were safe." He smiled briefly, comforted by the thought, before he was reflective again. "I thought it was over for me.

"I didn't want it to be. It wasn't that I was afraid of dying." His voice had taken a softer tone still heavy with meaning. "It was just that this time, I actually have someone worth living for."

His eyes were liquid, revealing all the things he couldn't say. I swallowed, wrapping both hands around one of his and holding it to my chest. I never wanted to let go.

"I woke up in the hospital. Had to stay there for a week."

As did I.

The queen herself visited us." I was lost in his smile. "Gave me a medal for saving her grandson's life." He indicated the elegant ribbon hanging on the left side of his chest with ill-concealed pride.

"I'm alive because of you, London." He leaned forward so that our foreheads were touching. He smiled. Keeping our heads together, he continued. "In many ways, you saved my life. Of course I had to live, eh? I needed to hold you in my arms again." He raised our intertwined hands to my cheek.

"The prince asked me if there was anything he could do for me." He leaned back and looked into my eyes. "I asked him to help me find you." The green in them danced. "I had difficulty explaining things without sounding like I was mad. He remembers you. The one that doesn't listen to reason." He laughed.

I was bewildered.

"How did you find me? I was looking for you and I couldn't find you! I thought you lived in a different universe!"

"You said you were in California," he said with undisguised glee.

I looked at him blankly. Not comprehending.

"Remember how I had thought that you weren't human?"

I nodded. "You thought I was an alien that lived off cotton candy."

He was in the middle of saying something then stopped suddenly and laughed. "I never thought you were an alien!"

"Yes, you did," I accused him. He didn't stop laughing even as he spoke. It made it difficult to understand him. "An alien? I didn't say you were an alien!"

My eyes narrowed. I couldn't honestly say that he did, but at the time, I was certain that it was what he had thought.

"An alien," he scoffed. "Of all things ..." He shook his head in disbelief. "Not an alien, London. I thought you were my personal angel. You appear out of nowhere, talk to me about personal things that I couldn't normally speak to anyone else about, and then you disappear into nothing! You are ethereal."

He smiled fondly. "I wanted to believe that you belonged to me. You were mine and no one else's." He turned my arm over to expose the scar that ran up my arm. "Remember the night we were on the roof?"

"Yes, my one irrefutable evidence of your actual existence."

He looked away from me, as if what he was going to say would be unpleasant for him. "That night, you said that it was almost winter … in California. The United States of America. You existed in a world that we shared. You were a person. You couldn't belong to me. I couldn't claim that you were just mine."

I was about to interrupt but the expression in his face pleaded for me to allow him to finish. I kept my silence. "You deserve better than what I can offer. I thought that the right thing to do was to let you go. There was nothing I could give you that could compete with what you've given me.

"When it all came down to it, I couldn't do it. I couldn't let you go. Where did that leave me, eh?" He smiled ruefully. "I have to be better," he clarified. "Even if I spend a lifetime trying." I marveled at everything he was confessing.

"Where are you from?"

He grinned, my hand still on his lips. "New Zealand. I'm a Kiwi!"

New Zealand?

Things I didn't think to consider were coming together. His strange accent. The unfamiliar places. The time difference. The wrong seasons. Little hints that I chose to ignore, were practically drilling little holes in my head. All this time. New effing Zealand.

He laughed out loud at my expression. "Mundane, eh? Not quite the fairy tale wonder world you had originally imagined I was from, maybe?" He looked apologetic.

"It's not that," I said, growing quite angry with myself. "New Zealand?! That's helluva lot closer than a parallel universe!"

"See? Maybe knowing a bit of current events would have been valuable." He teased. Forgetting myself, I swore. His eyebrows flew up in surprise and amusement at the fury behind the curse. He didn't rebuke me.

"I could've found you a lot sooner," I whined. "I didn't look past this country! I barely looked past the school! Trust me to accept the theory that you're from a different universe over the possibility that you were in a different country! What kind of an idiot am I?!" I had wasted a ridiculous amount of time. I could've saved myself all this heartache.

He looked at me shyly. "You aren't buggered that I'm not from some mystical, magical place?"

I was still angry at myself that it took two seconds before I understood what he was asking.

"Ethan, I'm just relieved that we're on the same planet!"

He pulled me in a tight hug, laughing softly. "I'm here now."

"Yeah, you and, like, 20 agents! What's that all about?"

He shrugged. "It wasn't my idea. I think that was all the Secret Service. Not saying much, though. I suppose anyone with a computer and internet access could've accomplished the same. You're fairly easy to find, eh? Not many people with your name.

"I thought I'd fly here on my own, but they arranged for me to receive diplomatic immunity upon arrival." He shook his head at the memory. "I almost rabbitted when I saw the two agents and a police escort at the airport. I thought I was being arrested!"

"Happens often," I teased. His lips twitched. He didn't deny it.

"You have to admit," he said with grudging admiration, "The Royal Family knows how to return a favor."

"You were almost killed," I reminded him, unwilling to be so forgiving.

"I can't really be mad at him," he countered, bringing his hand up to my face. As always, I instinctively leaned toward it. "He helped me find you after all."

There was a knock on the door. Davis stepped in. "Sorry to interrupt. The girl's father is here."

It took me two seconds longer than it should've for me to realize that I was the girl in question, and it was my father about to enter the room. Ethan was faster. He let go of my hand and stood up. I stood in front of him. Dad followed quietly, though his eyes were filled with contained anger and suspicion. Anger gave way to relief when he saw me.

"Sweetheart! Have you been hurt?" I stepped forward and gave him a reassuring hug. "I'm fine, Dad," I assured him. "Better than fine, actually." I smiled. I couldn't contain it. Ethan was alive. The change in my mood was enough to hold Dad temporarily at bay. It wasn't difficult to see that there was life back in my eyes. For that, he'd be willing to negotiate.

"What's going on?" His eyes narrowed at Ethan.

"Dad, um, remember yesterday when you were asking me who Ethan was?" I gave him time to process. He did and he didn't like it. I tried to be confident about this declaration but I was embarrassed by everything Dad had to endure without proper explanation. "This, um, this is Ethan."

Ethan stood in attention. He was unable to salute properly or even extend a hand to Dad due to his sling. It should've been awkward but without being ornate about it, Ethan's military training kicked in. He kept his eyes straight ahead and spoke to introduce himself in a crisp, clear manner.

"Cadet Ethan Mattis of the New Zealand Defence Force, sir."

"Edward Evans," Dad replied, uncertain.

"Yes, sir." Now given permission to address my father, Ethan made eye contact and spoke respectfully. "I apologize for the intrusion into your home, sir. I had hoped to approach you in a less disruptive manner but certain people in my government made that difficult for me to do so." There was something to be said about decorum. The formal demeanor that Ethan immediately adopted conveyed nothing but respect. It was respect for my father's authority. It was appreciated.

"What's this about?" I could tell Dad didn't have any idea what Ethan was saying but was still trying his best to follow along.

Fighting a smile that only I would be able to see, Ethan continued formally, "I'd like to take your daughter out to dinner, sir."

It was difficult not to laugh at my father's expression.

"What?" It was all he could say. I bit my lip.

"If I may, sir," Ethan repeated patiently, without a hint of sarcasm. "I'd like to take London out to dinner."

Dad stared at him without a word. Ethan waited patiently. I couldn't take it anymore.

"So, um, Dad," I said, not wanting to give him the opportunity to think about it and say no. "I won't be out too late. You'll be fine finding your own dinner, right?" I remembered that the dinner I bought him, carefully double bagged, was outside, unceremoniously discarded and ignored. Probably flattened.

He was busy watching Ethan. Ethan didn't move. I tugged on Dad's arm until he finally looked at me. I didn't trust myself to say more. I hoped he could see that I was not going to stay here but was willing to give him the semblance of some type of parental control. "Yeah, OK," he replied slowly. "You have your phone? Call if you need me?" I nodded, relieved.

"Let me know where you are," he added. If that was all he required, it wouldn't be a problem.

"Of course, Dad. You know I will," I promised. I gave him a quick peck on the cheek and mumbled into his ear, "Thank you." It was completely unfair on my part to ask this of him. Not after everything I've put him through. He was being far more generous than I deserved.

Ethan stepped forward. "Thank you, sir. I'll take care of her." I saw Dad frown, second-guessing his decision to let me have this freedom. Ethan didn't flinch. It was as if he was expecting it. "See that you do," my father warned him. Ethan nodded, understanding fully and accepting the responsibility.

I walked out, feeling Dad's eyes follow our progress to the car.

Dinner

"Where am I taking you?" Ethan asked me when we got into the back of one of the black SUVs.

"To dinner?"

"Yes, but where?"

I shrugged. I didn't know. I didn't care. I wasn't even hungry.

"A bit of help, London," he pleaded. "I've never been outside my own country. I don't know where anything is."

"There's a pancake place down the main road," I suggested questioningly.

"Pancakes?"

I laughed. "They sell other things too!"

"Like eggs?"

"Can't drive one-handed," I teased him when he leaned back and the convoy started moving.

"What makes you think I can drive at all?"

Wait. What?

He raised his eyebrows, daring me to ask more. I didn't.

"Good thing you have the Secret Service to drive you around now."

He laughed. I leaned against him and he wrapped his arm around me. "My London," he whispered in my ear. The gentle vibration traveled right down to my stomach. It was a pleasant feeling. I took a deep breath. The smell of him was just tantalizing.

"You're right," he said out of the blue.

"About what?"

"That bracelet does look better than the one I got you." He was looking down at my wrist. I laughed. "Well, it didn't have much of a competition."

He shifted so that I had to sit up while he reached into his sling with his left hand. He grinned at me then pulled out his knife, still closed. I was going to rebuke him but I caught a glint of silver around the dark metal. Wrapped around his knife was his ID bracelet.

"Your trinket is probably still sitting on the dummy floor," he said, though didn't seem particularly saddened by its loss. "Soldiers are rank. I'd leave it be if I were you." I helped him unwind the silver.

"Maybe you'll wear this instead," he offered humbly.

"Where did you get it?" I asked as he fumbled with it.

"I've always had it," he said, his eyes busy on the bracelet's tiny clasp. "It's the only thing I've had from my childhood. The only proof I have that meant I once had someone love me."

Enduring life doubting something like that was unimaginable to me. It was too much for me to have. I touched his cheek with my palm and made him look at me. I searched his eyes. "Are you sure you want me to have it?" I wanted him to see that I understood that this was not just an ornament. I understood that it was not an easy thing to part with.

"I'd like you to wear it," he said meaningfully. "So that you'll have proof that someone loves you."

I held out my wrist. I didn't need the rubber band for it to fit. It was just my size. I helped him put it on me. There was no way he'd have been able to do it one-handed.

It was a physical representation of the hold he had on me. The silver chain wrapped around my wrist was an echo of the love wrapped around my heart. I was bound to him. Irreversibly.

"Ethan Robert," I mumbled, reading the engraving on the plate.

"Don't start," he said, putting his chin on my head as I leaned back on his chest. I laughed.

I called Dad when we got to Caden's, making sure that I was dotting the i's and crossing the t's of our verbal agreement. He still sounded suspicious but he didn't try to stop me either. The man was a saint. I would have to make it up to him somehow.

I don't know what attracted more attention; the obvious Secret Service agent scouting out the place or Ethan in his full dress uniform. People stared at us even as we took our seats at a booth in the back.

Cindy looked at me wide-eyed when she came to take our order but was uncharacteristically incurious. Perhaps it was Davis' steely look that discouraged her from asking questions. I don't honestly remember even ordering but we must have because she jotted down some things and walked away.

"So," he said, when we were alone. "We're finally on a date."

I looked down at my hoodie, jeans and Chucks. I grimaced. There was a small, dark stain on my hoodie that may or may not have been from this afternoon's hot chocolate. I hadn't had any desire to make myself presentable since I had gotten back home from the hospital. I hadn't even brushed my teeth since this morning. Not exactly date material. Meanwhile, he was looking his best. The inequality was beyond obvious.

"Not how I imagined I would look for it."

He reached for my hand across the table. It delighted me to see the thin silver line around my wrist. When I reached back it made me even happier to feel his hand in mine. "No," he agreed, his eyes never straying from my face. "Fully better than a dream."

I don't know if it was because he had said it earnestly or because I wanted to believe it. But his words made me feel 10 times better. I blushed.

He let go of my hand when our order arrived. I took a couple of bites of chicken before I noticed that he was having difficulty eating with his left hand.

"Did you need me to feed you?" I teased. He lifted an eyebrow at me, his expression sarcastic. "You can throw a knife with deadly accuracy 50 feet away from your intended target but you can't eat left-handed," I continued, enjoying myself.

"I'm not trying to impale myself with the fork," he said in defense. I laughed. "How did you survive the past two weeks?" I fed him off my plate. He took the bite, a playful expression on his face.

"Cheeseburgers," he said after he swallowed. I laughed.

The rest of the meal seemed unreal. Our reality had been defined by insanity or impossibility. Having dinner with him, talking about ordinary things, made this all the more sublime.

It was a real date. No one was shooting at us.

We paced ourselves, talking about things we had never had the luxury to share before. The weather. New Zealand. School. We compared songs we listened to and books we've read. It was not much of a revelation that his library list were mostly non-fiction historical biographies but I loved that we could talk about it. We talked about the lunch choices at the barracks and favorite foods. Knowing small things about him excited me. I wanted to know everything.

We laughed a lot.

We split dessert.

The hourglass was frozen, allowing me to experience every sensation with individualized attention. Every glance. Every touch. I was seeing the molecules of my life finally come together. Building me. Healing what was shattered.

I was surprised when it was time to go. I had fully accepted that the clock had stopped for the world to allow us to have this. The restaurant was emptied of other patrons. Cindy was waiting by the register. He paid the bill, apologizing for keeping her late. She invited him to return for breakfast.

"Time to go home," he said with regret. Then with a twitch on the edge of his lips added, "We'd better get a move on if you want to get to your father before he involves the police."

I shrugged, unconcerned. "Let him," I said, nodding toward Davis. "They're on our side."

Nightfall

Dad had all the lights on in the house when we arrived. He may have purchased a couple of more when we were gone because it was brighter than I remembered. More an airport beacon. Less like someone's home. He was sitting in the front room, obviously waiting for us. Ethan let go of my hand before we walked inside the house.

"Hey, Dad." I gave him a kiss on the cheek. He put an arm around me, holding me possessively beside him as if to say, *don't forget that she's my daughter.* Ethan hung back a respectful distance. It seems I wasn't the only one who could feel the change in atmosphere.

"Sir," he said.

Now that Dad has had time to absorb the situation, he was more prepared. "Have a seat, son," he indicated the couch across from him. Ethan dutifully sat, still in attention. The third degree was about to begin. I looked apologetically at him. He spared me a quick, reassuring glance before giving my father his full attention, as was expected.

"New Zealand," Dad began.

"Yes, sir."

"What brings you all the way here?"

Ethan didn't miss a beat. "London, sir."

I smiled at him even when he didn't look at me. Dad frowned. "How did you two meet? The Internet? Some dating site?"

"Dad!" I protested, mortified. He remained unmoved. This was going to be difficult to explain.

Ethan was more confident. "No, sir. Not the internet. We met shortly after you had moved here." He kept his answer honest, but left out the details. "When we weren't together, things just weren't right. I came here to find her." My father considered this a moment, then harrumphed. I don't remember ever hearing him make that noise before. I struggled with suppressed laughter.

"So much so that you had to involve the Secret Service?"

The laugh escaped before I could stop it. I threw both hands over my mouth. Dad didn't look at me, but Ethan shot me a dirty look. He blushed furiously.

"That wasn't part of my plan," he admitted in a strangled voice. He shifted in his seat and looked at me for help. I bit my lip. This was an opportunity I did not want to waste. I dove right in.

"Apparently, on the way to finding me, he went ahead and saved the life of the Queen's favorite grandson by taking three bullets to the chest." I was having fun with this. Ethan was becoming more and more uncomfortable.

Dad did not expect that. "You took three bullets to the chest?"

"Um, not to the chest." He swallowed, seemingly painfully. "Two to the arm, one in the shoulder " he added, his voice becoming smaller and smaller. He looked like he was burning on the spot. "Sir," he added belatedly, cringing at the oversight.

"He took down a terrorist group that was holding him prisoner. Taken style. He was a regular Bryan Mills with particular sets of skills. Notice that fancy medal hanging on his chest? That's how he got it. The queen pinned it on him herself." Dad zeroed in on it and I saw Ethan stiffen under his scrutiny. He was not half as pleased as I was.

"To thank him, they set him up with a plane ticket and the president's bodyguards. He is, after all, a national hero now." I almost choked on the last word. Ethan's was silently livid, which made it all the more hysterical. I could practically see the angry glyphs shooting sharply out of his head.

"Is that true?" Dad asked Ethan.

Ethan swallowed. "I'm not a national hero, sir." He did not dispute the rest.

"The queen herself, huh?"

"Yes, sir." He refused to look at me.

Dad turned to me. "You knew all this?"

I stopped laughing. "I knew he was shot," I admitted haltingly. There was dawning comprehension in Dad's eyes. Why I had called out Ethan's name and why I couldn't talk about him afterwards. He realized all this from that one sentence. He understood how I had fallen hard.

"I only found out now that he survived it." I met Ethan's gaze. The power behind his silence strengthened me. The silence, heavy with emotions, filled the air.

Dad broke it. "Are you in town for the holidays?" His voice took on a decisive tone.

"Yes, sir."

"Do you have a place to stay, son?" I dared to look at Dad. I had an idea where he was going with it but I was afraid to hope. I had no right to hope.

"Not yet, sir. I was going to find a place tonight."

Dad scoffed. "It's late. Find a place tomorrow. If you don't mind sleeping on the couch, you can stay here for the night."

"I don't want to intrude, sir." I gave Ethan a dirty look and mouthed out the words "shut up". He refused to acknowledge me.

"You've already done that. Go get your stuff." Dad stood, indicating that the conversation had come to an end. He took two steps then realized he had forgotten that Ethan didn't travel alone. "What about your body guards?"

Ethan stood as well. "They aren't my body guards, sir, despite the impression London gave you." I stuck my tongue out at him from behind the safety of my father. "I would think that they've completed their assignment. I've been safely delivered to her." He smiled at me. "They were supposed to help me find a place to bunk."

"Well, you've found a place. Let them go home to their families."

"Yes, sir. Thank you, sir." He stepped out to get his stuff and speak to the agents. Dad and I were alone.

"Dad," I began, not really knowing what to say. I had an overwhelming amount of grateful love that I couldn't quantify into words. "Thank you."

He snorted. "I'm not entirely naive," he said. "If he wasn't going to stay here, I could see you sneaking out to see him." I hadn't considered doing that but I couldn't find it in myself to deny it either. "I'd rather have you both where I can keep an eye on you."

His eyes locked on mine and his expression hardened.

"Where did you meet him?" he asked again.

My stomach tightened. I wasn't used to lying to him. I tried to act nonchalant. "We didn't meet on the internet, Dad. Don't worry." Obviously, I didn't exude the same confident ease that Ethan demonstrated because Dad wasn't buying anything I was selling.

"I didn't ask where you didn't meet him. I want to know where you did meet him."

"Um …. in the middle of a forest?" My answer was more like a question. He lowered his chin and fixed me with a look that told me that his patience wasn't nearly as infinite as it had initially seemed. I winced. I chewed my lip and tried to look everywhere but at Dad, hoping to find the words to explain the unexplainable. There was nothing. How could I reason something I didn't understand myself?

"I know this doesn't really help my case in not sounding like a complete lunatic and I swear I'm not lying. I can't understand it myself. I did meet him in the middle of a forest but not anywhere near here. It was more like, well, like …"

"Like a dream," Dad finished for me in a quiet voice.

I stopped in mid sentence, finally looking back at him. His hardened expression was replaced with one that I've never seen on him before. It was a mixture of nostalgia, sadness and understanding. An impossible amount of understanding.

"How --?"

I blinked and a man I almost didn't recognize stood in front of me. Dad visibly aged, tired, and haggard. I had introduced unexpected stress into his life that neither of us were prepared for. Consumed in my own world of selfishness, I couldn't see what this was doing to him.

Until now.

He slumped back into his chair and covered his eyes with one hand. I sat on the coffee table in front of him and waited. Something significant was about to happen, though I couldn't predict what. I heard the clock ticking in the other room and the sound of engines outside the house. I forced my breathing to be steady.

What I'm sure felt much longer than what was reality, he lifted his eyes and sighed.

"You are just like your mother," he said in a faraway voice. It was a statement I'd heard often growing up. Sometimes he said that in frustration when I challenged him in ways that no one else would. Other times, it was meant as a compliment. I didn't know the context at this moment. "Did I ever tell you how I met her?"

I shrugged. "Locke told me. You went to college together, right?"

He smiled softly at the memory. "There's a little bit more than that. It was my freshman year in college. The committee that I was a part of had volunteered to clean up the neighboring lake shore.

"I was leaning into the water trying to reach out for a floating pop can when she showed up. Scared the hell out of me. I fell in." I smiled too, hearing this story for the first time but not understanding what this had to do with anything.

"She helped pull me out of the water, laughing the entire time. I was furious." On the contrary, he didn't look angry at all. His smile had turned into a grin and the lines on his forehead that had made him look older seemed to recede. He deserved this trip down memory lane if it would ease some of the burden I've put on him.

"But your mother ... she was something else. Before I knew it, it was the end of the day and I had nothing to show for it. I spent all that time chatting with someone who was single-handedly responsible for me catching bronchitis the following week," he laughed again. He paused for a beat then looked me in the eye, his expression more serious.

"She disappeared without a goodbye. I tried looking for her. I went through the entire school body trying to find someone that matched her description. I checked with neighboring schools. Just in case. Nothing. It's like she never existed."

I held my breath. This was all starting to sound familiar.

"It was two years before I saw her again. The next time I did, she was a freshman at the university I was in. She walked right up to me on the first day of the semester as if we just met the day before.

"I found out then that when I met her, she was a junior in high school. Seventeen years old."

Just like me.

"And from a high school all the way on the other side of the state."

He let the implications of that sentence settle before he continued.

"She said she had a dream. She dreamt of a boy that fell into the water. It was a dream for her but it was reality for me."

I straightened on the coffee table, staring off into space.

Just like my mother.

"What is this, Dad? Some kind of mutant power?"

He laughed. "It's a gift, Sweetheart. Some kind of magic. It's as if you have the ability to realize what it is your heart is looking for." He leaned over and kissed me on the forehead. "Whatever kind of power it is that flows through your blood from hers, it's not something I would dismiss. It's the same power that brought your parents together."

"Why didn't you ever tell me?"

Knowing this would've made this whole process easier. It would've answered a lot of questions. It would've eased many doubts.

He shrugged. "Really, Sweetheart? How can I tell you? How could we tell anyone?"

The irony of it all. He stood up and I met him with a hug. All this time. He would have been the one to understand it all. I could tell him everything. "Dad, I thought he was dead." My voice broke at the last word. He patted me in the back. "He's not, Sweetheart. He's here now. It's going to be fine."

He coughed, took a deep breath and said, "It doesn't mean he has a free-for all pass. Your brothers will be here tomorrow. They'll help me out with this guy of yours. Keep him in line."

"Dad!"

"Or maybe after seeing how grouchy you can be at breakfast, he'll leave on his own." He laughed. I stuck my tongue out at him.

"If that doesn't scare him away, your hair in the morning will." He was on a roll.

"Stop it!"

He gave me a decidedly fatherly look, pointed right at me and said, "I don't care how magical this whole thing is. He's not allowed in your room."

I nodded, rolling my eyes but smiling. It was not an unreasonable request.

"Fine. Well, I'm going to turn in for the night. I have to fetch Liam from the airport early in the morning." I gave him a peck on the cheek and hugged him.

"Thanks again, Dad."

He kissed me on the forehead. "It's nice to have you back."

My heart light with this discovered knowledge, I half danced out the door and met Ethan on the front steps. He had an almost empty duffle bag slung over his shoulder. The headlights of the Davis' car washed over us a moment as they turned around and drove away. I took Ethan's hand and waved after them. When they turned the corner, Ethan faced me.

"This is mighty right of your father," he said thoughtfully.

"Yeah, I know. He's the best." I wrapped both my arms around his and leaned against him. He stood a little straighter than normal.

"I don't want to abuse his trust," he said seriously. I pouted. He laughed.

"Come on," he said. "It is late. Get your sleep. There's no need to tire yourself out now," he said with a grin.

I hesitated. He picked up on it right away.

"What's wrong?" he asked quietly.

"Well," I looked away, feeling like a loser. "It's just that … having you actually here. It feels more like a dream than any other time I've been with you. What if that's all it is? What if I've finally snapped? I'm afraid that when I open my eyes, you won't be here."

He dropped his duffle on the front steps and twisted me around. He waited until I met his eyes. He was illuminated by the light from the porch. His hair, a little longer than it had been the last time I saw him, glowed with a strange tinge of violet. It only enhanced the dreamlike state I was already in.

More and more like a dream.

He brought his hand up to brush my cheek.

He whispered my name in a way that made it sound like a song.

His hand went from my cheek to the back of my neck, under my hair. Holding me in place with his eyes, he brought his face ever closer to mine until I was overwhelmed. Just as I had been the first time he stood this close to me. I closed my eyes, feeling his breath on my lips.

I was fully aware of his every movement. Fully aware of my own. I put both arms around him, pulling myself to him while I pulled him down to me.

Until that explosive moment when our lips met.

At that moment, I was aware of nothing and everything.

It was the merging of both my worlds. Worlds that I had thought to be far apart and impossible to reconcile were blended together in unimaginable beauty. Everything that we had gone through together and the agony we suffered apart found its purpose here and now. They were the threads that bound us. The magic that would keep us together no matter how far apart. All the pain and the hopelessness were formidable, but not impossible.

I knew that I would do it all again for the epiphany of this moment.

I couldn't wake up from this dream. Not only because I would never want to but because I would never have to. The dream was real.

I was no longer sleeping.

When he broke the kiss, I opened my eyes slowly, almost reluctantly. When I did, my vision was filled with only him. There was powerful emotion burning beneath his eyes that I would've feared if not for the courage I also took from them. I once again had a taste of the certainty of his love that I knew still lay beneath the strength of his passion. All my fears were put to rest in this security.

"I'll be here," he promised. I believed him.

Above us, the infinite stars with their infinite possibilities promised nothing but love.

Thank You

Lorenz Laureola
Stepping into Dad's shoes and having so much faith in me

Logene Laureola
Being a supportive big brother

Bel Laureola
Putting up with the family

Peggy Lacson
The support and encouragement that only a mom can provide

Victor Lacson
Providing support halfway around the world

Kari Glenn-Fitzgerald
Purchasing the first copy and having faith

Marianne Ambrose
Attempting to steal the first completed draft

Beth McGowen
Beta reading Reverie in its entirety within 4 hours

Ellie MacKellar
Target market beta reader with thoughtful notes

Kari Pohar
Acting like I was a published author long before I was an actual published author

Eleanor Giron
Offering to bring a veggie tray to future book signings

Michelle Katigbak-Alejandro
Celebrating all the #WINs

The Grayslake Arts Alliance
Bringing together a supportive group of artists

The Grayslake Area Public Library Writer's Group
Being an advocate for local writers

David Rutter
Sensei editor extraordinaire

About the Author

ZEE LACSON

Zee was born and raised in Manila, Philippines. She grew up with her dad, brothers, and grandparents. She lives in the North suburbs of Chicagoland, IL with her husband, twin sons, and fluffy dog.

She is an engineer by education, a photographer by profession, an artist by practice, and a writer by soul.

She drinks good coffee and appreciates fresh sushi. Just not together.

This is her first published work of fiction.

9 781735 135816